Chandra —
—a signed-
an intriguing
What is

All best.

TOMBOLA

FORTY-THREE SHORT STORIES

Paul Purnell

Paul Purnell

Grosvenor House
Publishing Limited

This book is published by
Grosvenor House Publishing Ltd
Link House
140 The Broadway, Tolworth, Surrey, KT6 7HT.
www.grosvenorhousepublishing.co.uk

A CIP record for this book
is available from the British Library

ISBN 978-1-78623-399-8

Also by the same author

'The Hireling'

'Scaramouche'

'The Storm'

'Dangerous Cargo'

'The Kazak Contract'
(First of the James Ballantyne series)

'The Tontine Trap'
(second in the series)

INTRODUCTION

I have called this book of stories 'Tombola' because it is a medley of differing styles and subjects. You can dip into it and find something interesting every time.

Despite what my publishers tell me, I firmly believe there is a demand for short, punchy fiction. Every commuter, parent and bedtime reader needs a short read for their enjoyment. The iPhone, iPad and Kindle have changed the landscape of modern living. Reading requires a new 'espresso' format to satisfy the impatient reader.

If I am right, a large potential readership has no convenient format to boost their imagination and enjoyment. If one of these stories does not appeal to you, I am sure the next one will.

Paul Purnell
paulpurnell.com

CONTENTS

Tombola

DAY ONE

Wayne collected his gear and waited at the front gate. The winter air was bitterly cold and he shivered in a skimpy T-shirt and jeans. His bony frame showed through the thin material.

"Right! Pick up your gear and follow me," said the senior Screw, as he took the main gate key from his chain. The wicket gate swung open. Wayne stepped through carefully. He wanted to savour his first steps to freedom.

Two years had passed since the day he stood in the dock at Old Bailey and was sent down. Two years to pay for a stupid mistake. That was the day he vowed never to carry a knife on a job again.

He checked the cash they gave him on release: a twenty-pound note with no change.

Very handy! he thought. *How do I get a ticket from the fucking machine with this?*

White City tube station was a half-mile walk and he dumped his gear in a bin on the way. He began to breathe more easily as he got further and further from The Scrubs, but the noise of traffic and the speed of the vehicles came as a shock.

When he got to the tube station, there was no ticket office – just a ticket machine. He jumped the barrier and climbed up to the platform.

Clocked up one already, he mused, *still it's their fault – no way to pay anyhow.*

Soon the train ran underground and from then on he found it hard to sit still. The gloom and the noise plus the crowd pressed in on him. He could feel the pulse in his temple throb, his throat felt dry and he crossed his arms as if warding off an attack. He could stand it no longer, so he jumped off at Queensway, pushing through the barrier after the person in front. This part of London was unfamiliar and it was a surprise to see the green of Hyde Park just a short walk away. Its bright open space made him blink and he paused on the pavement and looked around.

"Watcher looking for, darlin'?" A voice behind him made him turn and a girl with a pale face and dark red lipstick was walking up to him. He tagged her – peroxide blond hair – leather bomber jacket – torn jeans – for what she was.

"Saw you wanderin', and felt you needed a little company sweetheart."

"That's true. How's business?"

He was curious and felt glad to be speaking to her though he had no money to spend on her.

"Never mind that, it's cold, just let's chat and 'ave a cup of tea. I live around the corner so you can make your mind up after that."

It was amusing to chat to this brassy tart and he could spend a few bob on a cup of tea – no worries – he'd break it to her later he was no punter. She put her arm through his and he felt the warmth of human contact run through his body. He realised how much he'd missed it for the last two years.

They walked a few yards to a workmen's cafe on the corner of Queensway. Inside, he went to the counter to get their teas and she sat at a corner table. The men eating at the counter watched her as she sidled into her seat and crossed her legs, dangling a shoe from one of her feet.

"It's a bit early for trade isn't?" – Wayne was no chat-up master – "I mean, how often do you get fixed up at this time of the morning?"

It was half past nine. He felt as if it was later but realised he'd been up since five getting ready.

"Depends," she said looking him defiantly in the face. "The Arabs stay out all night and come around at any time."

Wayne bit off the remark which came to his lips: What sheikh was likely to go for a brassy cheap blonde? So he just nodded.

She began to gain confidence.

"So what's your line of business then?"

"I'm between jobs at present but I do a bit of this and that, you know."

He looked down and watched her reaction with a sidelong glance. She bent her head to meet his gaze.

"You're just out of the nick ain't you?"

Again, he nodded.

"There's that look about you. I missed it when I spoke to you, but I can see it now."

"Then you know I'm skint and you're wasting your time!"

She smiled and to his surprise she looked almost pretty but the hard lines around her mouth and eyes returned quickly.

"Don't fret yourself. It's too bloody cold for business anyhow."

He smiled at the reality of her life and thought to himself: *I'll never be brought this low – I've got to get some bread somehow.*

"What's so funny?" she bridled at his grinning face. "You're not so clever, doing time. I never been inside and don't intend to neither."

He wiped the trace of his smile away.

"You don't understand, I'm thinking of the life I'll lead when I get a break."

"What sort of break are you talking about? Your chances of a good job are nil."

She's no optimist, he thought wryly.

"No, I mean when I can get into a good deal with no questions asked – if you get my drift."

He looked at her to see if she really understood what he meant.

She sipped her tea and looked around. The other customers had all gone, only the fat man behind the counter remained and he was deep in *The Mirror* at that moment.

"Happens I know someone who could help you out, if you like." She looked him in the face.

"Depends if you can cut it with 'im to keep your end up."

Wayne sat back in surprise. Was this tart well connected? Walking the streets in the morning and well connected?

He took a long sip at his tea.

"How come you know someone on the go?"

She stared at him and he noticed for the first time how green her eyes were. It had been a long time since he'd felt the kick of sexual feeling.

"Well, maybe a friend has jobs going, but not for strangers."

He realised at once her "friend" was more than a pimp – maybe connected with the drug trade – they usually were.

"Is he about?"

"I could give 'im a bell if you want. What's your name?"

"Wayne," he didn't feel like giving out more info, "tell him I'm fit."

She smiled at this. "Yes," she said, "I can see that."

He grinned and cadged a cigarette from her while she tapped her iPhone. After a short wait, she spoke to somebody and he couldn't quite make out what she said as she held her hand over the phone.

"He says wait here and he'll find you."

"Fair enough, I've nowhere to go at the moment. How will I recognise him?"

"Just 'ave a guess."

They talked a bit about how life had changed in the last two years and he noticed how she glanced at the door every few minutes.

Ten minutes past and the door pushed open. She looked up and said, "You took your time... this is Wayne I was talking about."

Wayne took a keen look at the man who walked in. A big black man about six three – his skull shining in the fluorescent light – broad features and heavy brow – a look of malignant power. He was dressed in a dark double-breasted suit and wore a silk T-shirt – no collar. On his fingers were two big gold rings like knuckledusters.

He sat opposite Wayne and turned to the girl dismissing her with, "Cherie, get us a coffee will you?" She slid out from the table and went to the counter.

After a pause, Wayne took the first step.

"Maybe you need some help on a job? I might be interested."

The big man frowned. "What makes you think I'd take you on? Cos she says so?" He nodded towards the girl. "Who the hell are you?"

Wayne shrugged. "I'm just a workin' man who likes the good life and can get a job done, if you get my meaning."

The black man scrutinised Wayne's getup – old T-shirt and jeans. He grinned. "Sure, I can see you live the high life!"

Wayne frowned. "Look, if you want to talk business, go ahead – but don't take the piss. I'm just out of the Scrubs and looking for work, so if you ain't got some, then say goodbye, drink your coffee and shove it."

The man's features relaxed and the fixed, hard look faded.

"Cool it," he said, "just playin' wiv you. What was the crime you didn't commit?"

His mouth opened in a grin as wide as a piano keyboard.

"I got involved in a heist from a supermarket. Did two of a four-stretch."

"So what was your job?"

This is like a fakkin job centre, Wayne thought, *next he'll be askin' me for my national insurance number.*

"I was backup outside but got caught with a knife. I'm never goin' tooled up again."

"Depends," said the man and looked out of the window.

"Max!" the girl called out. "Want a slice with it?"

The black man got up and said to Wayne, "Hang on a minute while I sort somethin' out."

He walked over to the girl and Wayne could see he was questioning her. She nodded her head and he came back over to the table.

"Look, till you get your own gaff, you can camp out at the flat, watch the punters and check 'em out for me. OK?"

Wayne realised this was a check-over. *Fair enough,* he thought, *I'd do the same, and it suits me.*

He nodded and went to pay the bill at the counter.

The blonde was still there. She nudged him. "Well? Set you up alright?"

"Yeah. Thanks." He felt small taking a favour from her.

"Suit yourself," she said and shrugged.

The big man never drank the coffee. He got into a big four-by-four Jeep and blipped his horn as he steamed away.

They left the café and walked a hundred yards to a large block of flats just off Queensway. He began to regret dumping his gear as they reached the front hall. His scruffy outfit gave the game away in this posh area.

To his surprise, the flat was not at all what he expected. It was on the first floor and they walked up the carpeted stairs into a large apartment which looked over a private square. The furniture was modern and clean.

"Max says you can stay if you watch the punters for me. Is that OK with you?"

Wayne felt a bit of an apology was needed; she was not such a scrubber after all.

"Fine," he said, "I was a bit off just now, got to get used to things again."

She smiled briefly and showed him a small bedroom where he was to stay.

"I'm goin' to get changed and meet a client. I'll be back about one I reckon. So I may need a bit of a cover when I get back."

He didn't quite understand what she meant, but nodded.

As she disappeared into another bedroom, he took the time to have a good look round. Outside in the square were several big cars, BMWs and Mercs, even a chauffeur in a cap waiting for some big shot.

Off to the city, Old Chap? he mused. *Still, plenty of cash about in this place.*

The bedroom door opened and Cherie walked out, a different woman. His eyes registered the shock. She wore a smart black suit and her hair was dark red. Her high-heeled shoes gave her inches in height and made her legs look a mile long.

"Whoa! Now I know how you can afford to live here!" he said.

She smiled, pleased with the remark,

"A girl has to work – the place belongs to Max."

She took a last look in the hall mirror and told him:

"I'll be back about one, maybe with a feller. If you hang out in the small bedroom that's best."

"Understood," he said and watched her as she tip-tapped out into the hall.

The phone in the living room was tempting, so he dialled up his brother in Liverpool. They chatted for some minutes but Wayne never said what he was up to – just said he was chilling in London.

"Look, do you know anyone down here who needs a bit of help? Cos I need a start, if you get me drift."

His brother knew exactly what he meant and promised to give him a heads-up if a job came along.

Reckon I'm stuck here for a while, he thought, *could do a lot worse.*

He snoozed on the leather sofa and it was the buzzer at the main door that woke him. Instinct kicked in and he dived for the small bedroom door just as the front door key was turning in the lock.

It was a humiliation he'd never experienced before: to be listening to a whore and her mark. They said very little as money changed hands and within minutes he could hear moans from next door as Cherie worked her magic on the punter.

God! She's a good worker! he thought. *She deserves an Oscar.*

But he covered his ears to muffle the sound; somehow it was hateful to hear Cherie having sex with a stranger. He never asked himself why.

Then, from the bedroom, there was a commotion. Cherie shouting – a man's voice raised – the noise of furniture being shoved aside.

He pushed open the door. A dark-skinned man was wrestling with Cherie and grabbing at her purse and shouting in some foreign language.

Wayne took him from behind in a double armlock and frogmarched him to the door. The man was in his shirt sleeves and his jacket lay on the big bed.

Cherie threw it after him as he fell out into the landing, still shouting. Wayne gave him a kick and slammed the door.

He looked at her face. It was puffy with a bruise forming under her right eye. Lipstick smeared her face and the red wig she had worn was on the floor.

Wayne said, "You have a tough life, girl. How often does this go on?"

She didn't reply but ran to the bathroom and began to bathe her face in cold water.

"Bastard tried to fleece me. Look at me now! Can't go to work like this!"

There was nothing he could say, except: what did you expect from rough trade? So he said nothing and stayed out of her way till she had done her first aid.

Back again in the living room, she had changed into a tracksuit and her hair was tied in a scarf. Wayne could see the real woman and it was pleasant. She looked softer somehow and more sensual.

"Shall I go for some beers?" he said

"No need, there's plenty in the fridge."

So he brought out a six-pack and handed a can to her.

They sat quietly for a while just sipping the beer and he felt light-headed after just two cans.

Just shows you what two years in the pit can do to a man, he thought wryly and waved away the third can she offered him.

Outside, the weather was clear and bright.

"Do you mind if I get a bit of sunlight? It's what I've missed most inside," he said and she nodded looking up from the magazine she had been reading.

"Treat yourself. I can't work today anyhow."

Stepping out into the street, Wayne felt a keen wind blowing down from the park and again wished he'd not dumped all his kit in that impulsive way. He tucked the T-shirt into his jeans but felt the keen wind slicing through the thin material. Outside the tube station was a charity container for discarded clothing. He rummaged inside until he pulled out a sweater and an old vest which smelt OK. He pulled on the vest and the dark blue sweater and strolled down the street. No one paid any attention to him. It was good to be out and invisible. After twenty minutes, he returned to the flat; he climbed the stairs to the apartment feeling good.

As he reached the first floor, a scream echoed along the corridor and he saw at once that the door to Cherie's flat was wide open. In two strides, he was in and could see that backs of two men manhandling Cherie. Her legs were bare and one of the two was ripping her tracksuit from her body. The second man turned to face him and he recognised the disgruntled punter he'd tossed out.

The man held a knife in his hand and the blade gleamed in the soft light. He uttered something in a foreign language and moved in to use the shim on Wayne. They grappled as the knife was aimed at Wayne's gut but he managed a wrist hold and prevented the blade from reaching his stomach. They were face-to-face and a moment came when Wayne's instinct kicked in. A "Liverpool Kiss" broke the man's nose and the force of the blow spurted blood over the man's face. He reeled away and that gave Wayne time enough to grab the nearest object – a lamp – and smash it down on the sprawling body. The man cowered on the floor, blinded and semi-conscious.

The knife had dropped to the floor and Wayne grabbed it without thinking. A surge of energy ran through his body as if it had been stored for two years and now burst out of control.

He stabbed at the second man once – twice – again and again, till screams penetrated his brain and he stopped.

He was panting and his heart pounded rapidly. He registered Cherie was screaming and looked down at the man on the floor. He lay writhing on the beige carpet, then he lay still. A slow stream of dark blood snaked across the floor as if searching for a way to escape.

"What 'ave you done? What can we do?"

Cherie's hysterical words broke into his mind and he began to think.

She stood in the doorway of the big bedroom holding her torn clothing to her body. Scratch marks tracked across her bare shoulders and her face was white as alabaster. She looked at him for a long second, eyes wide with shock.

"Get Max quick! He's got to do something!" she said.

Wayne grabbed the phone before realising he had no idea of the number. He handed it to Cherie and she fumbled with the numbers, eventually getting through.

"Max! Get here quick! Something has happened. No! Wayne's here, but you gotta come!"

She put the phone down and pointed to the man near the door.

He was shaking his head and beginning to stir. Wayne took the cord from the lamp and tied his wrists behind his back tightly. The man sank back onto his back, blood oozing from his damaged face.

Exhausted, Wayne slumped into the nearest chair and wiped his hands on the front of his ragged jumper. He trembled with the nervous effort from the fight but his mind was clear. He was in a desperate situation. He could not trust the big man and he had no mates down here in London to call on.

However, the black pimp would have to help because the fight had been on his pad; he couldn't have police nosing into his business – could he?

Cherie had shut up by now and sat hunched on the bed in the big room. She did not change out of the torn tracksuit and Wayne figured she wanted to show Sam how badly she had been attacked.

Blood had seeped into the pile of the carpet but did not spread very far. Wayne pulled the body of the dead man into the kitchen and dumped it on the vinyl flooring.

He closed the front door and then checked the wire binding the second man. The man's face was puffy and masked in dried blood; the eyes half closed.

Footsteps pounded on the stairs and then Sam burst through the door.

"Jesus! What you been up to? You silly sod!"

"Don't blame me! These two tried to rape your woman. What was I to do?"

Sam's eyes bulged. "You didn't 'ave to slice 'em up did you?"

Wayne spread his hands wide in a gesture of helplessness.

"Listen! I come in and two guys are bustlin' your girlfriend – what am I to do? Join in?"

"So tell me what you were doin' outside in the first place?"

Wayne saw it was useless to argue with him in that state, so he called to Cherie, who was still sitting crouched on the big bed in the main bedroom. She came in slowly making the most of her appearance.

Christ! What a diva! Wayne thought. *Better than Eastenders.*

The big man put his arm round her and patted her back with his huge paw.

"Calm – calm – I'll sort this out, babe."

Turning to Wayne, he said, "You! Fetch some black bin bags and give me a hand."

The two of them stooped over the body and wrapped the hands and head in plastic.

Wayne could scarcely credit what he was doing, but it needed sorting, so he obeyed. Then they cut away the stained carpet and wrapped the body in it.

Cherie stood immobile at the bedroom door, her hands over her mouth; her white shoulders still visible in the torn tracksuit.

"Sam, what you goin' to do with him?"

She gazed at the wounded man, inert on the floor. His eyes were wide with horror but he was unable to speak.

Sam looked at Wayne and his eyes gave no hint of what he meant to do – the stare as cold as a cobra. Then he shifted his gaze to the helpless man on the floor.

"Don't fret. We'll think of something"

It was still mid-afternoon; there was little traffic in that quiet, respectable quarter of London. They carried the carpet-wrapped body down the stairs and into Max's Jeep, struggling under the weight of the dead body.

"Tinted windows – very handy," said Wayne.

Sam ignored the remark and slammed the rear door shut.

One of the residents passed at that moment, looked at the pair and the flashy car, then moved on, shaking his head in disdain.

Back upstairs, Cherie at last began to recover her senses. She wiped up the face of the injured Arab and did her best to clean up his clothes. His hands were still tied and he began to speak in some foreign language. It was plain he was pleading for his life as a babble of words poured from his mouth, interspersed with tears.

Sam pulled him upright and frogmarched him down to the vehicle.

Wayne hesitated on the stairs, hoping he could stay out of it, but the big man turned and looked at him.

"Get yourself down 'ere. You caused this fuck-up and you'll see it through."

He was in no mood for an argument so Wayne followed down.

Sam drove west till he reached Shepherd's Bush then found his way to the motorway. Wayne sat in the back next to the cringing Arab. Not a word was said – even the wounded man stopped babbling. As they drove along, Wayne had plenty of time to reflect bitterly on his first day of liberty.

Christ! I had it good in the Scrubs compared with this. How can I get out of here?

The thought stayed in his mind as the car reached Heathrow. Sam turned off the motorway and joined the stream of cars and vans heading for the airport. It was getting dark and the November sky was like a grey blanket. Further on along the slip road, he diverted into a service area where several large containers lined the road. They had the names of airlines printed on their sides and Wayne recognised them as the old baggage boxes used to load passenger luggage on long-haul flights.

The car pulled up level with the third one. They both got out and Sam pulled the cadaver out of the back of the Jeep. It fell to the floor with a thump.

"Give us a hand."

They both managed to heave the body into the container. There were other bundles and bin bags in there and a stench of rotten material. They quickly shut the lid and backed off.

Wayne began to doubt whether he would survive much longer. Life on the outside had taken a wicked hold on him. He trembled. Was it just the cold? Or was it fear? For a moment, he longed for the rigid normality of prison life. He was far from the mean streets of Liverpool that he knew; he had no cash, and now he was flung into a crime scene he had not foreseen. The lure of a pretty woman and a cushy life had put him at greater risk than he had ever faced before. He had to think quickly to exit this nightmare.

Back at the Jeep, he searched the wounded man. His wallet was in his back pocket and he pulled it out, it seemed bulky. Carefully shielding it from the big black man, he counted the notes. The man was loaded. There was more than five hundred pounds in fifties in there.

Life was looking up! A plan was forming in his mind.

Wayne went round to the driver's side of the car and spoke to Sam,

"Look, give me twenty minutes with this fucker and we can forget about him."

Sam studied his face. Wayne put on his hard man stare and pulled the knife he'd taken from the dead man.

"It's a dead end and the noise of the planes covers everything."

As if to confirm what he said, a 747 roared overhead, drowning out both speech and thought for a few seconds.

"You up to it?"

Wayne nodded and put the knife away.

Sam stared out of the windscreen for a minute, turning over the idea in his mind.

Come on you fucker, make your mind up! Wayne was racked with suspense. Would he agree?

At last, the big man nodded.

"OK. Take him down there and do it. But don't come back here. Get back somehow to the flat and I'll settle with you there. Got it? Change your clothes too."

They pulled the man out of the car and Wayne grabbed him as he nearly fell into the road jittering with fear. Half pulling, half carrying the man, he walked him down into the obscurity beyond the meagre security lights. The Jeep started up and pulled away at speed.

Wayne stopped as soon as he saw the Jeep was well away. He kicked the wounded man and brought him down to the ground.

The man squealed with fear, but Wayne didn't wait to explain.

Like a greyhound, he was away down the dark passage towards the lights of Terminal One. Clambering over a wire fence, his ragged clothing ripping as he went, he reached the departure terminal. Running upstairs he scanned the departure board.

The check-in queue for Liverpool was not a long one but every second stretched out into minutes as he stood in line. When he reached the counter, the check-in girl took in his grubby torn clothes and asked coldly, "What do you want, sir?" The "sir" had a wealth of scorn in it.

"Give me a ticket for Liverpool – quick."

"Would you fly First Class or Economy?" She was amusing herself on a dull evening.

Wayne pulled out the wad of fifties and said, "First Class, you Muppet!"

Her mouth shut like a cat-flap and she tapped the details into the computer with heavy strokes and shoved the ticket across the counter. He gave her a sarcastic smile and ran to join the crowd filing down the passageway towards the departure gate. Just before he boarded, he found a phone stand and rang his brother.

"Hey, Ryan. I'm on my way home. Tell Mum I will be back in an hour and get some brew in. I'm out."

He climbed the steps to the plane and sat in the big leather seat with a sigh.

"Can I get you anything, sir?" The pretty hostess smiled.

"No thanks, just get me home quick!"

Looking out of the window, the sun shone briefly above the clouds then sank out of sight, the day was over. Wayne glanced at his reflection in the glass. Staring back at him was a slick young criminal. He hated him.

THE TANGO LESSON

George sat on the top deck of the bus. His seat was level with the windows of a pub. A woman in a scarlet dress leant out of the window peering down into the street. He could see the room behind her lit by a bright glow, as if a party was in progress – music played and couples flitted past behind her. Before he could make sense of it, the bus moved on and the incident was over. He slumped back in the seat and rubbed his eyes feeling all of his forty-two years at the end of another workday. Next evening, he took the same route at the same time but the bus went past in a second and the pub window was shut.

He put the scene out of his mind.

When he got home, his mother put the tea on the table as usual and sat down opposite him. She wiped her wrinkled hands on a tea towel and looked across at him.

Here we go he thought, *another bleeding lecture.*

"Why don't you go out a bit more Georgie? You're always under my feet and yet you're earning a good wage. Enjoy yourself!"

Her voice had a piercing tone and it grated on his nerves.

"Do you think a packer gets a good wage? Working from eight a.m. to half past five in a grimy warehouse? It's a treadmill, I tell you. I'm fagged out by teatime."

She rumbled on for a few minutes but he didn't listen anymore. He read the *Evening Standard*, and switched on the telly. But when he went up to bed, he found himself thinking back to the mysterious window and the lady in the scarlet dress. What was going on that night?

*

The following Tuesday, he decided to find out. He jumped off the bus a few yards down the road from the pub. It was the Wheatsheaf, one of the big Victorian pubs with Assembly Rooms upstairs. Outside the Saloon a notice read: "TANGO CLASSES TUESDAY 6 PM". He climbed the stairs and heard unfamiliar music coming from the room above. It had a slow beat and an accordion played the melody in an extravagant way. Through the swing door, sound poured out from a loudspeaker. Dazed a little by the noise and the swirling couples, he stood in the doorway wrapped in his old mac and holding his cap in his hand.

The music stopped and a little woman came bustling over to him and took him by the arm. Her black hair, obviously dyed, was pulled back into a bun,.. She wore a tight blue dress and very high heels so she tottered as she led him to a table.

"You're a little bit late, but Gloria will look after you."

He could see the lines round her mouth wrinkle up like parchment as she smiled. Her body was as fragile as an old china doll in an antique shop. George had no time to explain that he was just curious. Everything moved so fast he couldn't keep up.

"Hello, I'm Gloria," said the lady sitting at a desk, a petty cash tin in front of her. "That will be five pound for the first lesson."

Her mouth was a cherry but the outline of her lips seemed a bit blurred. Her eyes under their long false lashes were lost in dark pools of mascara.

He was too embarrassed to protest; she expected him to pay, so he got out his purse and selected five coins carefully.

"Just sit down, dear. Take off your coat and Doris will be over presently."

He wondered what his mother would say when he got home late for his tea.

He pushed the thought out of his mind.

The class was reforming for another dance and the little woman in the tight dress clapped her hands and shouted:

"Now change your partners and let's try a little harder – just glide – glide." Her thin voice rose high above the chatter.

The beat of the music began again and George watched as the dancers gathered on the floor. The male dancers clasped their partners tightly and it seemed like the women were trying to keep them away. Some of the men gleamed with sweat as they shuffled about. The women struggled along as if pushing a heavy load.

Several untidy old men sat round the room looking on expectantly, their knees spread out as if claiming a space. It reminded him of musical chairs when he was small and everyone waited for the chance to grab a chair when the music stopped. Eyes scanned the women hoping for the slightest hint of approval.

Then his attention was attracted to a younger woman who came over to him. She was the girl in the red dress he had seen the week before. He remembered her long blond hair tied back in a ponytail and her slim figure.

"Have you been here before?" she asked.

"Well no, not inside," he said.

He realised it wasn't the right thing to say because she frowned and cocked her head.

"What do you mean?"

He stood up and muttered the first thing that came into his head but she paid no attention and took his hand. He felt the warmth of her soft touch as she guided him onto the corner of the dance floor.

At close quarters he reckoned she was about his age yet had worn well. He was amazed at the way she propelled him about like a parcel.

"One – Two – Slide. One –Two – Slide."

He moved awkwardly. His partner scarcely reached his shoulder but she kept up the chant as they ploughed through the other couples.

One or two avoided them with a quick change of direction but most suffered the crunch of his foot against their heels or toes as they moved around.

When the music stopped she dropped his hand and wiped her palm against her dress in a furtive way.

"That'll be enough for one session," she said firmly and walked away to the other side of the room.

He called after her, "Doris!" She turned and seemed puzzled. He stuttered, "I just want to say thank you."

She walked back. "For what?"

"For giving me a dance," he blurted.

She laughed and he noticed for the first time that she had a nice smile.

"You're a funny one! I dance with all the newcomers."

"Well I mean..." but he couldn't say what he meant. So he stopped. She smiled again and her eyes smiled too.

"Maybe I'll see you next week then."

It was more a question than a statement. George nodded without speaking. He put on his coat and took his cap and went out into the dark.

*

During the week he wondered if it was worthwhile turning up the following Tuesday. He felt embarrassed by his clumsiness and the way she had to push him round the floor. Besides, the other men in the class depressed him; it was like joining a queue at the Job Centre. They were a sad bunch and he would be just the same if he went back. But as the weekend arrived, he kept thinking about the woman in the scarlet dress and how she smiled at him.

On Saturday he bought a new shirt in the market and came home with it hidden under his overcoat. He told himself one last go would be OK, if he kept himself away from the general group of old losers.

On Tuesday, he left home with the new shirt still in its wrapper. He put it on as he left the factory at the end of the day.

At six p.m. he was there. The room was empty. He sat for minutes before he heard the sound of high heels tapping their way upstairs. Through the door came Doris and she seemed surprised to see him.

"O hello! Wondered if you would come back."

She went to put her coat away, not expecting any reply. He stood up but couldn't think of anything to say, so he sat down again.

As she came back he saw she wore a different frock – a bluish colour but it looked good on her. He stood up again.

"You know it costs seven pound for every session after the first?" He nodded as if he knew.

"Well, you can pay Gloria when she gets here."

One or two other older men arrived soon afterwards and clustered near the door. One of them nodded to George but he pretended not to see.

The music started and Doris took his hand and led him into the middle of the floor. When he recalled what she'd done last time, he wrapped a handkerchief round his hand which held hers and she seemed surprised. She smiled and he felt a confidence he'd never sensed before as they moved off in the dance.

There was no one to run into as they circled the open space in the centre of the room. She guided him as before but slowly the rhythm made sense and he began to enjoy himself.

By this time the room was filling up with the usual assortment of eager older men and apprehensive women. When the music stopped she dropped his hand and turned away.

"You need to practise more. Ask Alice," she said over her shoulder as she walked away. He saw her take the hand of a tall man with slicked-back hair and a sharp grey suit who smirked as she led him into the middle of the floor. She paid no attention to George as she whirled around. George bit his lip as he saw the odious man could dance a bit.

He worked out Alice was the little woman he met the previous time and she was dancing with somebody, so he sat down at the side of the hall and waited.

Gloria waved to him and pointed to her table. He went over and handed her a ten-pound note. He saw a glass of gin stood half empty at her elbow. She gave him his change she said, "Enjoyed your dance with Doris did you?"

"What d'you mean?"

She smiled thinly and said nothing but he knew there was something in her smile which was hostile. She didn't look at him again. When he had sat down nearby, he saw she was using a stick as she limped away

The man sitting next to him leaned over and said, "Poor old Gloria – such a queen." He chuckled and wiped his mouth with a grubby handkerchief.

"What d'you mean?"

"She was the number one teacher till she had her hip done." George studied the man. He was bald with long wisps of grey hair brushed back along the sides of his head. The tips of the hair just reached each other at the back. He needed a shave.

George said, "How long have you been coming here then?"

"On-and-off about three years."

"So you got the hang of this tango thing by now."

The man pursed his lips and cocked his head to the side, his eyes gleamed and he smirked at George.

"More or less," he said and turned to watch Doris as she twirled, hugging the figure of the tall man as he moved her round the floor.

The music stopped and before the dancers had moved off the floor, the man was up and walking over to Doris to speak to her.

She stood for a moment and glanced at George. She gave a wan smile and George leapt to his feet pushing the older man aside.

"You said I could have the next lesson," he lied

"Yes, that's right. Do you mind, Tom?"

The bald man grunted but George grabbed her hand and stood waiting for the music to start. He forgot about the handkerchief. Then they were away, moving together to the beat.

He held her close, feeling her body moving with him to the rhythm of the dance. The soft warmth of her back and her lithe movements sent a surge of excitement through his body. He couldn't believe it when the music stopped. It seemed unfair.

"That was much better," she said letting go of his hand. "You are relaxing more now."

"It's only because of you," he blurted out.

She looked away and didn't smile.

"Maybe you should dance with Alice next time."

"No! I want to dance with you!"

His outburst startled her and she drew back a pace.

"You can't," she said, "it's the rules, I only teach the new ones."

For an instant, he wanted to protest. He wanted to tell her that he had never felt so happy in his life when he danced close to her. Then he saw her turn and smile at the old man she had rejected and take his hand for the next number.

He got his mac and walked to the door. Doris whirled by, turning the greasy old man in time with the music.

"See you again next week?" she asked.

He didn't reply but pushed through the swing door and went out into the dark. Outside, a drenching rain had begun, seeping inside his mac and soaking the collar of his new shirt. He felt for his cap but he couldn't find it. He waited at the bus stop and when it arrived, he sat upstairs as usual. He saw his reflection in the glass, a damp figure with his scant hair plastered down across his forehead.

But he was smiling.

IN THE BEGINNING

I don't know what He was thinking. I've lived in that garden for quite a while on my own but He thought it would be a good idea to make another creature like me, except I have a willy-ma-jig and "she" has none.

Surprising, because he said to me that I would have free will and all that stuff. I thought He meant I could decide things for myself. Instead he has landed me with a WOA-Man so that most of the things I want to do are made difficult.

For example, I like to do a bit of gardening so I built a nice little shed and put a few things in it like a comfy chair made out of sheeps'wool and a jug made out of a gourd so I could have a little drink on occasions.

Oh No! WOA-Man said "What do we need a shed for? We need a shelter when it rains and a store room for food." Forgetting that we have acres of fruit trees and dozens of farm animals roaming around, so we can get what we want with a snap of the fingers.

And another thing, who does she think she is, bringing that snake into my shed? I had a word with HIM about that.

I said:

"What is that slippery thing doing here in the first place?

He gave me that patronising smile and said "The Lord knows best and I have made the earth and all things in it, and it is good"

Does He realize that she encourages it to sit with her under the big tree outside my shed?

I caught them whispering the other day and when I asked what about, the reptile just slipped away without a word. She said it was just a joke but I felt they were plotting something to upset me.

Then that night she snuggled up to me and asked me what I wanted most? I said "you know what I want but you're never in the mood."

She simpered and cuddled up to me so I couldn't resist could I? But when it was over, she told me that I was too timid and I could get a lot more out of Him if I showed a bit of spirit.

"I like a man with a bit of spirit "she said in a meaningful way.

I wondered what man she was talking about because I was the only man about in these parts as far as I could tell.

Two days later that damned snake was round again coiling about her neck and whispering in her ear. Worst of all, he had picked one of the apples off the big tree.

It was a beauty, large as a pomegranate and red as a ruby.

The serpent rubbed its surface with his slinky skin and it took on a shine like a mirror.

"Now you've done it "I said "You know it's off limits to eat them."

"No it's not" He simpered "He said we should not eat the fruit <u>on</u> the tree so I've picked one off and that's ok"

"Of course it is" chimed in WO-Man "Anyone can see that"

That did stop me in my tracks. I recall His warning that we should not eat the fruit, but was it "ON" the tree or "Of" the tree?

I didn't want to ask Him again in case He got stroppy but I saw the two of them nibbling, so I thought the harm was done and might as well take a bite. It was juicy and sweet and the best thing I had ever tasted. I've had mango and pineapples and strawberries and all sorts, but nothing compared to this.

Her slimy friend gave a sinister grin "I told you so" he said "Let's have another"

Before he could slink up and grab another--- Whoosh! Himself was down on us like a ton of compost.

"Gotcha"He bellowed "You won't be told. Now you've done it"

"Just let me explain" I said "we weren't sure if..."

But He cut me off mid-stream. He was in a right strop and went on shouting:

"I am fed up with you and that hideous snake. I wish I'd never made you. This free will business has got out of hand." He waved his arms about and pushed us towards a big gate I hadn't noticed before. He slammed it shut after us and we found ourselves here.

"This place is a bit bleak but Hell... we'll survive."

THE ARTIST AT WAR

"Stand up straight" The sergeant roared "you're in the Army you 'orrible thing" The new recruit moved just a little more upright then subsided into a comfortable stoop. He was a dark haired thin man of thirty eight.

"What's your name? You 'opeless 'eap?"

"Frank Brangwyn ...sir."

"Don't call me Sir, I aint no Sir, I 'm Sarnt Driscoll an' don't you forget it"

The first day of Army life had not been kind to Frank. He had enlisted with the Artist's Rifles in London but somehow he found himself at a training camp in Yorkshire. How did it happen? He had no idea, but wished he could change his mind. Could he go "Conchie" like his friend Bertrand Russell? No! It was not in his nature to rebel and he believed this would be a just war against the German Kaiser. All he hoped for was a chance to show support for the Empire and some part in the fight against the Huns. But this was something else, a world of shouting and mindless routines led by soldiers who regarded the volunteers as idiots and victims.

At night when, at last, the routine bullying and continuous noise ceased, he brought out his sketch book and doodled pen portraits of the characters he met. Driscoll became a dragon with a mouth full of teeth; Captain Foster, the officer in charge of his Company was a languid ostrich and the troop corporal Jenkins a Pekinese dog yapping at everybody's heels. The other recruits enjoyed the fun and soon his cartoons were circulating among the squads who shared the same training course. It was inevitable that some dunce would leave them on show someplace where the staff would find them.

During the second week he was told to "appear on Regimental Orders." the following morning. Corporal Jenkins explained this meant he was up before the Captain and he'd better be in best kit or else.

Next morning "Left Right--Left Right-Halt--Left Turn"

There were his cartoons on the desk in front of the officer.

"Did you draw these?"

"Yes Sir"

"Very good, I had no idea you are Frank Brangwyn the artist. What on earth are you doing here, training in Yorkshire?"

"Well" he began "I don't know either but they sent me here."

Foster leaned back in his chair and smiled.

"What would you say if I wrote a note to the War Office that you are available as a war artist? Would it suit you?"

Brangwyn nodded his acceptance and felt tears brimming in his eyes at the thought of finding a release from the drudgery he had endured for the last weeks. All the humiliation and pointless discipline had worn him down but he felt ashamed of this outburst of emotion in front of the officer.

The War Department was in Whitehall and he reported to The Official Record Office, still in his unbadged basic uniform.

"Your Yorkshire training was useful?"

The enquiry came from an officer considerably younger than himself and dressed in immaculate uniform of one of the top cavalry regiments. He smoked a Turkish cigarette through an ebony holder and wore a monocle which he played with from time to time.

"We have rather a different regime here" he smiled archly "I have to find jobs for the Belle Monde who offer their services to the Nation."

Frank took an instant dislike to this effete young person.

"I am not one of your Belle Monde; I enlisted like thousands of others to help the country at war."

"Well, so you shall." His arrogance was insufferable.

"I am posting you to First Army Headquarters at Arras as an official war artist; you can have three days leave and then report to them.

Frank left the office without saluting although he had learnt well enough what was correct. Promotion to War Artist meant an automatic commission, so he arrived in Army Headquarters in new uniform but no idea of his role. He reported to a Major Symens who explained the job involved creating sketches or simple line drawings of the men at the front line.

"Good for Morale, y' know" Symens twirled his waxed moustache to emphasise the point "But not too much blood and guts."

He smiled nodding to Brangwyn as if they were old comrades.

"I'll do my best" Frank assured him "But I will draw what I see."

"Of course, do what you think is right, but remember we are supporting the folks at home not writing a Penny Dreadful"

He chortled at his joke and offered Brangwyn a glass of sherry. Frank accepted gladly, knowing it was unlikely he would get another till he came back to England.

His first "expedition" took him to a field hospital near Mons about twenty miles from Arras. The sound of shellfire boomed incessantly, but far away. The wounded, lay in makeshift wards. It was a scene which stirred his soul. These men accepted pain and loss as they waited quietly for a release which would most likely be death. He drew the lines of grey men and shadowed in the canvas covering which shrouded them.

In the next weeks he went to the front trenches at Ypres and saw for himself that life there was a survival against terror. The gunfire from both sides roared continuously overhead. Corpses in shell craters; horses slaughtered in harness; guns and gunners in fragments and huddled groups of troops sleeping in muddy trenches like dogs in dirty kennels. All these images he sent back to Arras.

Immediately he was recalled and confronted by Symens.

"Brangwyn, I reminded you at the outset; we did not want images of suffering or other dreadful stuff from you. What has got into you, Man?"

"What did you expect? Scenes of Christmas cheer across No Man's Land?"

Symens shifted in his seat and gazed out of the window as if to gain control himself or get guidance from outside.

"Look" he paused and dropped his voice, "all we want is some views of the country from our side. Maybe a picture of our troops manning the trenches. Or..." he was gathering steam-

"what about a sketch of one of the aerial Observation Balloons? They look splendid in the sunlight."

Frank simply said "I didn't see one but I heard one was shot down only two days ago."

He glanced at Symens to check whether he sensed the irony in the remark.

"Well" Symens continued, unaware of the barb "I can't send these back to London. I'd better get advice from further up."

And he dismissed Brangwyn with a wave.

Within a week Frank Brangwyn was transferred back to England and detailed to travel the North Country sketching the stolid workforce producing the guns to fight the Boche and the sturdy farmers, who fed the Nation, at their ploughs.

His War Sketches never reached the Public until 1934.

By that time the nation knew The Great War was "The War to end All Wars." and his sketches were used to prove that such horrors could never happen again.

Germany re-armed the next year.

THE HIRELING

It was 24th July and the day of the Hiring Fair, the highlight of the year for the folk of Charlbury. Before seven o'clock the square filled with farmers trundling in on their wagons. The stoves of the victuallers sent spirals of steam up into the morning air as they got ready for business. The Magistrates had licensed the Moonraker from 8 a.m. and an impatient crowd shuffled and gossiped outside the locked door.

Farmer Broadmead stood eyeing the growing number of labourers collecting in the square. He needed four to be sure of getting the corn in.

"Happen you'll be suited by mid-day Master," his man of work said.

"Dare say, Silas, but no toper from the alehouse will suit me," and he nodded to the crowd outside the Moonraker.

Farmer Broadmead was a man of sixty with a round ruddy face and a solemn air. He had been a widower some five years and lived in a large farm outside Charlbury with extensive stock and land. Everybody respected his upright manner and he maintained a vigorous lifestyle. This day he wore his best clothes, a velvet coat with a check waistcoat and tan cloth breeches. His topboots shone as bright as liquorice and his straw hat was braided with ribbon.

He knew the importance of 'front' on this important day. Every farmer in Dorset and beyond would be competing for the best labourers.

The men, in their turn, put on clean smocks and wide-brimmed hats to show themselves to the hirers and to impress the ladies and farm girls who flocked to Charlbury for this special day. The ladies stood apart in a group and the girls chattered and giggled as they paraded up and down the sides of the square in their best frocks.

On the Green, at the edge of the town, a musical hurdy-gurdy man had set up and soon its wheezy tunes drifted down to the busy square, promising dancing and fun when the hiring was done.

The July sun burned away the mist and bargaining began.

"What tools do ye have?" Broadmead asked one of the men. "Can ye thresh as well as scythe?"

"As well as I did last year, Mester. I worked a three week for ye and mended tools after the harvest." The man's nut brown face and arms were proof of his trade.

"I'll tak thee on same terms, give us your name."

The man of work wrote down the fellow's name and the deal was done with a handshake. Broadmead never saw the young man slipping into the ale house to celebrate, else the deal would have been off. All down the street the same simple process was repeated and as the day wore on, the number of men for hiring diminished as the parties settled terms and went their way.

By five o'clock Broadmead had found his four labourers and was about to leave when he saw a man sitting on the kerb twitching a stick and looking down at his feet. He was the last man and yet he did not approach the farmers or waggoners. Broadmead crossed over to him.

"Have you no trade?" he asked.

The man glanced up and shrugged.

"No luck for me today Mester, I'm no labourer and there is no call for my skills."

His limbs were thin and long, his eyes had a golden tint, and when he doffed his hat respectfully, his dull red hair looked like the fur of some animal.

"Then what's your trade, man?"

"I fettle poultry Mester, and no one has wanted me so far." He looked down but watched the farmer out of the corner of his eye.

Broadmead was a decent man and took pity on the fellow.

"No man should be idle if there is work to be done. Come to the farm tomorrow and we will get you employed."

The slim man knuckled his forehead and his eyes followed the farmer and his man as they set off home. A grin slowly formed on his long, narrow face and he slipped into the shaded part of the square and disappeared.

That night the town came alive with laughter and dancing. The alehouse doors were wide open and on the Green the girls and lads danced to the tunes from the hurdy-gurdy man. Beneath the trees out of sight of the dancers, the red-haired man sat on his haunches observing the frolics of the young people. Occasionally he licked his lips with his long tongue and scratched himself with his sharp fingernails.

Early the next morning as the men pulled back the shutters at Broadmead farm, they were surprised to find the red-headed man leaning against the farm gate as if he had been waiting all night. Shown the duties, he set about cleaning the fowl house at once. His tasks kept him at a distance from the general labourers as they worked out in the fields from early morning till after dusk. The harvest was good and the weather uncertain, so Broadmead wanted the crop gathered in the shortest time. At night the fowl keeper set up his bedding in an empty shed and fed himself. He never took his meals in the farm kitchen, even when Bridie the cook invited him.

"Sure you need a hearty meal Mister, after them hours in the coops?" she urged, but he just shook his head and stayed outside.

Soon the other men ignored him and got on with their work and their usual fun. But there grew a sense of unease among all the people on the farm about the stranger and his ways.

In the Moonraker that evening, Jethro, the main hand, asked, "Do ye know where he eats? Is it in the shed or in the fields?"

No one knew.

"I saw 'im back of Long Wood last night," said one of the hired men. "He was skipping and running like a wild thing and he catched a hare I do believe."

They stared at each other but no one said a word. Then one of the ancients piped up: "Likely he's a Green man come back to the woods."

"Away! Old man," retorted Jethro. "'S a story to frit young babies, not a real happenin'."

"Tis no tale, my father met one, years ago and he warned me on it. Them is spirits in guise o' men and wicked too."

This raised a laugh and soon the whole company forgot the old man's memory and turned to other things.

Outside in the dark street the light from the inn door threw a beam onto the cobbles. Backed into the shadows of a doorway the Redman crouched as still as a pillar of stone and watched the scene. His golden eyes gleamed and his hair stood on end like a brindle dog. Someone opened a door nearby; disturbed, his eyes flicked in that direction and he sidled away.

The harvest went well but the fieldworkers had no time to waste as the storms of August blew in from the ocean. Strangely, the news on market day dealt less about the good tidings than about losses of farm stock. Several farms had been raided over the harvest period and slaughtered cattle and poultry left dead in the yards. No one could explain these happenings and no one had seen the killer.

Broadmead listened to the tales and began to concern himself about his own stock. He said nothing but realised all the farms thereabout had been attacked except his. During the night he kept watch over the yard and the barns. Some instinct kept him awake. About three in the morning he made his rounds of the farm. All seemed quiet except for the rustling from the poultry sheds and an occasional call from a night bird. He walked softly past the shed where the fettler slept; the door gaped open. Peering inside, plainly, the man was not there. Broadmead went back to his house pondering what it could mean.

Next morning Silas knocked at the kitchen door before breakfast.

"Master, have you heard the news from Belchurch?" Silas was beside himself with excitement. "The herd of Mister Fenwick have bin killed, evry one."

"When did this happen?"

"Last night, well after midnight."

The farmer stood still. Fenwick had the finest herd of Herefords in the county and was a particular friend of Broadmead. What should be done? Could there be a connection between his strange workman and these happenings?

Later he went to the poultry house to talk with the fettler. The man was collecting the eggs. There were marks on his hands and arms.

"Show me your arms," Broadmead said.

The man sprang up and held them out. They had deep scratches along the forearms and dried blood still stained the skin.

"Merciful God, how did you come by these wounds?"

"No harm, Mester. I fell among the briars when catching that feisty cockerel."

Staring hard into Broadmead's face, he dared him to challenge the story. His eyes were unlike other men's eyes; they had a black centre within the golden orb, reminding Broadmead of a fox.

The farmer turned away but said, "Go to Bridie and get them seen to."

His mind was in turmoil and he needed time to think.

"Yes Mester." The man nodded and turned back to his tasks. The farmer never saw his furtive grin.

Later in the evening the farmer checked with the cook whether she had washed the wounds. Bridie knew nothing about it.

Broadmead, a fair-minded man, decided he must take steps to find out the truth. He waited till after midnight, then, dressed in dark clothing, he left the house by the back door. The moon bathed the farmyard in a soft light. Nothing stirred and he moved carefully out of the yard to a spot where he could see the shed where the man slept and the field where his cattle lay. Hours passed so slowly and he began to drift into a half state between awake and dreaming. He would drift away then jerk back into life as his head dropped or some owl screeched.

During one of these wakeful moments he saw a figure running across the paddock away from the farm. It ran in a strange manner as if using its arms as forefeet, hunching forward like an animal and leaping or hopping across the meadow. Its thin figure crouched for a moment and turned towards the buildings, checking to see if it was followed. Moonlight fell on its features as it twisted to look behind. The farmer recoiled as the face of the figure was revealed. It wore a mask which covered the entire head – dark green and horned like a stag. The eyes peering out of the mask were bright gold and the head turned slowly, searching the countryside for a target.

Broadmead crouched stock-still until the shape moved away into the woods, then he ran back to the farm and locked all the doors. His first thought was to raise an alarm but it would take too long to wake and arm men at this hour. What was familiar about the figure? Then he remembered the Redman and the way he sprang up when asked about his injuries.

When dawn broke, Broadmead went out before any of the servants had risen. Making for the shed where the Redman lived, he took with him a cudgel but kept it hidden in his sleeve. His plan was to check on the fettler. He knocked loudly on the door – no answer. He knocked again and shouted. The door sprang open and the farmer jumped back in surprise. The fettler put his face round the door.

"Mester. What time is this? Is it so late?" he said. "What's to do?"

There was an impudent tone to his questions and his face was sly, as if he guessed Broadmead's thoughts.

"I need to sell some fowls today, catch me a dozen for market."

"As quick as you please," replied the man and he bowed and touched his forelock with exaggerated courtesy. Broadmead hid his anger at the impudence of the man and walked away without another word.

He drove to market and learnt of the slaughter of sheep in a nearby village. He thought of what he had seen and decided he would stop this cruel destruction himself. He loaded his twelve bore and filling a cartridge belt with more ammunition, sat in his parlour waiting till the servants were all asleep. Every tick of the old clock by the front door wasted a second and added to his impatience. Midnight struck and he could stand the waiting no longer.

Gathering his dark cloak, he put on his old grey hat and stepped silently out into the yard. Far away he heard the cry of an owl but there was not a sound from the yard or the barns. He made his way to the same spot and waited. The door of the fettler's hut gaped open; he was abroad. Broadmead moved into the meadow nearest to the woods where he had seen the figure and cautiously trod along the edge of the wood. He cocked the gun and his finger caressed the trigger as he moved. A sound in the woods like the snapping of a branch underfoot made him swing towards the hidden depths in the trees. A figure was racing towards him. He crouched; he raised the gun and fired. The blast flashed like a shaft of lightning in that dark space and the noise seemed like thunder. Screaming with pain, the figure stumbled forward and fell at his feet. Broadmead dropped the gun and knelt beside the man. It was Silas.

"Good Christ! What were you doing here?"

But Silas was already dead. The blast had taken him in the chest at short range and his body had taken the full shot. Broadmead walked back to the farm, leaving the body in the bracken at the edge of the wood. There was nothing he could do for the man and the matter had to be passed to the authorities. He waited quietly in the farmhouse till the servants awoke and then called a man to summon the magistrate. When he arrived they went together to the woods and recovered the body of the dead man.

He told of his fear for the cattle and why he went out armed. The inquiry showed Silas had gone into the woods to search for an intruder without telling his employer. The inquest found the death was 'Misadventure'. Broadmead kept to himself his knowledge of the hireling.

When questioned about his movements that night, the Redman shrugged his shoulders and replied: "Just walkin', Mester," and not another word.

Tormented by his secret knowledge and by the death of Silas, Broadmead kept to the house for days. He neglected his usual rounds and even missed the next market day, leaving everything to Jethro, the oldest hand.

"Will you see Mr Farlee?" Bridie asked. "A doctor can maybe help ye?"

He waved her away, knowing that his ailment had no physical cure.

Night after night he wrestled with himself. What could he do? Without proof he was helpless. Gradually he faced the task of confronting the fettler himself and finding the truth. By day he knew the man carried out his duties well enough so to find the truth he must confront him at night outside his dwelling.

"Jethro, I want you with me tonight to check the livestock and poultry with the poultry man." He said he was concerned with the news of the attacks and they must take precautions.

"Bring a net wi'you and a stick."

He did not explain the real reason why they were needed. Jethro arrived at midnight as instructed. Both men set off to the shed where the fettler lived. It was empty. Inside they could see bedding arranged on the floor.

"No bed?" Jethro seemed puzzled. "Looks like a dog's pit." He pointed to a pile of feathers and wool; it looked as if an animal had settled there. The farmer made no comment but simply gripped his cudgel tighter.

The moon was waning and had lost its brightness but there was enough light for the men to find their way to the fields where the cattle were kept. They sat under a hedge and waited.

A fox barked nearby but the men sat still. It barked again, nearer, and Broadmead stirred. Something in the sound was different – more shrill. He looked towards the dark gloom of the wood trying to pierce the shadows. A figure moved quietly out of the trees, tall as a man but crouching forward like a hunting animal.

"Good Christ!" Jethro swung round to face the creature and as he did so the horned mask gleamed at him with its golden eyes.

"Stand off!" shouted the farmer. "We've weapons – be warned!"

The apparition stood stock-still for a second then slowly, so slowly, it lifted its mask and stood erect. Jethro held his net with both hands.

"Go back, you devil – back to your hellish world!"

He raised the net as if to push the Green Man away. But the moonlight fell upon the face from the mask and Jethro dropped the net. Staring out at the men was the vulpine face of a creature with the narrow long jaws of a fox. Its eyes burned with golden fire. It sprang at Jethro – its teeth ripping at his throat – twisting him from side to side as it savaged him. It snarled and red foam dripped from its maw. Broadmead struck out at the creature, time and time again, but its dense fur seemed unharmed. Then it dropped the dying man and turned its eyes upon the farmer. It spoke in a strange voice as if words were being forced through a throat unused to speech.

"You scar the earth with your men and your greed enrages us. Take back this message. There is a price to pay for every sacrilege..."

The terrified farmer fell unconscious to the ground. When he awoke the creature had gone but the reality of what had happened struck him like a blow. Staggering back to the village, he raised the alarm and within minutes a hunt started for the Green Man. They found Jethro's body and a trail of broken branches leading away to the deep forest, but no man could be persuaded to pursue it.

"Call in the militia, Broadmead," said farmer Fenwick. "I want this fiend brought to justice." They did so and combed the forest end to end and set fire to the shed where the creature had lived, but nothing was found.

There were few regulars in the Moonraker bar until the memory of Jethro's death faded. Still, no man would enter the big wood after dark, nor would they speak about the Green Man again. The locals saw how

*

Tombola

Broadmead declined after the death of Jethro and Silas. The farm was neglected and after a few years, it was sold at auction for a pittance. Farmer Broadmead retired to a cottage a distance beyond Belchurch and lived alone. From time to time Fenwick called to see him.

"Will you see the priest? Mayhap he will bring you peace."

Broadmead shook his head. "I'll never rest while that creature still lives in my mind. Can it be we are despoilers of Nature? Are we guilty according to their laws?"

He lived on in this weary state for several years and died alone. The country paid its respects but soon forgot him.

Some said the episode was the superstition of country people who took against a stranger, blaming him for their troubles; but those folk never explained how Jethro died or what or who killed the cattle.

I SHOULD HAVE

Saturday night and the lights were bright.

Jenny said "Rocky's goin' to be there, so you'll come too, right?" She's like that; a bit shy and still wants back up.

"But how can you pull a boy like Rocky when you don't put out?" I said.

"Just come will you? I'll die if that cow Josie flashes her knickers at him."

So I tagged along, got the new lashes out, nicked her sister's push up, and made a bit of an effort. She looked like a check out girl on steroids but you can't say so can you?

"Do I look alright?" She said.

"Yes, let's get going. Spray some Nuit de Paris behind your lugholes and you'll be a princess!" I said.

We arrived just after ten and headed straight for the ladies for a chat. No point in showing out before eleven; well, the boys can't face us before they've had a skinful. Josie was in there, glugging WKD, cos she's basic and giving us evils.

"The cleaners arrived then?"

I slammed her one in the gob for starters and within a second we was clawing and screaming the place down. Jenny, as usual, stood by, hands in her mouth, staring at the two of us.

"Gimme a hand you silly moo, Don't just stand there!" But she did F.A.

By the time the bouncers arrived, the place was crammed, including Rocky and his mates. He took one look at Josie and me and grinned.

"Hen night at the boxing club?" He asked and shoved off back into the bar.

I picked up my bag and peeked in the mirror; Dracula was looking back at me.

Mascara streaking down my cheeks, hair gone Jurassic, tights a mess.

All Jenny could say was; "Oh. Lindy! You look dreadful!" She's a good friend in a crisis.

We did our best to clean me up and went outside. The boys were all in by now and the lights went down, so I reckoned I might get away with it. Then Jenny pulled at me.

"Oh Lindy!" She said, and she began to sob.

Over in the darkest corner, Rocky sat wiping Josie's eyes and putting his arm round her fat shoulders. He stared at me and gave me the finger. Classy!

I grabbed Jenny and made for the door. What's the point of helping your mates?

I should have stayed home and watched Strictly.

HARLEQUIN

It was 2018 and Harlequin was bored. He put aside his mask and carnival clothing and changed shape for fun.

Sitting in a Knightsbridge Costa, he checked over the girls chattering around him. Two blondes in Pashminas, long boots and flicking hair; No. A brunette; hair dye too dark, faux fur coat; constantly on her I-phone; No. The girl with red hair? She arrived carrying her Latte and searched for a seat. He looked up and smiled, moving along the bench seat to make room. At first, she glanced elsewhere but he had chosen carefully and kept space on his table. With a diffident smile, she sat down carefully placing her china mug on the table. He glanced at his Times and then caught her eye.

"Busy time--have you enough room?"

She murmured something in reply which he didn't catch. He noticed her hands were long and thin and the way she held the drink, as if a precious thing, so delicate that it might break if she put it down.

"Much better in a china cup, don't you think? I hate those plastic beakers!"

She looked at him for a second and nodded but she said nothing.

He leant forward, not too far but, just enough to engage her attention and try his best smile--the one he used to show his sincerity. His blue eyes gazed straight into her eyes.

"Can I ask you a question?" He spoke gently and he waited for her reply.

"What is it?" She looked back, curious.

"I have the feeling you are a musician," he said, he held up his hand and smiled again--"don't tell me yet! I want to know if you find that too intrusive."

"I don't mind," she said and put the mug down on the table. "I'm just working in the Art Gallery in Montpellier Street, I'm no musician."

He put on a grimace, showing his even white teeth as he bit his lip. "Oh Dear! I know you are artistic but certain you were musical!"

"How would you know that?"

"Because I'm a natural!" he laughed and ran his hand through his wavy blond hair. "I'm never totally wrong. You must have some connection with music."

"Well, I sing in a choir at home but not down here."

"I knew it, will you allow me to boast, if I say I was part right at least?"

She laughed and he noticed how the corners of her mouth lifted as she smiled exposing her neat white teeth and heart shaped lips.

He moved to leave. It was time to go; first step done. He folded his Times and stood up. She didn't see him slip a paperback book onto the floor near her feet. He smiled again, said goodbye with a wave and made his way out into the Brompton Road. He moved away swiftly once he left the coffee bar, to make sure she could not catch him and return the book on the spot. That would be annoying. He had left his mobile number and assumed name on the fly leaf to set up the next move.

The afternoon went by slowly. He sauntered through Harrods, noting the glitzy displays and vulgarity which he deplored. Once or twice he marked an admiring glance from the glossy women as he wandered from one department to another but his mind strayed to the girl in the coffee bar. It would be more fun to corrupt her than spend time with some rich socialite accustomed to the vices he habitually abused. Sometimes he longed for the bawdy life of the Medici Popes and their rowdy catamites and licentious cardinals. These modern times were tame, but interesting.

On Friday of that week he spent the morning in the Art Galleries of New Bond Street, away from Knightsbridge, but full of the latest trends in expensive art. He bought catalogues for several upcoming exhibitions and studied them. At the Albemarle, he gave one of his cards to the receptionist.

"Yes Mr Harlekan, we will be open for you on Friday, of course." He nodded and left.

On Monday, he scanned the Costa to see if she had returned. She had not rung him to return his book and he wondered if she might have missed it. He went in and sat at his usual place. The clientele seemed identical. He wondered if there was some time warp at work; the blondes and the covens of smart ladies chattering appeared to be the same. Then she walked in. Her auburn hair pinned up on top of her head and her long neck accentuated by pearl earrings. She looked round and saw him and smiled shyly. He waved to her to join him and she hesitated but gathered up her cup and came over.

"I wanted to catch you," she said," I found this book under the table last week. Is it yours?"

"Thank God! I am reviewing it for the Guardian," he lied "I have a deadline!"

He asked her whether she had read it and she shook her head.

She blushed and lowered her eyes in confusion. His eyes glinted with malicious delight as he saw the effect he created.

"No, I didn't forget," she said "I hoped to find you here again, so here it is." She handed over the book without another word.

"Does this mean you forgive me for my intrusive questions?" He laughed and grinned easily to relieve her embarrassment. "Look, I am thrilled you thought of me and so kind of you to return the book yourself. You don't know how much it means."

She sipped her coffee and looked up at him for the first time. He liked her large green eyes and how the light from the room caught the deep red tints in her hair. She really was a prize.

When she got up to leave, he offered to walk with her the few hundred yards as far as Montpellier Street. They spoke about her work in the gallery and the exhibition on show there.

"Look" he said "Can we meet some time this week? I'd like to show you a Paul Klee I've seen on the Albemarle Gallery, which I like. Would you come?"

"To buy?" She said.

"Yes, I have a small collection and enjoy adding to it." He spoke as if it was a matter of minor interest and noted the effect when she opened her eyes with surprise.

"Do come" he said "can you make Friday afternoon?"

"Well, yes I suppose. I could get away at about four."

"It's a date." he said. "I'll come round to the gallery and collect you. I'm James Harlekan, by the way"

"Jane Seymour."

They exchanged mobile numbers and he took her hand as he left, just a moment's contact, but enough to signal his interest. She gave a brief wave and he walked away. The smile on his face was not one he wanted her to see.

Friday morning he chose some expensive jeans and a cashmere polo neck for the occasion. He spent the late morning and lunch at his club and decided to walk through Green Park to Montpellier Street. It was a warm day and the silky air reminded him of other times. Like the day he seduced the Duchess of Alba in 1576-or was it 1578?--and killed the Duke in a duel the following morning. The summer days with Nero at his palace with the Nubian Princesses; what fun there had been and such fearful consequences! Modern times were much quieter but still, there were pleasures to be had.

She was waiting outside the gallery when he arrived. He hurried forward.

"I walked through the park and forgot the time, I'm so sorry!"

"Well, we close early on Friday. Most people have gone away for the week end." People, meant the wealthy Knightsbridge crowd.

They took a taxi to Piccadilly and chatted on the way about favourite painters. She adored Hockney and disagreed about Francis Bacon and they arrived at Albemarle Street in a few minutes. A young man was waiting for them.

"I hope we haven't kept you. Most people want to get away on Friday afternoon."

Harlequin offered his hand and the smart-suited fresh faced young man semi-bowed.

"We always have time for an enthusiastic client." He said and showed the way into the gallery. It was carpeted with fine rugs and the room breathed a mellow atmosphere of luxury. Fine French empire furniture mixed with a few modern pieces decorated the floor and they were conducted through into the gallery itself where an elderly man with a goatee beard awaited them. He wore a grey suit and a Hurlingham Club Tie with its purple garish colours. As if he had known him for years, he greeted Harlequin, pressing his arm in a familiar way.

Champagne and canapes were laid out on a Pembroke table and they were helped to them by the younger man. It was amusing to see the antics of these mortals with their minor cupidity, prostrating themselves for money. Under soft spot light, two paintings, mounted on easels, caught the eye with dazzling colours splashed across the canvas.

"So fine," said the elegant older man, "he took several years to recover from the war, you know."

"But his output was prodigious," said Harlekan, "I prefer his later work and I'm looking for smaller late pieces for my collection."

The old man nodded sagely, "Yes, I understand, so much more sophisticated, would you say?"

"Agreed." He turned to Jane "What do you feel from these two? Do they resonate with you?"

She said "They are museum pieces, not for a small private collection, if I am allowed to say so."

"Of course you can, dear lady, you show a very wise judgement, if I may say so." The old man smiled at her with gritted teeth.

"Anything later?" Harlekan dismissed the two masterpieces with a wave of his hand.

"Well, we are sure to have something to intrigue you within the next few weeks."

Harlequin smiled at this. He recalled the old men in the souks on Casablanca used the same phrase when they had nothing appealing to sell.

"By all means let me know while I am in London." He offered his hand and wished them both good day.

"What conceit!" he said as he escorted Jane across Piccadilly. "Let's wash the taste away with tea in Fortnum's"

She laughed and was relieved that he had valued her opinion and agreed with it.

Soon they were chatting freely and time passed quickly.

"I suppose you have plans to go down to the country this week end?" he dangled the prospect of further meetings with a smile which quickened her heart.

She blushed and Harlequin noted the charming colour that came to her cheeks. For a single second he felt a twinge of compassion for this immaculate young woman, but the impulse to torment and win was too strong to resist.

He took her hand and held it gently. "I can't imagine what is happening to me" he said "I feel as if we've known each other for a long time, yet there are so many things I want to learn about you."

She looked into his wide blue eyes and left her hand in his while he spoke.

"Could we meet again soon?"

"I don't know what to say" she said, "we are strangers; I suppose yes," -here she looked down--" I would like that too."

He held her hand for a second then released it.. He busied himself with the tea things, making sure he was inept so she would take over. Predictably, she enjoyed the simple task and he smiled appreciatively.

"Well, am I too pressing if I ask, would like to go to see the new film at the Academy tomorrow night?"

She smiled, "I'd love to. I wanted to catch it and haven't had a chance."

"That's wonderful," he said and dropped the subject for the moment.

They talked about her family in Wiltshire; Daddy at the stud farm and mother as a JP in the local magistrate court. Then he told her lies about his foreign background and banking interests which kept him travelling most of the year. She accepted all of it and he enjoyed the fantasy as she gazed at him with innocent credulous eyes. When the time came to leave, he hailed a taxi and she gave her address in South Ken. On the way, he made arrangements to pick her up at seven for the show at nine p.m. He gave her a peck on the cheek as she left the cab and she waved as he pulled away.

He was comfortable. Pleased with progress, he gave the cabbie instructions to drop him at Shepherd's Market off Park Lane. This was an area he had known since Georgian Times. Of course it had changed! But the gambling houses and high class brothels still flourished. Just the clientele was different. Instead of dandies in silken hose and blowsy tarts, there were Arabs with limitless cash and their entourages. The girls were different too; cleaner and more luxurious.

He knocked at the door of number 17 and a black man opened the door carefully, then he smiled broadly.

"Welcome back Mr Harlekan. Good to see you! Your usual table?"

"Thank you Bob, can you get me some company?"

He spent the rest of the night with two beautiful Russian girls and plenty of white powder to sustain him. Strangely, in the still moments of the highs, he felt it was all too familiar, too repetitive and stale. He left at three o'clock and made his way back to Albany off Piccadilly to sleep a dreamless sleep. He awoke at four in the afternoon and ruminated on what to wear and how to arrange his evening entertainment. His flat had been furnished to his taste. He had always enjoyed the voluptuous silks and colourful drapes from the Ottoman palaces of Persia. They brought back memories of exotic nights, wild escapades and perfumed women, captives for pleasure. He ordered new sheets of silk and chilled champagne for the evening. Then he bathed and chose his clothes with care.

At seven precisely, he arrived at her door, a single rose in his hand. She stood in the doorway and held it like a precious jewel marvelling at its glowing colour.

"It's a summer rose from Provence," he said "I sent specially for you."

She smiled and offered her cheek shyly as gesture of thanks.

"So lovely!"

His heart gave a strange skip. What was wrong? He ignored it.

She wore a simple dress of plain blue with a belt of black leather around her slim waist. Her hair was loose and as she moved it flowed around her pale face in a glossy wave. He handed her into the cab and he watched her graceful figure as she sat besides him. Something was wrong. His fingers tremored as he sat alongside her; he gripped the door handle of the cab to steady himself. She chatted excitedly about the film and never noticed how silent he was. When they reached

The Curzon, he got out first. He felt better as he touched the ground. Nothing to worry about, then.

The film was a black comedy created by some avant-garde Italian director. She laughed in all the right places and he enjoyed the fact that they both saw the crux of the film in unison. At one point, she rested her head against his shoulder and her soft scented hair brushed against his cheek. It was a gesture he had never felt before--a natural touch, not a deliberate move as he had done a thousand times before. Something strange and yet exciting. Again, the little throb made his heart beat out of time. He became a little dizzy and sweat gathered on his forehead. He wiped it away and sat upright. She touched his hand, concerned,

"Are you alright?" she said, "you seem uneasy?"

"No. I'm fine. It's just a little hot in here."

It soon passed and they enjoyed the rest of the film. As they left, she took his arm naturally and he sensed the warmth of her body next to his as they strolled towards Piccadilly. It felt good and he returned her smile as they made their way among the Saturday night crowds enjoying the late summer evening.

"Where are we going?" She asked

"I thought you might like a bite to eat at Albany, it should be fun on a warm evening."

"Where's that? I haven't heard of it. Is it a restaurant?"

"Well not exactly, just the most special place that few people in London know about."

He smiled his special dazzling smile and tucked in her arm protectively.

"Wait and see."

The Albany is set back from Piccadilly in a courtyard with elaborate gates away from the bustling street.

Built as apartments in the early nineteenth century, it remains, perhaps, the most exclusive address in London. A uniformed porter saluted as they came in to the oval courtyard and Jane wondered how she had missed the elegant building which she must have passed a hundred times. Lights gleamed from behind doors of mahogany and glass; beyond were Persian carpets and gleaming brass fittings.

Jane stiffened a little as she wondered at the luxury of the scene. She had imagined some dining Club with a noisy society crowd but this was all in exquisite taste but so silent and dignified, a little daunting.

"Come and see where I live." He said and threw open the door to his apartment. They walked in and she gazed at the opulent drapes and bright colours of the room with some surprise. It was exotic and luxurious at the same time; as if she had passed out of modern London into a world of Arabian Nights.

"It's fascinating," she said and he took her arm and guided her to one of the sofas arranged around the fireplace.

"I can be lonely here," he said, "but it suits me, I have to write, you know."

He spoke as if it was a burden that weighed him down, "Deadlines can be a curse!"

He took up a phone on a side table and rang for room service. Without consulting her, he ordered cold salmon with mayonnaise and thin white bread.

"Are you hungry?" he smiled and kissed her hair as he passed by on the way to the kitchen. She felt nervous but excited.

"Yes, I'm famished!"

He returned with a bottle of dry sherry, cold from the fridge and poured two tall glasses of the pale yellow wine. They drank and discussed the film while waiting for the meal. Gradually, she relaxed and began to enjoy the ambience of luxury and isolation which the apartment provided. When the meal arrived, they both ate with appetite and laughed a lot.

Harlequin joined her on the sofa as he filled her glass a second time and helped her to more food. She sat close to him and afterwards, he played a little on the piano in the alcove of the room. She told him how much she enjoyed it and asked him to play something romantic.

"Will you come and sit beside me, to inspire me?" He said and he recalled a night when he had seduced one of Edward the Seventh's mistresses in this very apartment with the same ploy. He had to leave London for a season as a result, but the scandal had been worth it.

She did sit next to the piano stool and he had the chance to see her in the warm lamplight. Her hair was soft and waved in a natural way unlike the sophisticated styles of the women he was used to. Her skin was radiant, but with a glow of good health and her green eyes reflected the light in such a way that he saw his own reflection clearly in them.

He began to play something he recalled but could not remember its name; she got up and danced, moving gently to the rhythm. "I know this," she said "It's Ivor Novello."

He watched her as he played, her feet tracing a delicate pattern across the carpeted floor; she was enchanting. She had the grace and a lightness of spirit which only existed in an innocent soul and was spellbinding. He played on with some difficulty but his mind began to falter. He gasped for breath and his fingers would not follow his commands.

She stopped dancing immediately and ran to him. He stumbled from the piano and she helped him to the sofa. His face was ash grey and he sat back against her arm as she cradled him. "What happened?" She cried "Is there something I can do?"

He shook his head, although his mind was in turmoil. He knew what the trouble was affecting him.

"You must go," he said, "Forgive me, I have to be alone tonight. Can you ask the porter for a cab?"

"But I must stay; I can't leave you like this!"

He moaned, with every word she said. He writhed with pain and she trembled as she held him in her arms, feeling desperate to do something to help. He knew that every minute she stayed would be like a torment. Her innocence and untouched beauty was like a caustic poison scorching his soul. He turned his face away and felt the transformation begin.

"Go! I said go!"

He looked down and the shame of deceit welled up inside him. She hesitated, uncertain how to deal with this stern unexpected order. Gathering all his strength, he stood and turned towards her.

"Now GO! The Comedy is over!"

She shrank at the sight of his face. A mask covered his eyes and his face was a pallid narrow shape with painted lips and pointed teeth. His head was covered in a black skull cap and he stared with a luminous glare. Then he crouched down on the floor and sobbed.

He knew that whatever pain he inflicted, he suffered eternally; knowing pure innocence was sublime and unobtainable.

PLAYING THE GAME

Monte Carlo? Listen! I'll tell you about Monte Carlo.

I'd set it up good. Everything seemed just right; the timing, the punters; the setting. How could it fail? The casino was full and the croupiers on duty. The Cote d'Azur never looked brighter.

I planned this for over a year. Finding the right player is always the difficult part. I need glamour and skill; star quality and good knowledge of casino games. After months searching the gaming houses of South America, I found Mario in a flophouse in Buenos Aires. He was thin and dirty but I could see his style had not deserted him. He still possessed that spark he had as a first class gigolo. He smiled when I outlined the game to him and I'd found the man.

Alexia was never a problem. Her auburn hair and full breasted figure had been a feature of six or seven magazine covers before she fell out with Harvey Weinstein and lost her contract in Hollywood. When I rang her she was 'resting' in a motel in downtown San Diego, a long way from the bright lights. She had been 'resting 'for quite a few years.

"You sweet man! Of course I can make it to Monte! I'm having a break from filming and would be happy to help. What's the gig?"

I outlined the plot and she jumped at the idea; two days later she was in Nice looking at dress shops at my expense.

As they sauntered along the boulevard leading to the Grand Casino, I knew they looked the part. Mario wore his tuxedo with elan, his long black hair pulled back into a shiny knot like a bull-fighting torero and his slim figure completed the image. He smoked a cheroot in a jade holder and strolled with the studied ease of a rich sportsman. Alexia took his arm and they made the picture of a celebrity couple as they walked up the long flight of steps to the main entrance. I was their chauffeur in black cap and dark suit, carrying an aluminium briefcase.

"Good evening," The major domo bowed and presented an orchid to the beautiful Alexia, "May I ask you to sign in and I will take you to a table."

His smile was warm but his eyes were like flints. I warned Mario that the staff would check on them and I provided him with the name of a Spanish bull fighter who was fighting in Mexico at that time.

A dark suited clerk took me aside and examined the briefcase; it contained one hundred thousand US dollars. His fingers flickered over the notes like the touch of a butterfly, then he nodded to me and I closed the lid. We were in.

The money belonged to me. If you think I have a hundred thousand dollars -think again! It was made for me by Luigi Macron in Lille. Of course it would not fool a Treasury Official but good enough for a quick show at the guichet of a casino and it worked perfectly. The clerk issued a chitty for chips to that figure and I drew them from the counter and handed them ostentatiously to 'my Boss.' They made a pretty pile as he sat at the big roulette table. I positioned Alexia at the far end of the same table with a few chips so that when she leant forward to play, she accidentally showed her cleavage. When she did, no man could watch Mario and no woman would take her steely eyes off her.

My role was to spend time in the basement like a good servant, chatting and gossiping with the others. I held the briefcase tightly since the Company would not accept responsibility for punter's assets. I sat apart and no one watched me as I pinpointed the fusebox for the lighting system. The plan was to switch off the interior lighting and 'top hat' the winning numbers at the best table.

Give me a moment and I'll explain.

If you can quickly add extra chips to the winning counters, then you can make thirty five times the stake on each coup. It takes quick hands and good timing but two working together make it easy. How do you make the switch? Kill the lights for a second and it's done.

We had set it up for midnight plus five minutes and I watched the clock.

Just before I moved to the switch I felt something was wrong.

The staff around me began to gather round the screens showing the gaming tables. Then one screen zoomed in on the table where Mario sat. His hands filled the screen; in his fingers you could see three 100 dollars chips ready to flick onto winning numbers as soon as the lights went out.

What could I do? What would anyone do? I pulled the switch.

There was uproar in the basement and I slipped upstairs to the Gaming Salon, holding the briefcase. Within a few seconds, the emergency lighting came on and I confronted bedlam. What had been the sophisticated social scene, was a madhouse. At every table glamorous women old and young were grappling with each other or stretched across the green baize to reach any chips still lying on the table. A man in a wheelchair barged through the crowd to reach one of the Baccarat tables, scooping up chips on his way.

Alexia? I found her under the gaming table, half naked, struggling with an ancient crone who managed to snatch the chips Alexia had pinched from the croupier.

There was no sign of Mario. His chair was empty and his pile of chips had disappeared. The Casino staff were struggling through the swarming mass to reach the tables and rushing to close the doors to the Gaming rooms. I squeezed out just before they closed and ran downstairs with my briefcase.

Before I got my head together, a burly Gendarme grabbed me by the arm and shoved me out into the street.

"What's up Monsewer?" Says I,

He gave me a sickly smile, "About five years, I reckon." He pointed to the briefcase and the fake dollars.

"But I can explain," I said. He shoved me into a van and we drove off.

As we passed through the square, I peered out of the window. There, at a café, sat Mario with a large plastic bag; it bulged with what I knew to be casino chips. He looked content.

It all depends on the staff you pick. I struck out this time but in a few years I'll be out and give it another go. You've got to keep playing the game, haven't you?

SACRIFICE TO KALI

Sena squeezed out, past the tree trunk jamming the door. He looked up at the crushed roof with the great tree pressing down on it. A strange high sound like a voice came from the ruin and after some time he realized it was the house moaning under the weight of the tree. Slowly the walls buckled and at last, the structure collapsed. Only the brick chimney and the oven remained intact. The wind had lasted three days and he expected some damage, but not this. Bangladeshi knew how the great winds called The Brides of Kali visited these shores every year. He, like his father, prepared for winds that raged for days.

"Never build high" his father had said "be humble before the rage of Kali."

*

Two weeks before, the village elders decided to take the women and children away from the village. Carts and a bus rented from the company in Barisal, carried them off to the hills above the valley. Tents and shelters were set up for those who had no family to protect them. Jitna and the two children lodged with her uncle while Sena stayed down at the coast with all the men.

"Make sure you check the animals" she had said "or the stray dogs will get in. We'll be back home soon."

The children laughed and waved as they climbed into the bus.

The men set to, battening their roofs and tying down the cages which kept the animals and poultry. Jaffit, his neighbour had a goat.

"Sena, my brother, your house is brick and your yard is walled...."

"No!" shouted Sena "last year the goat smashed my gate and ran away. It will not happen again."

Jaffit turned away and spat into the dust. He said nothing.

The Head man had ruled the harm was natural and awarded no compensation but it rankled in Sena's heart and he did not forget.

For the next six days they fished as before, but with an eye towards the horizon where clouds bloomed high above the sea. They noticed the waves diminished and the swell did not rock their boats as usual. Yet the fish still jumped and twirled as they were drawn into the nets. Among the men, tempers frayed as the tension increased. When would the winds start? Had they sent the women away too early? Time in the deserted village seemed endless, with no good food or entertainment.

Then the winds struck.

Outside Sena's house the lanterns swayed in the branches of the great tree. A gust, strong and sudden, blasted in and tossed the lanterns out into the street. He scrambled to catch a table which flew away, sending the bottles and dishes spinning and rolling away down the yard. The dogs lurking under the table scuttled away whimpering like children.

He pulled down the shutters against the growing wind and went indoors. The familiar howl of the tempest rose as it gathered strength. There was nothing to be done but stay inside and check for breakages.

Then he heard the voice of the sea. Like a rumble at first, then growing louder and more menacing.

He scanned the ocean from his upper window, peeping out through a chink in the shutter. From there he could see as far as the beach where his boat lay. Everything was still, but the roaring went on.

Anil, his neighbour shouted up to him: "Can you see the waves?"

Sena: "No big waves just the sound of the wind."

But what was happening? The sea crept away from the land and dragged sand and stones down the beach with a rumbling noise. His boat yanked at its moorings straining to join the ebbing water and escape to the sea. Sena pushed out of the shutters that covered the door to the house and raced to the shore.

Halfway there, the first wave returned. It rose like a green wall flecked with timbers and debris and stormed up the street with a hiss. There was no surf, just the barrier of water pushing and whirling through the houses and trees. It caught him and threw him down, then rushed past him to find another victim. Salt and grit filled his mouth and water filled his lungs, driving the air from his body. He flung himself into the shelter of a broken cabin, which stood half submerged like a wooden outpost. He gasped and coughed to gain his breath. Soon his protection crumpled feebly into the mass of water and was snatched away by the sea.

The old tree in the garden was fighting to stay upright in front of the house, as if daring the flood to take it. Then slowly, so slowly, the great trunk began to tip as the water pushed against it like a battering ram. It came down on the roof of the house, piercing it like a giant knife.

*

Sena clambered back inside the ruined building and scurried to the kitchen space. He felt safer where the brick oven still stood among the floating wreckage of the house. He climbed on top and hugged himself to try to bring some warmth into his body. Outside, the noise of the sea and the wind dropped away. Every few minutes a thud shook the building as some large object shouldered its way past. Within an hour, the sounds change. Instead of the clamour of the sea and the howl of the wind, he sensed a different, quieter murmuration. It was like a snake stretching its slimy body along the side of his house. It moved from the mountains towards the sea. Through the broken doors and battered walls, a stream of brown mud, viscous and smelling of rotting vegetation coiled through the debris. Sena jumped up and stood helpless on the oven. The dark mass spilled over the floor and climbed the walls, sometimes bubbling as it engulfed a chair or the table. He stood stock still and prayed to Kali to spare him. Then the evil slime stopped and while it settled, he was left perched on the brick oven. As it ceased to move a skin of dark matter formed on its surface with a sinister sheen.

Cautiously, he climbed down from his perch. His legs were engulfed with the thick earthy mixture up to his thighs so that he moved as if toiling against a fast running stream. Objects hidden by the mud checked his progress but he got to the doorway without injury. Beyond the fallen tree there was nothing to see in the yard. The cages and outbuildings had vanished. Outside in the road, a half-submerged bundle lay a few feet away. Sena approached it. It was a body of a man. He turned his face away, not wishing to add to the weight of catastrophe pressing down on him. Jaffit's house opposite had gone. Just the broken strands of a Palm tree showed where the yard had been although the mud held shapes which might have been broken walls.

He called out several times but there was no answer. It was clear that his house with its wall and tree was the only structure to survive, even if a ruin.

Down by the shore were a few boats in a strange conjunction. Three fishing dhows crammed together as if seeking company to ward off the storm. When he got close he saw they were crushed against each other and wrecked.

Then his eyes scanned the foreshore. Could it be true? Was the shape at the end of the beach his own fishing boat? He raced towards it and fell on his knees when he realized it was his very own skiff. It sat upright in the sand, trim as usual but discoloured by mud and sand. He bowed his head and prayed to Kali the Cruel One. She had taken her sacrifices but spared him.

After a few minutes, he rose and began the tasks that he and his forefathers had done for centuries. The village had to be rebuilt; his family re-united; the dead buried. He knew man must carry on and defy the Gods.

INCIDENT AT CASA VERDE

Monroe heard the noise of the guns from a distance and broke away from his tasks to find out what happened. Sporadic gunfire meant an Indian attack but who they were attacking was a mystery. He knew of no outfit in this part of the Plain except the Casa Verde and they were miles off.

Following an arroyo which led towards the sounds, he reached the massacre as it occurred. There was nothing he could do but he waited, hoping maybe he might help any survivors. As the sun went down he approached the silent wagon. All around lay the corpses of the butchered animals -wagon horses, two cattle and a dog. The stench of carrion caught his throat although this was not the first time he had seen such a sight. At first sight, there were no bodies of men. But in the faded light he realized something was tied to each wheel of the wagon. Even Monroe bit his lip as he saw what had been done to the men who died at the hands of the savages.

It was next morning at sun up he made his mistake. If the raid was over, he reckoned, the war party would be miles away. A cook fire gave little smoke and hot food was essential after days of hard rations. He had almost finished up and dowsed the fire when the arrow thudded into his thigh.

In a rush he reached his horse and half dragged half mounted in a second. A lone Apache had returned to the wagon for some reason and surprised him. The blood from the wound dripped inside his boot so he eased his leg out of the stirrup. The pain went on but the warm trickle seemed better than the stiffness he had gotten used to.

After an hour he left the hard stone path and slowly weaved between the mesa trees and clumps of cedar wood to the lower plain. The hard trail jarred his wound and he was glad to reach the pampas where the going improved. He broke off the feathers and managed to pull the arrow through. The pony was ringed in sweat and foam streamed from her mouth as she struggled on. His guess was she would never make Casa Verde without a rest. They had to stop. Faint and in pain he slumped from the saddle and slipped down into the shade. Just ten minutes -just a short break for himself and the horse.

Something jerked him awake. A warrior in full paint was searching the scrub about 30 yards away. His pinto grazed nearby but neither seemed aware of the cowboy or his horse. The sun was high and he knew he lost precious hours in sleep. Could he reach his rifle in time? He moved slowly towards the saddle pack but the Apache ran screaming in his direction. With trembling fingers, the cowboy levered a shell in to his rifle. Before he could fire, the Indian was clawing at his hands and grappling for the gun. Releasing the weapon, he drew his skinning knife and rammed it into the naked gut of his attacker.

The Indian fell, turning on the knife as it thrust into his belly. He screamed like a wild animal as blood streamed from his body splashing over his attacker and down into the ground beneath him.

Monroe had worked for Casa Verde for three years now, riding the edge of range looking for strays. The solitary life suited him and he stayed out for days on end -living off game and the meagre rations he drew when he went back to the Ranch. The Apache didn't bother him normally,they grazed their herds and lived like him.

But now things were changing, a war party had formed and begun to roam the frontier between Casa Verde and Mexico.Magwa, son of the Ogarro Apache chief, spent too long herding mustangs for the tribe and watching for wolves. He was twenty two years old and still unblooded by combat.

Why did the Chief believe a warrior would exist like this? If the Elders could not see the weakness in herding like whitemen, then he must set out himself and bring others with him to master the Plains as they had done for many years. His brother Chaqua joined him and several other young men who had horses. The band took pride in living outside the village and foraging their own supplies. For days the band hunted buffalo along the High Mesa and honed their killing skills by challenging the great beasts of the prairie.

One morning, they fell upon a solitary wagon making for the Mexican border. Surrounding the party, they stayed out of range until the guns stopped firing and the whitemen stood silent. One of them came forward unarmed as if to speak with him. He rode him down before the man said a word. The others took this as the sign to move in and within minutes the group of pioneers was dead. From the wagon they picked up food and took the rifles as trophies.

That had been two days before.

Monroe's Appaloosa ran for more than six hours but at last dropped exhausted. The pony could not carry him further and he had to end it. For a long minute he reflected how she served him well for three years and he owed her his life. With regret, he slowly drew his knife and cut her quickly, not daring to use the rifle.

Sitting beneath the narrow shadow of a tree cactus, Monroe pondered his options. He had to move on, but which way? He checked his rifle and water bottle -there were shells and water. His wound was now old and crusted with a scab of blood, painful in a dull way but he reckoned he could walk for a bit. The only thing to do was to keep going east towards Casa Verde. He hoped to come across some strays trapped in one of the culverts along the way.

The sun stood high above him as he trudged forward. The heat struck down like a hammer on his head and shoulders. After an hour of slow agony he knew he would never make it to shelter. Dropping down behind a granite outcrop he gave himself to the wonder of sleep, free of pain. He remained there till dusk when the cool air from the Sierras began to blow away the heat of the day.

Waking with a start, he sensed another presence nearby. Nuzzling in beneath the rock, a mustang was searching for feed or water. Monroe knew full well these wild horses were herd animals and never roamed alone. He opened his flask and poured a little water onto the flat rock surface. He kept stock-still as the animal nuzzled then scooped up the liquid. Monroe talked quiet words to the horse such as every wrangler knows and slowly he handled the beast till it stayed quiet in his company. Stiffly, he rose and with his hand on its mane and leaning on its flank, he stepped out from the rocky shelter.

In the moonlight he saw other horses, some grazing and others still. As he appeared, some raised their heads in alarm but the mustang with him seemed to calm their instincts. From the centre of the herd a voice shouted a curse as the horses shifted.

Monroe hollered: "Be easy, help me."

A figure rose out of the ground some twenty feet away. "Keep still-drop your gun or I'll drop you" A harsh voice and a dark figure moved slowly towards him. Light shimmered on the silver barrel of a handgun. Monroe showed him his wounded thigh and told of his Indian encounters. The wrangler was a lean tall man called Wyatt.

"Sure as hell you're the luckiest man in New Mexico-I only came over here to graze and move 'em straight down to Fort Victory. Not stayin' more'n one night in this damn'd place."

Wyatt looked at the wound and saw the arrow head had passed clean through the thigh.

"My, My" he said "nothin' I can do -best clean it and leave it alone."

He poured water from his canteen over the wound.

"What you goin' to do now ?" Monroe asked "Apache is scouting me for real."

Wyatt scratched his beard and sniffed the wind.

"Let's us get the hell away from here leastways"

They decided to strike out for Fort Victory at once. Their direction took them south east away from Apache country. Monroe kept the mustang who found him---he reckoned it was a lucky charm and its easy action spared his leg somewhat. It followed the lead mare willingly. He carried his rifle on a sling across his back and held on with a neck strap. Bareback was no pleasure but he had no choice. The two men hardly exchanged one word as the day wore on. Wyatt was everywhere, hazing in the young and chiding the lead mare as he moved them on. Monroe kept looking at the plains behind them, straining to see any dust.

That evening, they staked out the leaders near a thin stream running down from the Sierras. Monroe took first watch. He felt glad to do some duty for this laconic man who spoke few words but had shown kinship with him.

Apart from the cries of the night jar and the yap of coyotes, the night seemed still. The mustangs were his best alarm -if any animal approached -human or beast -they would spook at once.

By midnight he switched places with Wyatt and snuck under the blanket. He slept deeply and woke with the cold of dawn seeping into his bones. There was no sign of Wyatt. The mustangs were scattered and just the lead mare stood tethered nearby, with wild eyes and straining at the hobble.

He knew what the Apache had done. They intended to hunt him in their own special way -by torment and slaying every means of survival. The loss of Wyatt meant that poor man had suffered torture just because he helped their enemy.

Monroe screamed and swore with anger but within minutes faced the hard fact that his survival now lay in his own hands and he gave little more time to the man who died. He took the mare away from his location. Her whinnying for the herd was a constant danger to him. He walked her with difficulty to the rocky outcrop above the camp. He circled the rocks, leaving no prints. Below him the rest of the small herd had returned to the spot they shared the night before.

There was a gap in the stones where he got a sighting of the camp and waited. The day grew long, the shadows moved slowly. By late evening he dozed upright but a small sound from below brought him back to life instantly. Below him were three Apache warriors, shining with war paint and sniffing the air near the dead fire.

Only three? Monroe realized the hunt had become personal, not a contest for the general tribe. He took his rifle quietly in his hands and caressed its walnut stock. One shot and a painted warrior was spinning downwards into the dirt. Before he could reload the scene below transformed. Mustangs scattered and two Indians dived into the scrub. Monroe fired again and one of the men stopped moving for a second then snaked away into the shadows leaving a trace of dark blood behind him.

He reloaded and turned to examine the cold rocks all around him. Any attack would show in silhouette above him so he pointed the rifle that way. Time passed and the silence of the prairie was suffocating. Like a leopard, Magwa sprang down on him in a mighty leap from above. Monroe's gun barked and the shot hit something but did nothing to stop the rushing attack. Knife in hand, the warrior flung himself at Monroe and lifted him off the ground with the force of his leap. They skidded together down the slope, the cowboy under the body of the Apache, twisting in a spiral of hate as they each tried to free an arm to strike. Monroe felt the slime of blood on Magwa's right arm and twisted it to force it down. His gun had vanished and he could not reach his knife. All his strength went into gripping his enemy in a strangle hold with one arm round his neck and with the other grasping for the Indian's knife. Gradually the strength drained from the arm of the Indian as he struggled for life, but Monroe still locked him in a death embrace for several minutes. Shaking with exhaustion, at last he relaxed and the body of the Apache slid lifeless to the ground.

He climbed back to his hideout and recovered his rifle. The Repeater was still loaded. He limped down to the floor of the canyon. The blood trail snaked like a dark ribbon in the moonlight. It stopped at a brush cover some twenty yards from the campsite. He flushed out the last of the Apache brothers, Chaqua,. His eyes pleaded for mercy and he spoke in a tongue which seemed to beg for his life. Monroe shot him twice; once for Wyatt and once for the joy of it. He did not bury him, knowing that the Apache believed a warrior unburied never reached The Great Prairie. Their bodies would be picked clean by coyotes.

He took the mare and turned slowly eastwards. Within a day he reached the Casa. As he limped into the hacienda there was a commotion but he got down by himself and half fell into the bunkhouse.

"Where in hell have you bin?" they all wanted to know, but he was too weary to relate it all to the crew. He just said "I met some Injuns and got away."

It was three days before he sat astride a horse and his leg always gave him gyp when it rained, but he went back to the range without another word. He looked for the body of Wyatt, as a Christian should, but he never found a bone of his body to bury.

THE CLUB TIE

(MCC is the Middlesex Cricket Club the
exclusive club of Lord's cricket ground.)

It was in September 1989 I met Gilbey at the Plaza Hotel
in Bangkok. He rang me to say he was the new rep for
Tudor Gin in the Far East and would I like a drink?

The Plaza Hotel was large and flashy. Flaky gold
paint was everywhere. The red plush banquettes sagged
wearily from years of hard use. Dusty chandeliers
drooped overhead, lending a faint hint of a glittering
past. The girls who lingered in the Director's Bar were
the type who liked you on sight, if you were loaded.
They looked pretty under the dim light. They never
improved on closer acquaintance.

As I waited in a booth, a Gin Fizz in my hand, I saw
this figure pause at the bar, looking about for somebody.
A thin man about six feet tall wearing a suit which had
been Savile Row but was now Skid Row, with missing
buttons and frayed cuffs. He wore a Panama hat with
a greasy headband. It sat on the back of his head
exposing his large balding forehead. The striking note
of his outfit was that he wore a grubby stiff collar and
tie. The tie was an MCC tie although the strong colours
had faded and it was spotted with various stains of
different hues.

I looked over in an enquiring way and he moved
down the room towards me swaying and weaving on
his long legs.

He reminded me of a baby giraffe taking its first
steps. In his hand he carried a paper shopping bag.

"Lovely to meet you" he said and he held out his hand, tilting just a little. His hand felt moist and hot and I made an effort not to wipe my fingers on my trousers after our handshake.

"Thought I'd search you out cos I'm new to Bangkok and people say you know everyone here."

It was, at least, a frank introduction and a true one. I had lived there for twenty years working with several different regimes and making a quiet profit from each one of them. I knew quite a bit about the locals.

He saw my cocktail and he clicked his fingers at a passing waiter.

"Same again for the Maestro and a large one for me"

I spoke for the first time: "Is this a good pitch for your sales?"

He grinned. "Lord, No! They sent me here to wither on the vine, me Boy. Our Gin is foul...wouldn't touch it if I was you. But some of the locals sup it up like kittens, so no need to work."

This was the first time I had been called "Me Boy" since I was a teenager but there was a glitter in his eye, He was horrible but watchable at the same time, a tropical Svengali.

Lowering his voice to an intimate level he put his mouth close to my ear. I smelt that Gin on his breath.

"They say the girls here will do anything for a US dollar."

"I wouldn't know" I said, although I knew Craisie Maisie, standing at the bar, specialised in massage and extras.

The waiter brought our drinks and we chatted for a while before he pulled from his paper bag, a huge 2 litre bottle of his Tudor Gin.

"Put it away for God's sake, you'll get me barred from here" I snorted.

"Just try it" he urged "after a while you get used to it."

He was an expert at siphoning gin from hidden bottle to glass and we both had a large one. I mixed mine with the remains of my original drink and the effect seemed ok. He had knocked off the original drink and had nothing to drown the taste. He downed it in two gulps.

"I like this place" he said "Got a touch of class."

He took in the bar girls and the fading gilt furnishings with an expansive look like a rajah surveying his palace.

"What's it cost to stay here?"

"About four dollars an hour" I said "but no one stays more than two hours, if you get my meaning."

He chortled and swigged his glass, eyeing the girls intently.

"Maybe I can get a room and do a deal with the manager to stay on."

He raised himself with a slow practised effort as if the task was a difficult one.

"Hold my bottle would you?"

He moved slowly towards the bar as if he was treading through thick jungle grass and reached the bar.

"I want a suite of rooms-your very best and be quick about it"

The fat barman looked impassively at him and said nothing. He pointed his finger at the office near the front of the hotel.

Gilbey disappeared in that direction leaving me with a huge bottle of gin hidden under my table. I was trapped and if I wanted to leave there was no explanation for the bottle. I sat, curious to see what happened next.

Ten long minutes passed without a sign of him. I began to think he had left me with the baby, or rather, the gin bottle, and sloped away.

But then I heard sounds coming from the hall. Raised voices and excitable cheers, not threats and screams, Marching through the hall was Gilbey arm in arm with the surly local manager. In all my time he'd never said a civil word to me.

The man was singing some gross song about The Foggy Foggy Dew and Gilbey was harmonising in a gargling sort of voice.

"Hoo Hoo!" He shouted "You'll never guess! William here is a member."

"What the hell are you talking about?"

"I just told you" he tried to show some patience. "He's a member of MCC"

"Yes" said the manager" I've been a member for years. Come up to my apartment and we'll celebrate."

I was mystified but keen to share in the secret, so I followed them up, as did Craisie Maisie and a couple of the bar girls. The 2 litre bottle came up with me. Long into the night and the early dawn, we partied with the girls who brought a few friends up to entertain us. The gin soon disappeared and we moved on to Arak and ate curry from a communal dish.

One hundred cocktails later I looked at the badge hung up on the wall of William's room.

It read "MCC ...Motor Cycle Club Bangkok."

I looked at Gilbey, he smiled and gave me the faintest of winks.

ESCAPE FROM SYRIA

As the bus drew up at the Hungarian border, Faid realized that his chance of getting into Germany had gone. A Border guard in a helmet stood by the driver and shouted "Passports Quick! Quick! "The front passengers began to fumble for their documents-- some in a genuine search-others pretending and hoping vainly to plead with the guard. Watching the sour expression on the man's face Faid knew he had to do something or be arrested.

He slipped from his seat to the back row, squeezing in between the three passengers already seated there. With a quick twist the emergency door opened and he was out, through the hedge, running fast and swerving through the fir trees. From the road the sound of shouting and movement followed him as pushed on but when he stopped to rest, no one was on his track and he was alone in the depth of this forest; but he was still in Serbia.

*

Six weeks before, in Aleppo, Mr Rashid the headmaster summoned the staff to discuss the crisis.

"Last night, my brother was taken" said one.

"They want my son, I cannot stay" said another.

They all looked down and then someone spoke, after an awkward pause,

"But you, Faid, you have no family.

He said nothing. It was as if he was the accused and sentence had been passed.

He smiled weakly and nodded. It was true. He was the latest teacher to arrive and he understood the fear that made these family men tremble.

"So be it, I will stay."

He realized if he left, the school closed and the insurgents had won.

Within a day, Faid said goodbye to the other teachers and began his lonely task.

In a swirl of dust, two days later, a pick-up truck loaded with masked men drove into the schoolyard... One of the men carrying an AK47 strolled over to the class under the trees. He wore dark glasses and a scarf over his face. Faid wondered why a Jihadist needed to hide his face.

"Who is in charge?" The tone was casual and arrogant; the man curled one hand round the sling of the gun.

Faid nodded to the man; "I am the only teacher here-the others have gone."

"Well, we will take boys for the cause and make men of them, inshalla"

"But they are only fourteen, they know nothing of war."

The masked man said "All the more reason to train them. Come! Get out of my way!" He stepped in front and motioned to his men to take the boys. Seven were pulled from the group and herded towards the truck.

"Stop!" Faid shouted "Their parents are good Muslims. They must be told what you do."

The masked man said nothing but levelled his gun at him and flicked the safety.

Then he turned and got into the truck. The boys looked back, some of them realised the meaning of what had happened. One or two began to cry, others smiled as if embarking on an adventure but most sat dumb as cattle.

It's hopeless. Faid reflected *I cannot stay in these conditions. If I can get to Europe I will be human again.*

The last of his savings went to the man with a van travelling to Turkey. He took nothing with him and started the long trek to Germany, following a trail set by thousands. This bus was through Serbia was to be the last stage into the European Union.

*

After so many hours in the bus it felt good to be in the open air. The afternoon sun penetrated the gloom as he trudged on hoping it was towards the frontier. Within an hour he reached a track leading out of the trees. There were a few tyre marks on it and he reckoned he would find some shelter or even a hut somewhere.

By the time he had walked about ten kilometres he began to doubt his calculations. The faint sound of a motor coming from behind made him stop. The truck was old, dirty and piled with bags on the open cargo deck. He waved and it stopped about five metres away.

The driver was a big man wearing a sack over his shoulders and he examined Faid through thick glasses. He leaned out of the open cab, a shotgun slung across his back. He said nothing but he gestured with his head as if demanding to know what the young man wanted. Faid waved his arms towards the road ahead, miming that he was lost. The man scanned him up and down slowly, taking in the jeans, sweater and rucksack, then pointed to the spare seat alongside him and moved off as Faid scrabbled into the cab. The driver never spoke a word as they rattled along and his shotgun never left his shoulder. From time to time he glanced at his passenger taking in his dishevelled, unshaven face and his threadbare clothes. Too exhausted to speak or communicate with him, Faid leant back against the hardboard panel which formed the back of the cab.

He awoke to the sound of brakes squealing as the driver swung sharply into a gateway and stopped. They had arrived at a cabin. The roof sagged in places and smoke curled up from an opening marked by a black stain on the thatch. The driver trudged up the path and waved Faid to follow him. Still, not a word had passed between them. The interior smelled of smoke and sweat with the odour of food intermingled.

At a table in the middle of the room sat a woman in an apron plucking a chicken.

She stood up and spoke in some language Faid did not understand. It was not German which he had learnt during his university days, he supposed it was some dialect of Serb-Croat.

The man pointed to a chair by the table and the woman brushed the remnants of her work onto the dirt floor, and then brought a cooking pot and three plates to the table and they gulped down the meal of dark meat and root vegetables. Faid broke the silence with a thank you in German and the woman nodded in reply.

"You are welcome" she said "but you no stay here now -you go."

Her hesitant speech expressed a fear more than the words she spoke.

The old man addressed her sharply in the unknown tongue.

"He says you are danger to us but he will show you the way to Hungary,"

Thanking her, Faid gathered his jacket and rucksack and made his way to the door. Outside, the farmer pointed to a barn. Gratefully he nodded his thanks and settled down between hay bales. Sleep came easily.

At daylight he was ready before the farmer had appeared. By six o'clock they were on the road but the grey morning offered little hope of a bright journey. The old truck wheezed down the unmade road and turned into the highway, joining a stream of vehicles.

Faid tried to talk with the driver: "You like forest work?"

The old man wiped his moustache with his sleeve and began to speak in that strange language.

None of it made sense but he gabbled on as they drove down the road and seemed to enjoy the one sided conversation. Faid nodded to encourage him and an hour passed quickly.

A sign "Koszeg" came up and the old man indicated that they were at the end of the journey. He pulled in to a layby near a river bridge and pointed across to the far side. The bridge was controlled by a barrier and guards slouched against the parapet, their rifles stacked against the wall. Pointing to the river, the driver gestured waving his arms in a swimming manner. As they separated, the farmer embraced Faid and slapped him on the back. He turned and without another glance, backed the lorry and set off grinding the gears as he went.

He examined the river. A surge of water foamed up against the bridge pillars and the noise of the water tumbling through the arches drowned other sounds.

There was no way he could get across even though he was a competent swimmer. He sat in the cover of the trees down by the bank and considered his options.

"What are you doing?" a hushed voice said, in arabic. "If you stay there they will catch you!"

Above him a young woman crouched at the top of the bank looking down on him. She was dark haired and wore a woollen cap pulled down on her head. Slim and pale faced she urged him with gestures to join her and he climbed up to meet her.

Standing beside her was a young man in blue overalls, he smiled and said "We can see you want the same thing as us" and pointed to the other side of the river.

"That's just a half day from Germany!"

Faid grinned in return; it felt good to find companions in the same situation.

"Where do you come from?" he asked

The girl laughed and said "Probably the same place as you-my name is Aziza and this is Sule we're from Aleppo." The news delighted Faid

"I trained in Aleppo! I come from Anadan--welcome friends!" all three embraced and laughed excitedly.

"Come" said Sule "let's be serious. How can you cross this river?"

"I believe that the bridge is the only way, the river would swallow you like a whale!"

Aziza frowned "How is it possible?"

"By driving through in some vehicle -we need a lorry or some such...

Sule thought for a few seconds "Let's look in the town there must be something there."

Faid shrugged his shoulders, "I have been spotted already so I'm not going in there"

"I'll do it" Aziza said "if I take off my ski jacket I can pass as a tourist...perhaps!" she laughed but it was clear that she was as nervous as the others. The two men said nothing but as she left Sule shouted "Be careful!" She waved and her slim figure disappeared into the town.

The border guards sauntered about on the bridge and took their break in a small guardhouse at the near end of the bridge. Within minutes, from the direction of the town they could hear running steps; female steps; Aziza scuttled down to the ditch where they hid.

"They saw me on the bridge-quick! We must move!"

Taking her by the hand Sule ran along the ditch away from the sound of pursuit. Faid dived for the cover of the thick bushes which lined the bank and lay still. Pounding boots ran past him as a group of soldiers charged along the culvert. He heard the sharp crack of rifle fire once -twice and then silence.

The marching boots passed him again and he could tell by the sound of their voices that the patrol was excited, as if they had enjoyed a successful hunt.

Raising his head slowly he saw two of them gripped Aziza by the arms and marched her towards the guardhouse. Her face grey with fear and her clothing torn. There was no sign of Sule.

By this time, it was twilight and the bridge was illuminated. Other guards were struggling with some cumbersome object; at least three of them were dragging it towards the guardhouse. For a brief moment the lamps showed what it was - the lifeless body of Sule. Dark bloodstains showed through his shirt and his head hung down like a broken doll. There was a pause as if the men were undecided what to do but then

Faid choked with horror as they pulled the body to the parapet and tipped it into the swirling river below.

For some seconds Faid lay stunned. This was Europe, the refuge where people rushed to escape ISIS and Assad. This was where he dreamed of safety. Yet murder and hatred lived here just as at home. A great anger against these men seized him and he climbed up the bank and slipped into the street. He looked for some weapon to take revenge, his mind unbalanced by what he had seen. Then he recalled his original plan and saw a way he could achieve both escape and maybe revenge at the same time.

In one of the side streets adjacent to the bridge, the feeble light of a small bar shone into the road. A taxi stopped outside and the driver stepped into the bar leaving the engine running. He went to the counter and was buying cigarettes. Faid raced to the cab and slammed it into gear before the driver knew what had happened. He turned into the main street leading to the barrier at the mouth of the bridge. There was no time to think-the bridge was yards away- the red and white of the barrier loomed before him-the engine raced as he aimed the car at the faces of the sentries screaming at him.

The taxi smashed into wood and bodies as it charged along the span of the bridge, grinding debris under its wheels. He reached the far end of the bridge before the fizzing sound of bullets passed overhead. He ducked below the windscreen and felt the car crunch along the parapet of the bridge and cannon across the road as it reached the far end. It rammed against the wall leading to the bridge, steam shooting from the damaged engine but Faid drove on. Within half a kilometre the engine seized and the car ran gradually to a halt. He sat dazed for a minute his ears ringing with the sounds of the splintering escape. Then he heard the noise of a vehicle racing up behind him. He began to clamber out of the crumpled door.

A head appeared at the broken windscreen:

"Quick! Come with us. Get out!"

He was bundled into a van with no rear windows and struggled to make sense of what was happening. They drove off at speed with his new companion peering out of a gap in the rear door.

"Inshalla, they will give up when they see the wreck." He laughed and grabbed Faid's arm in glee. It was then Faid noticed he held a pistol in his right hand.

"Who are you?" His senses warned him of new dangers.

"We are your brothers. We followed you across the bridge!"

"We have saved you from internment" said a voice from the driver.

His head was turned away from Faid so all he could make out was the wild black hair and the ragged beard. Beside him sat a young woman in a black hijab. Her eyes were cold and she said nothing but cradled an AK47 like a new baby.

"You want to reach Germany?" the question seemed more like a statement than a question.

"Of course, I want to escape from danger."

He looked at his rescuer, the one with the pistol. The man smiled and nodded.

"Of course you do, but we all have to pay a price for liberty my friend."

"What do you mean?" Faid felt sick, his dreams of freedom and safety were becoming fragile. Wherever he went he was soiled with violence and guns.

"Nobody can turn away from the struggle for Islam." The driver shouted above the engine noise "you are part of the conflict, my Brother, accept it."

He drove fast and carelessly, the van weaved as it raced along the carriageway clipping the verge and then the centre white line.

Faid sank down onto the floor of the van and held his head in his hands. His existence was meaningless. He had come so far yet failed to escape the terror masters. A great wave of anger swept his body as he contemplated a future dictated by Jihadi. All he had ever wanted was the life of a quiet man–a teacher who filled young people with hope and knowledge. Despite his hardships he was again a pawn in the hands of violence.

All energy drained from his body and he sat for several minutes in a state of despair. Slowly, his anger rose like a bile burning up through his body and he burst out in a wild scream of fury.

"Am I your weapon?" He screamed "Am I a man?"

He flung himself forward between the front seats and grabbed the steering wheel pushing the driver aside. The van began to weave as he pulled against the driver. He saw a truck coming on, its horn blaring in a wild continuous wail as the van veered across directly into its path.

"Allahu Akhbar" he shouted and the rest was silence.

LADY BELLAMY'S DILEMMA

Lady Bellamy wore diamonds.

"No well born gel would choose anything else!" She paused, "Of course, if he offered matched pearls that would be nice too!"

Jenny sat mute. How could she tell her mother what Jack had given her?

"But there are lots of other lovely jewels!"

"Such as?

The interjection stifled any reply. How could a ruby ring match up to her standards? But Jack was so sweet and kind. He looked so dashing in his scarlet unifom and he swore eternal love. Anyway, the ring was the envy of the other girls.

"I hope you bear in mind the family name? Your father was a dear man and died in the service of our Queen. You must never forget your father was 'The Hero of Mafeking'

"No Mama, I think of it daily! How could I forget when you remind me every hour!"

"Go to, you pert child! Such common instincts! You'd do better to emulate the sweet young Dora who is the picture of decorum and virtue. Besides, she's the daughter of an Earl." That meant a lot to Lady Bellamy, the widow of a mere baronet.

Jenny ran upstairs to her bedroom and sat down at her dressing table. A petulant image looked back at her. What could she do? Her fingers crept unbidden to the secret draw where she kept her most precious things. The ruby ring sat there nestled in its little mahogany box.

"Lovely thing!"

She jumped with fright. Dorcas, her maid stood at her elbow.

"Sorry Miss, I couldn't stop myself! It's lovely isn't it?"

"Don't tell Mama! She doesn't know I have it."

'Course I won't! Be more than my place's worth. And he's a lovely young man!"

"Do you think so? Yes, and he admires me so!"

For a moment, Jenny forgot herself and exchanged her inner most thoughts with her maid; the gifts he sent her and how they met secretly. All the while Dorcas smiled and encouraged her to talk. Soon conversation turned to her mother's resistance.

"Her Ladyship is a very firm lady. And she needs to be."

Jenny looked askance at her. "What do you mean?"

"It's no matter." Said Dorcas.

"Yes it is! You must tell me at once! Why should my mother be 'firm,' as you say?"

"Well, I don't know how to put it," The old lady paused, uncertain how to go on, "mayhap she feels tardy about the past."

"About the past? Tardy? You know something to make my mother 'Firm'?"

Dorcas fidgeted; her fingers twisting her apron strings into a hopeless knot.

"Well my cousin Nancy came with her when she wed."

"Yes I know, but this was before my time and the girl never stayed long. I know all that."

"Too true, she never stayed long! Your mother was firm indeed!"

"What do you mean? Out with it!"

Dorcas looked down and the last shade of blush tinged her faded cheeks.

"Nancy was her dressing maid, like me to you. And she kept your Ma's jewellery from before she married. When she left, she was given all your mother's old jewellery, to be rid of."

"Well,so?"

"Nancy kept the best bit which was a garnet on a pewter ring. Not even silver!"

Jenny sat mute for a long time, then she spoke in quiet voice. "Who has the ring now?"

Dorcas said nothing but left the room. Within a minute, she was back and handed a small cardboard box to her mistress. Inside wrapped in brown paper sat a steel coloured ring with a crimson stone.

"Happen you might want it yourself?" Jenny nodded and without a word, took the ring and slipped it onto her finger, it fitted perfectly.

That evening, guests were invited. Lady Bellamy enjoyed her reputation as a hostess. The Fanshaws were there and most of the county families were represented at the table. Jenny came down after they had arrived. She looked dazzling in an evening dress of white silk and long white gloves.

"My Dear! What kept you so long? The guests have already arrived. Where were you?"

Jenny smiled. "I misplaced my gloves." She said, and moved to greet Bertie Fanshaw. Her mother's eyes followed her as she drew off her gloves to give her hand to him.

Tombola

The cheap garnet ring glittered in the candlelight.

"My Word! Where did you get this ring?" Bertie held her hand up for all to see.

Jenny smiled and turned to her mother.

"It's a family heirloom, isn't it Mother?"

SHE LOVES ME

I bought the dog at a pub in the Camden Road. An old man with a cloth cap and a fag in the corner of his mouth sat down beside me with a pint of beer.

He said "You look like a good judge, what you think of this animal?"

The mutt sat down beside the bench and looked up at the old man with a quizzical look as if she didn't believe what she was hearing.

"I can see you've got taste Sir" the old rogue went on,

"and a dog like this could save you a lot of money."

"Oh yes? How come?"

"Well, you see, she is trained to hunt truffles and she's worth ever so much in the trade."

I have an idea that there isn't much truffle hunting in Camden, or Islington come to that. So I said,

"Then sell her to some French bloke where the truffles live."

"No, you don't understand. This dog was owned by Mr Locatelli who keeps a café down the Essex Road. He went all over London testin' the truffles in posh restaurants. Saved them a mint I'm told"

He leaned closer to me and the smell of beer and dog added flavour to his next remark.

"I can't let her go for less than a fifty, but you look like a sensible type and if I may say, needin' a good companion. So make me on offer."

He gave me a wink to show we were chums and pulled the dog up on his lap. It was a small terrier type dog with a brown and white coat.

The special feature of this valuable animal was that it had only one eye and its tail was like a half chewed rope end. Still, there was a brisk look about her and she sat as quiet as a nun while the scruffy old man supped his beer and dragged on his fag.

I told him that I was a busker in Leicester Square by night and did guitar lessons by day but before I could say another word he cut in:

"There you are then; she loves a tune and can dance a treat."

Just as he said that, the little dog got down and began to jig on its hindlegs in time to the juke box playing in the corner.

Suddenly it crossed my mind that the mutt might improve my spot in the Square. Trade was cut-throat at my pitch and anything unusual would help. Before I really knew it, two twenties had changed hands and I was walking out with a string in my hand and a dog on the other end trotting behind me.

That night I went down as usual to my pitch by the big Odeon in the Square and set up the speaker. It was a Saturday evening so the place was crowded. I was into my third number when I realized that the punters were gathering around me instead of dodging my cap. Behind me the mutt was swaying to the rhythm and the crowd loved it.

My take tripled and when I got home I was as chuffed as Christmas. I bought steak and we ate better than the Savoy. This pattern went on right through the month and I didn't need to give music lessons anymore.

I got a plug on London TV and thought of changing my digs. The little dog was good as gold never an off day and cost nothing to feed.

Until the day before Christmas.

I was down the pitch in the early afternoon, hoping to catch the shoppers in a good mood when she shot off like a rocket down Wardour Street. My kit was all set up and the crowds were all around me, so I had to get on with the set or lose a day's pay.

That evening, I searched all over for the wretched thing- down Seven Dials and up as far as Tottenham Court Road—not a sign of her.

Christmas day, I traced the route from my place to the Square but still no joy. As a last resort I wandered down the Eagle, that pub in the Camden Road. There sitting on a stool next to that greasy old soak was the dog.

She looked up at me with a nonchalant gaze and never gave me a second glance. I took the old man by the collar of his lumpy old coat and swore blue murder at him.

"Give me back my dog" I shouted.

"I can't do that"

"Why not?" I bellowed

"She loves me" he cooed with a greasy smile.

At that, I aimed a fist at him but the blessed dog bit my ankle and the bouncer at the door lifted me out of the pub and dumped me on the pavement. There was no way back in.

I never found out if she could smell truffles.

MARCELLUS IN THE FOREST

The mist lifted and he could see the centurion raise his spear to signal the attack. A beat began like an iron drum and the cohorts slowly moved forwards, hammering their swords on their shields. He noted with satisfaction the rigid line of interlinked men advancing shoulder-to-shoulder. He trained them to stand together and fight for each other, every man protecting the man to his right. Down in the lower valley where the mist still gathered, all the tribesmen could see was an armoured mass descending upon them out of the clouds.

This was to be Marcellus's last mission in Germania. He had been recalled to his original legion, the Fifth. Three seasons in Sylvania at the beck and call of the incompetent Legate, Titus Aurelius, were nearly over. No more marshland expeditions - no more bogs and forests to avoid. It would be a joy to be in plain, simple country with a warm sun on your back.

He called for his third file centurions - the veterans who would thrust through the struggle and bring havoc to the enemy.

"Let the young men earn their scars, then push both lines forward to roll up these savages," he reminded them "The cavalry are covering your flanks so do not deviate."

Then he rode down the line showing himself to every cohort. He was a tall man with broad shoulders and a weathered face. His long nose and firm jaw revealed his patrician background and his keen grey eyes missed nothing.

Some accused Marcellus of arrogance and impulsive behaviour but his men fought for him with complete loyalty. The legions called him "Bignose". He wore the long sword of a cavalry officer and the purple-trimmed cloak of an ex-praetorian guard. However, he shared none of the highhanded arrogance of many of his peers.

Here and now his mind focussed on the coming battle. His plan was to engage the Tribes with a frontal assault and when they were firmly locked in, to strike with the cavalry from both sides. The idea was the inspiration of his cavalry commander, Arminius. Once a tribal leader, Arminius was the perfect example of Rome's policy, in which loyal tribes were integrated into the Army. He had shown himself to be an able and brave commander in several actions in this difficult territory and had been made a Roman citizen with authority and wealth.

The legions advanced out of the mist. The voices of the barbarians faded as the noise and discipline of the troops began to take effect. With a final rush over the ground, the legionaries clashed against the first rank of warriors. These tribes wore no armour but fought half naked with all the weapons they could find: swords, spears, clubs and knives. Few carried shields and these were made of wood and leather. At first, the tribesmen attacked with ferocious energy but as the steady pressure of the shield wall never stopped, they were driven back and back, until gaps formed in the files and those who had not fallen began to fight as single men against this wall of weapons.

Arminius, dressed in Roman uniform and mounted on a grey charger, rushed forward with his troop from the flank of the fight and began the task of cutting the barbarians down as they turned away from the front. He was a sturdily built man with the blonde hair and blue eyes of the northern tribes. He had the cavalry skills of his countrymen and quickly learned tactics from his Roman companions. Marcellus had come to depend on him as a loyal lieutenant.

Predictably, the tribal forces began to fall like a toppling wall and each man who ran away left his friends to their doom. Soon the rout was unstoppable with the horsemen of Arminius cutting down man after man as they fled. Within an hour the battle was over.

The principal centurion, Lucius Quintus, reported to Marcellus with the figures of casualties and prisoners.

"Forty-two men of the Valor cohort dead and thirty-five wounded, My Tribune."

"Gods be praised - can you estimate the enemy loss?"

"We are collecting the weapons now but Arminius has not yet returned."

Marcellus frowned. Surely Arminius realized that pursuit was risky? The possibility of losing contact with his troop in these circumstances was high. However, he kept it to himself.

Within the hour the cavalry had returned as ordered but Arminius was not among them. Enquiries showed that he had led the pursuit and had ridden ahead of his troop; no one saw where he went.

Two hours later he arrived in the camp, his grey horse lathered and heavily splattered with mud. He saw to his horse and then reported to the Tribune.

"Congratulations on a fine victory," he smiled, "even Titus can't deny this." Marcellus hid his concern since all had ended well and Arminius was a capable commander. Still, the episode struck an uneasy chord in his mind.

The routine assembly of weapons and prisoners took much of the next day and a report was prepared for the Legate. In that time Marcellus had no time to question Arminius about the strange absence and then, the march back to camp pushed the matter out of his mind.

The success against the Sabitae was conclusive and the other tribes in that area sent Elders to treat with the Legate. Hostages were taken and weapons confiscated plus the usual rendition of the remaining prisoners of war as slaves.

Titus was pleased. "So, at last my Tribunes have shown their abilities in the field. I feel my task has been done." He adjusted his riding cape and smoothed his curls, so carefully crafted that morning; a satisfied man. "I have decided that the return to winter quarters can begin tomorrow, I will take the lead and you Marcellus will follow in the rear-guard."

This order had already been prepared by the Camp Prefect Balbus but Titus issued it as if a fresh order of his own. Marcellus cared nothing for his Legate nor did he care whether he stayed in the rear or not, the one thing that mattered was the route taken.

There was a choice: the quickest route took the army along a road which broadly followed the river Weser through the flat lands of Friesland - the danger here was the possibility of meeting with hostile tribesmen from the north. The second route took the army through the Teutonberg forest which was longer but had less chance of confrontation.

The meeting, attended by all Tribunes and senior centurions of the three legions, clearly favoured the quicker route, arguing that their strength and recent victory would dominate any opposing force. As if to confound the advice of the senior officers, the Legate chose the forest way. Marcellus, with the main centurions, argued with him; pointing out the unknown aspect of the forest route and the time lost in doing so.

"I have consulted our Germanic commander who knows the route thoroughly and I say we take this route." Titus indicated Arminius who nodded in acknowledgement it was true, and since neither Marcellus nor any of the other centurions could contradict him, the route was settled.

The preparations took several days. Moving three legions with their baggage and heavy weapons was a major operation which involved every officer. Leather tents themselves took up much of the wagons. Then the heavy artillery had to be disassembled.

Arminius was detached from the main operation for the purpose of scouting the route and setting up suitable camp sites. "I'll see you along the way, Marcellus, and drink a few cups to Odin," Arminius joked, invoking the name of a northern God knowing this would provoke a reaction. Marcellus waved him away in mock anger, but he missed his company and spent most of his free time with Balba, who was an old companion. This allowed him to avoid Titus as much as possible. "What do you see as the main danger on this route?" asked Balba.

"I would say the narrowness of the track through the forest," Marcellus suggested, "if an attack occurred how could we form cohorts?"

"Well, this is not enemy country," Balba replied. "Arminius will see to the forest." and the talk passed to other topics.

The next day the Legate addressed his forces. His wore his dress uniform with its golden breastplate and his parade helmet adorned with twin eagles.

"Today, we will pass through the forest of our enemies. The power of the Empire now reaches to the edge of Germania. We return with the laurels of victory, to rest and enjoy the spoils of our conquests. Rejoice, your Standards will be honoured throughout the Province. A huge cheer greeted this. He pointed to the Three Eagles proudly held by the standard bearers of each legion, and the march began. The Teutonberg forest was a wild dark mass of great oak and fir trees. It stretched for forty miles in each direction, criss-crossed by narrow causeways and paths. At no place was it possible for two wagons to travel side by side and at night the army camped in file along the pathway. Marcellus noted that Arminius was always on the move and seldom attached to any cohort of the Legions. His reports daily were reassuring, so Marcellus set aside his concerns about security. Nonetheless, the rear-guard was made up of four cohorts of legionaries and two wings of auxiliary cavalry drawn from the Iberian forces rather than the native Germanic horsemen. Marcellus felt that foreign horsemen were best in this difficult country.

Lucius Quintus, twenty years a centurion, served as Marcellus's deputy.

"The forest is our enemy, Tribune," he remarked looking up at the gloom reaching down on both sides. "How can we protect the wagons and followers who are so far ahead?"

"Your caution does you credit but we are far from any tribal area," assured Marcellus. "And we have our own Germanic officer to act as our eyes. Besides, we are well placed to deal with any surprise from the rear."

Lucius had to agree with his commander since he was confident that they had taken steps to protect the rear of the column.

Still he thought with a column stretching for fifteen miles, we can't cover everyone. But he kept his thoughts to himself.

At the front of the column, Balba as camp commander rode with the vanguard of three centuries of legion soldiers, leaving the auxiliaries to protect the wagon and weapon train. Behind him the Legate and his retinue moved at an easy pace. Titus Aurelius chose to travel in a carriage drawn by two black Thracian horses which he had bought with a Roman Triumph in mind. Surely the Senate would grant a Triumph to the conqueror of outer Germania? He felt, however, that the choice of route may have been a mistake. He favoured a safe route since he regarded his period of service in this barbaric wilderness as now over. But the time it took to move and the discomfort of nightly camp in these dark woods was almost insufferable. He would complain to Arminius as soon as he saw him.

The second night on the march took the army along the narrowest path in the Forest. All about the winding column of wagons and foot soldiers sounds seemed enlarged. Birds calling and animals howling made a dismal background to their slow progress.

Then, to complete their misery, rain began to fall and progress came to a stop as packhorses and wheeled transport bogged down in the mud.

Balba had no choice but to order camp at that location. No fires could be lit since no dry wood was carried by the column and foraging became impossible.

Ignoring the Legate in his tent, Balba joined Marcellus at the rear-guard to discuss the situation.

"We are in a hellish position Marcellus, Arminius seems to have misjudged the likely problems. I am unable to scout forward in these conditions and the forest is becoming denser on each side."

Marcellus for his part promised to set extra sentries and the night passed peacefully, but morale dropped as fuel and food became the dominant thoughts in every soldier's mind.

In the grey light predawn, all this changed. A great roar bellowed out from the woods on both sides of the column and an army of Teutons hurled themselves on the sleepy soldiers below. Only the sentries were awake and active while the main body of legionary forces in their tents scarcely had time to grab a weapon before the wild-eyed barbarians tore through the sides and were upon them.

Balba sprang to his horse bare-backed and rode at once to gather his vanguard into a defensive circle. Quickly formed, this action soon diverted the attackers onto the centre of the column.

Their force, like a wave, engulfed the tents and lines of wagons mired in the black, clinging earth of the forest floor. Men cowered under the wheels and kicked out as the blades and spears of the attackers cut and thrust into their naked limbs.

Others crushed by the overturning carts screamed for help as their bodies became transfixed by the weight pressing down upon them.

All along this unprotected column of thousands of men, horses and equipment, every section was attacked from both sides.

In the rear, Marcellus and his cohorts were the last to be struck and the sounds of combat from ahead were signals of the horror which had begun. Wave upon wave of savages cut through the unarmed troops in the centre leaving the advance and rear guards alone.

Struggling to reach the main sections of the column, he looked to the hills rising out of the forest to the south where a lone horseman stood directing the furious tribesmen. Marcellus saw a figure dressed in wolf furs riding a grey horse. The figure stood still for a very short time and before Marcellus could take a second look, it had moved on to another location. Something about this lone rider struck him as familiar, but urgent action required all his attention.

The rear cohorts struggled against the pressure of attack as if pushing against a tide of men. Slowly iron discipline had its effect and the embattled rear-guard were able to form a defensive circle of shields and with their spears kept the mass of warriors away. The attackers realized that there was easier prey further up the column and began to move on.

They carved a path towards the Legate's carriage. His bodyguards closed around it but the horses reared and plunged with terror, creating turbulence among the men and increasing the confusion.

Titus sprang from the carriage and for once showed how even a coward can do something surprising under pressure. He counterattacked with just the few guards who remained standing and with such effect that the mob fell back as if in surprise. With those soldiers he created a small pool of resistance to impede the force of the ambush.

Above him from among the trees a voice called out to him in Latin:

"Your time has come, Legate. Die like a man or give yourself up to Germania."

The voice struck deep into Titus's heart. There could be no mistake - the voice was Arminius. Emerging from the shadows of the trees, his distinctive war horse pawing the ground, the traitor smiled the engaging smile which he had used so frequently in the past.

The Legate stood among his dwindling band and wiped the blood from his eyes. His carefully styled hair had lost its curl and sweat mingled with the strands that hung limply over his brows. Slowly, with a sigh, Titus drew his personal dagger - his pugio - and, after a moment of hesitation, thrust it into the space below his breastplate. Blood spurted from his mouth and he dropped to the ground covering his face with his robe. His body sank into the bloody mire that contained many of his troops and was soon trampled as the massacre moved like a wave along the line of trapped men.

Arminius, dressed as a Teuton chief with a wolf's head helmet and fur-covered armour, pushed down among the exultant men and pulled the XII Legion Standard from the dying grasp of the signifier who clutched it desperately.

"See my friends," he shouted above the tumult, "their standards are not magic and now they are ours." As he spoke he held the Eagle high so that every Teuton warrior could see the golden wings. Further down the column, beyond the Legate's section, other tribal leaders began the plunder, even though remnants of the Roman column were still fighting for their lives. Two more Eagles from the VII and the XI Legions fell into their hands while soldiers, slaves and camp followers were slaughtered without hesitation. In the narrow valley, filled with blood-churned mud, a long line of cadavers, stripped pale bodies, lay exposed for wolves and carrion. Their bones were to remain there unburied for forty years.

At the vanguard of the column Balba and his men kept off the weight of barbarian force until nightfall. By that time the ambush had turned into a feast of vengeance where tribal loyalty began to dominate. Booty became the object of the exercise with each tribe seizing as much as possible.

Balba and some forty men were still able to fight. They moved in a tight column further up the deadly trail away from the massacre. It was not fighting prowess which gave them relief, but the distraction of plunder down along the column. To the Teutons the easier task of collecting booty rather than killing became attractive. Balba's group made good progress towards the fixed camp five miles away which had been their original objective. By early morning, before dawn, they straggled into the fort where the full significance of the massacre had not yet unfolded. However, when merely forty men out of three Legions appeared, then the horror of the Teutonberg Forest was exposed.

As evening came and the light diminished, Arminius assessed the position and decided that discipline was impossible and released his own tribal followers to join in the booty hunt. He pulled away from the seething cauldron of struggling men. There were still Romans standing exhausted and dumb, like cattle waiting for the fate they could not escape, and Teutons saturated in blood, squabbling and fighting among themselves.

He rode calmly back into the forest to rest and see to his horse. Later he appeared at the feast. The rape of women, their clothes scattered on the forest floor, and their screams, added to the noise of feasting barbarians. Even the camp followers' children cast into the huge fires seemed to increase the excitement of the mob.

"I need to encourage the tribes to believe in their prowess," he mused. Still, he was repulsed by the ancient customs he had left behind, but forced to disguise the pity he felt for the victims. His aim was the destruction of Imperial power east of the Alps.

It was too early to take the numbers of the dead or the tally of booty wrenched from body and wagon. He reckoned that three days of feasting and riot would have to pass before reliable facts would be established and order restored. He had no idea if Balba or Marcellus had escaped.

The rear guard rallied to Marcellus in a solid group moving backwards in unison away from the tiring savages. Spears and arrows still penetrated the ranks but the impetus of the ambush was now gone. Roman discipline and steady movement gradually detached his cohorts from the mass of enemy.

"Quick! Each horseman will take two soldiers," Marcellus shouted. "Hold on to the saddle horns on each side and move - move!"

Discarding everything but their swords, each soldier grabbed a horn of the saddle nearest to himself and clung on, half carried, half dragged away from the devastation as the horsemen urged their mounts into action.

After a short pursuit, the foot soldiers of the Chirusci gave up the hunt and the remnants of the rear-guard gathered to regroup.

"The Gods at least gave us horses!" Marcellus shouted as he marshalled the men, trying his best to raise their spirits.

"What do we do Tribune?" Quintus, one of the last centurions, demanded. "We go to collect men and regain our Eagles." His reply lifted the spirits of the exhausted men, but as his eye scanned the weary men and blown horses he knew that little progress could be made till they had recovered. Setting camp in a high ridge of the forest they stayed unobserved for two days. Foraging for game and fresh water was their only task. After that interval of time it was clear that the Teuton forces had left off any search for the remnants of the rear-guard.

Marcellus called the three centurions and two optios among the survivors to a meeting.

"We have escaped the worst betrayal in Imperial history," he began.

"Nothing can be more important than to report to our leaders and restore the pride of the Empire as soon as possible."

"Tribune," Quintus interjected. "We are more than one hundred and twenty miles from Lugdunum, if we send a man with a fresh horse he could be there in two or three days at most."

"True, but you forget that those miles are straight through the country of the Chirusci. No, we must move together even though progress will be slower." To himself he recalled Augustus's maxim: "Hurry slowly."

They divided the weapons and provisions among the thirty-four men who had survived and began their march to Lugdunum, known to the Gauls as Lyon. It would be a long dangerous journey.

TEA AND SYMPATHY

Molly put on her green hat, the one she wore to Sheila's wedding, and locked the front door. It was just a short walk to the teashop but she took her time. Had it been a good idea to choose a spot so close to home? Anyway, too late now. He wouldn't know that and the shop was nice, she felt comfortable there.

What was his name? She wrote it on the back of her hand but she forgot as soon as she did so. Yes, Derek, an author. Quite a surprise, actually. His email looked written by a cultured person, he wrote well and seemed to have a sense of humour.

Mam always said 'You need a man with a sense of humour.' The only man Molly had known was the man she married, that Harry Picken, and he was no joker. Twenty four years of drudgery proved that. After he died, she never thought of a male companion again till Betty at the Social Centre talked about it.

"So easy to join up! Within a minute you can see who's online! I can show you how." Betty loved interfering; meant no harm but she did annoy sometimes.

Two days later Molly went to change her library books. She saw the internet machine by the front desk.

"It's called a P.C." Said the girl behind the counter. "Do you want me to show you how it works? She fiddled with the keyboard and a picture appeared on the screen.

"Now you can find what you want on Google" The word stared at her in a bold way. Below, a section with a blank space lured her on.

"Go on" said the girl, "type in what you want."

Molly sat down at the desk and waited till she'd gone. Typing had been her forte; thirty years in Mister Althorp's office taught her that, but she wondered what to write. The blank space challenged her. Her fingers hovered over the keys, awaiting commands. Before she knew it, the word 'meeting' appeared in neat script on the screen. She looked round quickly. Did anyone see? No, so she tapped Enter just like the girl had done.

Up came a list of names, and she clicked on the first one. The screen changed and a title 'Partners Choice' took over; all the rest of the items disappeared. From then onward it became simply a matter of following the instructions and picking the name. She clicked on. Such fun! She was on the 'Internet' like Betty and by typing she could make things happen! When the name of Derek came up, the description 'author' intrigued her and she tapped a message so the meeting was arranged.

Sitting in the teashop, she felt it may have been a mistake. She didn't know Derek. Why had she done it? Perhaps the excitement of trying something new? Or was it a subconscious wish to make contact? Any contact? She fidgeted and crumpled a serviette; it seemed to stick like gum to her fingers.

A voice shattered this reverie. The waitress stood arms akimbo at her side. "Is it tea for one?"

"No I'm waiting for someone. It's tea for two."

The girl repeated the order as if she found it unusual, but Molly looked away and ignored her. The café began to fill up with mothers and children, older couples and a few single people. A quick glance at each single man was all she could do. She longed for the tea to arrive, at least then she could busy herself with preparations but she couldn't catch the waitress's eye.

Then she noticed the blind man treading carefully through the maze of tables. He wore dark glasses and he held his stick in front of him like a waterdiviner. He tripped at one point and she saw the need to steady him as he approached.

"Are you alright? It's very crowded in here isn't it?" She felt a fool; how could he see ?

He nodded and said "Can you put me near a table with a single lady please? Are you the waitress? I'm looking for a Mrs Molly Picken." She froze. Her mind went blank. She hesitated while she did her best to make sense of it. How did he write the internet entry? Why didn't he say he was blind? An author? He waited patiently by the table. He made no complaint but just stood there with his empty eyes fixed on her.

"Mind your back, Love!" The waitress lifted her tray high and put it down between them on the table. Then she looked at him for the first time and took his arm and sat him down in the chair facing Molly.

"There you go! Just make yourself comfortable and the lady will pour for you, won't you?".

She looked at Molly in a deliberate way as if to oblige her to speak or do something, then she marched away to deal with someone else.

"Are you Molly?" His voice was low and pleasant. He leant forward but she sat back in surprise.

"Yes. I'm Molly Picken and you are Derek?" How banal her reply sounded! and added quickly, "I wondered what you looked like!" She felt even worse.

He grinned. "I can't help you with that. Maybe you can tell me!" He put one hand out gently to feel for the tray. "Would you like a cup of tea?" His hand touched the cups and traced the outline of the teapot and jug.

"Oh, Please let me!" Like a spell, she woke her from inertia and eagerly set about making tea and arranging plates for them both. He smiled and put his hands back on his lap.

"You're wondering why I didn't say I was blind aren't you? And how did I manage the internet?"

"Yes" She said and was surprised how easy it seemed to chat with him.

"Well, I knew if I said so, no one would reply, so I got the Warden to write it for me and see what happened. Maybe I did wrong?"

"Yes I think you did wrong! But never mind now, here's your tea."

He took the cup and they sat for a while without saying a word. Molly examined her mixed feelings of surprise and recrimination. He was here and real. What was the point in brooding over what had passed?

She looked at his clothes, the grubby jacket had buttons missing; his trousers were frayed old cords; he was a mess. It didn't matter. She felt glad she'd come. They talked about the town and the way things had changed; he told her he had been a sailor and a deep sea diver. How he spent years in the Far East and lost a fortune in India. She wondered at the contrast between her life and his, the wealth of excitement he had found and her quiet homespun history. He never told her how he'd become blind and she was too embarrassed to ask. It seemed unimportant as they chatted together. The tea grew cold as they talked on and when the waitress came back, clearing the table, she looked at Derek.

"Nice cup of tea, my Love?"

She ignored Molly. Molly took out her purse and paid the bill. No tip.

Tombola

There was some activity at the door of the café and two men moved purposely towards their table. They stood next to Derek and one of them said,

"Come on Derek, you can't keep running off like this. You're causing grief at the ward. You'll lose you Leave-outs after this."

They pulled him up by his armpits and began to move to the door. He turned towards Molly. His face was bright as a happy schoolboy.

"See you Molly, thanks for the tea!" She watched as they led him to a van outside and carefully guided his head into the back seat. He sat quietly as the vehicle moved and never turned his head.

The key made that familar rusty noise as she unlocked the front door. The hall was dark and cold. She hung her coat and went into the kitchen to finish the washing up. Everything was as she had left it. She dried the dishes and for a moment, just one moment, she pictured his worn smile and frayed clothes that needed repair. Her eyes softened as she recalled the stories he told. Could they be true? It didn't matter.

Then she sighed and put away the crockery.

THE STORM

It was a storm like no other. In Bridport, trees fell, roofs rippled and lifted, thatch groaned under the power of the wind and tiles flicked about the streets like knives.

High up on the ridgeway, some miles above the town, was The Beggar's Rest. For over a hundred years it had stood next to the crossway where two roads met. It was a familiar landmark hereabouts. Some people said it was a dangerous place – others said it was a refuge – so isolated and far from the town. Joshua Trim, the landlord, a large man with a dark complexion, ran his house with a firm hand. He spoke little and rarely went into town. Since the inn was remote and customers were generally scarce, many believed the smugglers, who brought in rum and brandy, spent time there. Tonight it was shelter for a throng of folk caught out by the raging weather.

Rain had begun soon after midday and the sky darkened in early afternoon so that travellers and the shepherds who worked the hills sought protection as the storm gathered strength.

"There's no help for it," Silas Newcome, a shepherd, said," I've penned them tight and God save them this night."

He took a seat by the table and sat quietly nursing a small pot of beer, hoping to keep his place as more arrived. He had hung up his crook above the great fireplace as was the custom.

Outside, the rain butts overflowed and the sound of splashing almost covered the howl of the wind which prowled among the chimneys and pulled at the thatch.

Little by little the tavern filled with the victims of the storm.

A farrier, Thom Able, still in his leather apron, stooped in and shrugged as he faced the Landlord.

"It's no use Maister Trim, the animals are frit and I can't shoe 'em like this."

Trim nodded and drew a jug of beer for the man.

"I duresn't try the road back down till it leaves off," said Able and no one gainsaid this point. With a nod at the shepherd, he sat at the other end of the big trestle table, astride the bench as if in the saddle.

Maddie, the publican's wife added logs to the fire in the great fireplace. Her hair twisted into a plain cap upon her head, her face and tired eyes betrayed the hard life she led. For a minute she rested in the inglenook gazing at the flames as the occasional raindrop dripped down the chimney to sizzle in the heat. Then she gathered her apron and pulled herself up, holding onto the corner as she rose. As usual, she closed her ears to the talk of the men in the bar.

By six o'clock, Sam Barker, Carter Brown and several other men had come into the inn shaking their capes and clogs at the door. Every time the door swung open the wind rushed in like an unruly dog nipping at their limbs and making the flames roar up the chimney.

Outside, the darkness crept over the world. The yard and the crossroad, just beyond, were obscured in the gloom. Joshua struggled out and hung a lantern above the door as a last defiant gesture against the storm. The wind howled a curse and flung the light about like a toy.

Inside, as the evening wore on, Carter Brown called for the fiddle and offered a tune.

"Who likes a ditty?" he asked, tuning up.

He looked about for a volunteer to start the round. Landlord Trim shouted, "The Maid from Barchester," and the old man began the familiar ditty slowly and gathered speed and confidence as his fingers warmed up. Soon the room rang with a range of voices, all stretching to join in the chorus they knew so well. The warmth of the fire and the drink added to the spirit of the evening. The wild night outside lost its terrors.

A loud knock at the door broke the mood. A second pounding hammered against the oak panels and brought the music to a halt. Trim pulled back the bolts and held the open door against the wind. Outlined by the feeble light of the lantern was a man in an oilskin cape. He wore a tarred tricorn hat, black and shiny with rain.

"Can I come in?"

Trim stepped back and nodded to the stranger. All eyes followed as the man slowly moved from door to room, shedding water onto the sacking mat near the door. A pool formed around his feet and where he cast his black cape and hat.

He was tall and thin and gave the impression of a man of consequence. His eye was proud and he stood upright, stiff as a soldier on parade. His dark woollen jacket and trousers were soaked and his boots caked with mud.

"I'm on my way to Bridport, but lost my way tonight on the moor. Can I rest here?"

Maddie Trim brought out a blanket from the kitchen and handed it to the stranger without a word. He stripped off his coat and sat in the inglenook stretching his damp legs before the fire, wrapping himself in the rough cloth.

Sam Barker, the tiler, spoke first. "Happen you missed your way out of Denby Wood? Tis a wild way and a lonely one. You chanced your luck on such a day as this."

The stranger smiled and said, "I came from Ilchester this morning and my business in Bridport is urgent for tomorrow, so I tried to cut across the moor to save my legs."

"Tis a good three mile from here," said Barker. "You'll mak' no further in this storm tonight."

"Agreed." The man eased himself down into the corner of the bench and called for a jug. He had a leather bag with him and laid it carefully beside him.

The fiddler tuned up again and the music stirred the company to a song. One of the carter's men, Dan Widgery, danced an erratic whirligig till he collided with the bar and went down in a flurry of arms, legs and spilt beer. Roars of laughter followed and even the solemn stranger broke into a thin smile. Next, Jimmy Rant took to the floor with his spoons and rattled away to accompany the fiddle which set the company clapping and stamping. Soon the stranger was forgotten and the guests settled down for the night.

Maddie Trim brought out a cauldron of broth and set it on the table.

"All's welcome to a bit of broth and bread tonight," she said, "no man should go hungry on such a night."

The general murmur of thanks was followed by the clatter of boots and spoons as each found a place round the table.

"Mind!" said Joshua Trim, "the ale and mead is to be paid for." This was acknowledged with grunts and slurps.

Then the tall stranger spoke up. "Landlord, put out a firkin of ale on my expense to thank you for the company."

A general roar of approval went up and Trim obliged by hoisting a barrel from the cellar onto the table and spiked the plug.

Soon the room filled with the noise of loud voices and occasional bursts of song as the night wore on. The stranger kept to his seat in the inglenook but joined in the general talk.

"So tomorrow is a big day for thee?" said Sam, as if the earlier chat had never been broken, "happen it is a big day for the town as well."

"What's that then?" said Gaffer Basset from the table side, his ear cupped to catch every word.

"Well the Assize is due and the sentence passed on the Barnstaple thief."

At that moment, the wind rattled and a shaft of lightning blazed across the window. All eyes turned to look. Outside, for an instant, the face of a man was pressed against the glass. Just as quickly, the image disappeared and a rapping commenced, banging urgently on the glass.

Trim sprang for the door and others followed. As he lifted the latch the door was flung open with the force of the wind and the body of a man burst into the room.

He was dressed in poor clothing for such a night. His long ragged coat was covered by a layer of sacking, such as used for the field harvest, his leggings and boots were covered in mud and they slid on the tiled floor.

"God bless you!" he said. "I saw the light an' salvation too!"

His face was pallid, unhealthy as if he had spent time away from the sun. and his long dark hair was plastered to his forehead by the rain. He looked at the assembly with a keen eye as if he suspected trouble. His eyes took in every face in close inspection, although he glanced away when eye met eye. There was certain ferocity in his stare rather like a wounded animal at bay.

"You're safe at last," said the dark man from the inglenook, "come and warm yourself by the fire."

The stranger nodded his thanks and threw down the sacking as he climbed into the nook and held out his arms to the warmth of the fire.

Soon steam rose from his drenched clothing and he pulled off the serge jacket that covered his shoulders.

Maddie brought him a blanket and took his steaming clothes away. For a second she looked hard at the man, and then she nodded to the table where the broth and bread lay.

"Help yourself, like all the others," she said.

Peter Hinchin, one of the drovers, handed a bowl to the man and said, "How come you was out in such a storm?"

The man gulped down a mouthful before he replied. "I lost a wheel on the Downs and saw the light."

Hinchin sniffed, his curiosity was not so easily satisfied. "Oh, where? I know the Downs like a pig's back – was it at the river bridge?"

The stranger supped again as if to gain time. "I don't exactly know," he began, "surely not at a bridge but high up near some trees..." He tailed off and took another sip of broth. Hinchin shook his head, puzzled by the vague description, but looked at the dejected man and shrugged his shoulders.

"Well, all will be clear in the dawn," he said and turned away to gather his mug.

Sitting together at the fireside, the two incomers began to talk as their bodies warmed by the fire and their minds freed up with the ale and the company.

"Good of ye to share the firkin this night," said the newcomer.

"My pleasure," said the dark man, "like you, I needed a refuge on this wild night. Where have you come from?"

"I come from," he hesitated, "Portsmouth, but stopped off in Bridport for a spell."

He turned to his companion. "What was your route and purpose?"

There was an audience throughout the inn to hear the answer. A hush fell as the assembly pretended to be busy but each one listened with one ear to the mystery man with the tricorn hat.

The man rose and stretched himself; he stepped out into the living space before the fireplace and raised his pot of ale to the crowd.

"Here's to the Storm and good company!"

A holler rang out in reply, "An' here's to you Sir," a general toast followed and the dark man smiled in a genial way.

"I'll wager a guinea to any man who can guess my trade in one question," he said and spread his arms out in a broad gesture.

Outside the wind still moaned and distant thunder muttered.

Trim's instinct told him the man was an "official" mayhap a Customs Man.

He offered, "Excise." The man shook his head.

Sam Barker shouted, "Press gang." The press gangs had swept through Dorset the year before.

Again, the man smiled and said, "No."

He pulled his leather bag towards him and said. "A clue to help you."

The room was now abuzz with interest and the barrel that the man had given was tapped again.

From his bag he drew a coil. Not a rough rope of hemp, nor a string of twine, but a pure white silken cord no thicker than a man's thumb. His eyes scanned the group with a glitter that they had never seen before.

"Merciful Christ! He's the hangman!" cried Maddie and she covered her face with her apron.

"A guinea to that good lady!" He smiled thinly and pulled out the coil that unwound like a beautiful snake emerging from the gaping case. A silence fell like a curtain across the whole room.

"An' tomorrow the man what stole Farmer Betwood's sheep is hung..." said Peter Hichen.

"I have a job to do. Yes, at ten tomorrow in Bridport."

He put away the rope and went back to the inglenook and sat beside the other newcomer. Fumbling in his pocket, he found a guinea and offered it to Maddie.

She shook her head and gathered up some crocks intent on leaving. Her eyes never looked at the man again as she left the room.

Gradually, the atmosphere in the bar returned to its former noisy level although the barrel which the hangman had given was empty. Still, some got together with the fiddler and a tune began.

Just then, above the roar of the storm, the boom of cannon sounded from a distance. There was a short silence in the room and then the fiddler began again.

A second time they heard the boom above the wind and rain. The music stopped.

The publican Trim said, "It's the prison gun!"

The whole assembly stiffened. The hangman stood and Trim looked at him.

He stepped out into the room and spoke to the whole group.

"The gun must mean the condemned man has escaped. I need a posse to search for him."

Trim looked to Thom Able the farrier. "Well Thom, you're the sworn constable, where's you staff? You need to find the man."

"I ain't got me staff with me on such a night! How was I to know the man would run?"

"Never mind the staff!" said the hangman. "I have the power to raise a posse here and now." and he flourished a silver badge from his waistcoat.

Another cannon shot from the prison rang out over the sounds of the storm. "Hold hard!" said the man with the badge, "I name you all for the posse. Anyone who defaults is reported to the magistrate."

A sullen murmur ran through the men. Several looked out at the rain and wind outside and shifted their feet.

"A guinea each man for the posse and a name to the magistrate for them that hold back."

This made a change in the mood and one by one the men began to gather their coats, capes and coverings to follow the dark man who commanded them.

The man from the fireside slipped out into the open room and gathered his sacking and coat. He was the last to follow out into the whirling winds and rain.

The posse spread out along the ways of the moors in each direction with shouts and calls to keep contact with each other. Soon they had disappeared in the darkness.

Alone in the inn, Maddie made up the fire and cleared the table. She went to the kitchen and began to wash the crocks when a light knock tapped on the kitchen door and the second stranger in the sacking slipped in and stood with his back to the door.

"I seed you knew me Maddie, from the first off, I got nowhere to go but here so what could I do?" He looked at her with pleading eyes.

"You're a marked man, Jo," she said calmly. "What can I do agin the Law?"

"It was no justice to hang a man for one sheep!" he spoke with some fire. "You know well I had been turned out and my childer starving..."

She dried her hands on her apron and gave a slight nod.

"It's true, we all expected transportation, but the Assizes is London judges and they show no mercy." She sighed and put her hands to her head brushing a wisp of her grey hair away.

Then she opened the great chest which stood below the stairs and brought out a heavy coat.

"There Jo, I can do no more – I haven't a piece of coin I can give you but a coat and a bit of food to set you on your way."

He grabbed the coat and waited while she cut a thick slice of bread and a piece of cheese from the larder. Wrapping them in an old newspaper, she handed the parcel to him.

He held her hands as she gave them to him and for a second their eyes met and her face softened, her eyes grew moist and she bit her lip.

"Go on Jo Gargery, you broke my heart once but I forgive you."

He held her hands for a moment but said nothing, and then he kissed her poor chapped fingers and went out of the door into the raging night.

*

By dawn, some of the men returned to the inn. Joshua Trim threw down his topcoat with a grunt.

"All night and no sign of him. The storm has had us beat."

He slumped down in his chair by the fire and stirred it into life with a poker.

Four of the men had come back to the inn with him and they crowded round the sullen fire warming their hands.

"Well," said Peter Hichen, "I'll gather that guinea this morning I can tell you. I earned it last night, howsoever it turned out."

The others grumbled along with him and determined to go that morning to claim their rights.

"I heard it were a man from Wellsfield what done it?" said Dan Widgery. He went on, "Poor man – him with them childer."

A general murmur of agreement passed among the men.

"Mayhap he will escape wide an' free!" said the landlord. "Now, who can settle for their drink?"

Maddie took the tally down from the wall and began to count the strokes on it.

She looked out of the window; a beam of sunlight crept into the room as the new day broke.

"Joshua," she said, "let's give a break to these good folk and celebrate the new day."

Trim looked puzzled but sighed. "Well boys, we did our best and this is a new day, so let's clear the tally!"

Maddie smiled and wiped the slate. "Yes," she said, "let's hope it turns out well!"

MANY HAPPY RETURNS

"Mind the door," said the shopkeeper as Jimmy pushed his way into the shop. The bag of clinking bottles banged against the panel as he lifted it up to the counter.

"How many this time, you monkey?"

"Only a dozen, Mister Wright," Jimmy smiled as he acknowledged the cheerful nickname.

"Lucky for you there's thirsty people hereabouts," said Wright. "Now tell me how much you want."

"That's twelve at tuppence returns, so that's two shillin'."

Every few days the same exchange occurred. Jimmy collected the empty Corona lemonade bottles and claimed the "Return" from the shop.

Everyone in Barnsley knew Jimmy. When the war finished, the local authority had a problem finding a place for him. An orphan from the bombing, he became a liability which no family would take on, at that time. Nine years old and small for his age, he was passed round the town several times. It was not deliberate cruelty, but the lack of resources; rationing and austerity made people turn away. He was just another problem too many.

He ended up in the children's home, but they couldn't keep track of his whereabouts and soon didn't try. He became his own man and liked it that way.

It got dark as he left the shop and he fingered the two silver coins lying heavy in his trouser pocket. It felt good. Down the street he went, into the fish bar and waited in line for his order of "penny crispings," the local name for the odds and ends left over when the batch of fish and chips had been fried. The warmth of the frying gave a comfortable feel to the shop and the smell of fried fish wafted out into the street. He scooped the hot bits from the paper cone hungrily, as he sat on the kerb outside.

He could hear the voices of people in the queue as they waited their turn.

"She's a miserly old witch," said one man, "I only asked her if she wanted her winders cleanin' and she got huffy wi'me, the old hag!"

"Same as before," said the next man. "Hasn't bin out for years, daft old bag!"

Jimmy guessed they were talking about the old lady at Number 24 – the house with the dirty windows and overgrown front garden – he passed it every day on his way to school, that is, every day he decided to go to school, which was not often.

Next day, he peered at number 24 as he went passed. It seemed as dark and blind as a mole. Ragged net curtains hung awry at the windows and no light shone. He took a quick look down the side of the house to see if any bottles were there. It was dirty and smelled of cats.

"Get out of my garden!"

A shrill voice caught him by surprise and he ran back to the front of the house, tripping over himself as he reached the corner. On the step stood an old woman. She had a broom in her hand and held it like a weapon – two hands gripping the handle like a sword. She was thin and grey, dressed in a pinafore of the same colour. Her eyes were red-rimmed as if she cried a lot, but she gazed at him fiercely.

"I just wanted your empty bottles," he realised this would not do.

"I give 'em to the shop regular." He could think of nothing better at short notice.

"What's your name, boy?" she advanced towards him and he stepped back but she blocked his way to the street.

"Jimmy, Jimmy Fraser."

"Where d'you live then?"

Jimmy guessed she wanted to report him or tell his parents and he quickly gained confidence since he knew nobody cared a jot about him.

"I live in the Home down Surrey Street."

She stopped and leant on the broom looking down at him.

He tried a grin to see if that would work but her expression hardly changed. Then she turned and climbed the front step. When she got to the top, she looked at him and said, "Well? You better come in and look for yourself"

Jimmy looked past her through the open door. The hall was a dark cavern leading to a flight of stairs. There was a stale odour of old food and dust coming from the hallway.

"I'll be going," he said and began to make his way towards the street, not running but moving quickly as he could.

She called him back.

"Look! I got you some bottles anyway." She held up three bottles of different sizes. He could see only one tupenny Corona bottle. He stepped up to her and took all three quickly as if she might snatch him with her withered hands like a witch in a storybook. She nodded and went inside.

As she closed the door she called out, "There'll be more next week."

He ran down Surrey Street towards the High Street and dumped two of the bottles in a bomb site. The Corona bottle he stashed in his secret hiding place where he collected his stock.

When he got back to the Home it had gone seven o'clock and the Warden shouted at him for being late but he didn't care; he was rich, with money in his pocket.

He kept away from number 24 while doing his rounds for days, but something brought him back to the house the following week. Was it the mystery of the old house? Was it a dare he made with himself? Or something to do with the isolation which he shared with the old woman? He persuaded himself he might get more bottles to swap and pushed the question aside.

This time, he rang the bell. There was no answer. He rang again and heard the sound of shuffling feet approaching the door.

"Go away!" her voice was shrill but weak.

"I come for the bottles," he said, "you told me to come back."

The door opened and he could see the outline of her frail body against the gloom of the interior.

"Yes," she said, "I've got a few here and you can have them."

She turned and he hesitated, then followed her inside. He did his best to ignore the stale smells. She went into the front room and sat down in a worn old chair and picked up a bag from beside the chair.

"Here you are," and handed him the bag with four bottles in it.

"Them's not all Corona," he said, "I can't swap 'em if they're not Corona."

She smiled for the first time and nodded

"Well, that's your job isn't it? You've got to sort them yourself."

He agreed and then in a moment of silence, he looked round the room.

On a table beside the chair were two photos of a young man in Air Force uniform.

"Is that your family?" he said, filling the awkward silence.

"He was called Jimmy, like you, but he didn't collect bottles!"

He picked up the bag and thanked her. She remained in the chair, as if the effort of getting up was too much, and he went out of the house and shut the door.

By the time Friday came round, the Warden discovered he'd only been to school that week on just two days. He asked for an explanation but Jimmy kept his mouth shut and stood with his hands behind his back.

"This has got to stop!" The man bent down and stared at Jimmy but the boy looked away as if ignoring him.

"Look at me when I'm talking to you, boy."

The man shouted and flecks of spit formed in the corner of his mouth. Jimmy looked at him. His eyes show no expression and he said nothing.

"You'll stay in for the whole of the weekend – d'you hear? Now get out!"

Jimmy nodded and left the room.

Saturday came, the Warden went home and the staff slacked off. No one took the trouble to check on Jimmy, so by Sunday afternoon, he slipped out and took his collection to the shop.

"Well," said Mister Wright, "you're late this week. Has the town run dry?"

Jimmy smiled his best cheeky grin, and said, "I was a bit busy this week."

He counted the cash for the bottles and bought himself some biscuits from the Broken Biscuits Tin which were not on ration.

The next week was Wakes week and the town went mad. Every street had a party and the pubs stayed open from 11 in the morning till midnight. Parades and Union Rallies happened every day and the neighbouring towns joined in. Jimmy busied himself. He collected all sorts of bottles – beer bottles – cider bottles and, of course, plenty of Corona bottles. He spent a long time separating the penny and tupenny returns from the rest. Then he did his rounds of the pubs and off-licences to collect. He saved the Corona ones till last, knowing that he was sure of his money. He collected his cash and forgot about number 24 till he made his way back to Surrey Street. It had been ten days since he last went there.

He ran up the steps and rang the bell. He rang again and heard the familiar slow steps approach the door. He called out: "It's OK Missus, it's Jimmy!"

She opened the door wide and he saw she had tears in her eyes.

"I thought you'd forgot me," she said, "and I kept your bottles."

"Well it's been Wakes week an' I've been collecting all over," he said.

"Tell me how many you got," she said.

A strange feeling of pity for her came over him, as if he was her nurse or friend. He had never felt this before. He had found someone who needed him.

"Shall I come in then?" he asked, and she led the way into the back parlour where he had been before.

She sat in her old chair and he told her about the fair and the rallies that he'd seen that week. She gazed at him with close attention, her sad eyes wide with interest. When he finished, she pointed to the bag by her chair.

"I expect you don't need these then," she held out the bag to show three Corona bottles inside.

Jimmy grinned and said, "They'll do! I can put them in the shop next week but not today, 'cos he's paid me already."

She made a croaking sound and he realised she was laughing, it must have been something she'd not done for a long time.

"Well, will you be back next week?"

"Of course, this is my regular round now isn't it?"

Again, he saw the glint of tear in her eye and he turned away embarrassed.

"Well, I'll be off. See you next week."

He skipped out of the room and down the steps.

The following week was wet and cold, a spiteful wind blew away the bunting and the flags left over from the carnival. People kept indoors and the town seemed to close down like a grey prison. Jimmy had money in his pocket and left his collecting alone for a while. He began again when the weather cleared and one of his first calls was at number 24. He rang the bell but there was no answer. He rang again and hammered on the door in case she was asleep, although it was late morning. Still no answer, so he went round the back, but the grimy windows and net curtains gave nothing away.

As he returned to the front, a postman was banging on the door.

"Do you know the woman?" he asked. "I've got a registered letter from the council. Has she gone away?"

Jimmy blurted out: "She never goes away – she never goes out."

The man looked at him and muttered something Jimmy didn't catch. Then he walked swiftly away.

"You stay here lad, we'll be back in a minute."

He reappeared with two other men, one a policeman. They peered through the letterbox and shouted, but there was just silence.

"Stand back, son," said the policeman, and he ran at the door and gave a mighty kick. A panel of the door gave way with a splintering crack. He put his hand inside and released the lock. The hall floor was littered with circulars and a few papers but the house was silent. The door to the parlour was open and the three men stepped into the room. Jimmy followed knowing that something must be amiss.

"You stay outside," said the postman, but Jimmy could see into the room and the figure of the woman lying on the floor. She was curled up as if asleep but he knew she was dead. Her face seemed younger than he recalled, as if she was at peace at last. In her hand was a crumpled note.

"What's all this?" said the policeman, and he pointed to the floor. Twenty empty Corona bottled stood in a row around the old chair. In the neck of each bottle was a pound note neatly rolled.

He took the paper from her stiff fingers and read aloud, "For Jimmy."

He turned to the others. "Who's Jimmy?"

"Me"

For the first time, Jimmy felt a strange, painful pricking in his eyes.

He realised he was crying.

CIRCUMSTANTIAL
EVIDENCE

A hush fell on the Court as the Prosecution Q. C. rose to cross- examine. He pulled his silken gown around him and looked across the court. James Comyn was a thin man with a large head. He stood with his shoulders hunched and reminded one of a predatory bird - perhaps a hawk or a kite.

Across the well of Court One, the Defendant stood tall in the witness box. His fair hair and blue eyes caught the light from the high windows of Old Bailey in London. Gavin Somerset had been accused of the murder of Lord Gower, his father in law.

Upon the body of the dead man was an important piece of evidence: a fragment of a typed letter with the words:

.."and misfortunately, we have lost everything..."

The first question seemed harmless. What was behind it? "Did you lose your parents when very young?"

"That's correct."

"And it caused you much distress?" "Yes"

The cross-examination continued on the same theme: "When you were twenty one, did you suffer an accident?" "True. I was ski-ing in Verbier and broke a leg."

The defendant, Somerset grew in confidence as he related past events.

"What was the reason for the accident?"

The calm quiet manner of the query had the jury straining to catch the question. An elderly man at the back leant forward and cupped his ear.

"Well, I suppose it must have been my own fault," - then he interjected -" but that was years ago! I don't see how it relates to this case."

Comyn paused to see if there was any legal objection.

There was none. Henry Pitcher, for the Defence, saw no harm in the line of questioning, although far from the facts in the case. His instincts told him to save his ammunition for more serious objections.

The questioning went on; he persisted in querying other mishaps during the young man's life, dwelling on his bad luck and misfortune. Pitcher began to feel uneasy. It seemed as if the questions were sympathising with the Defendant; almost sharing his misfortunes. His instincts told him there was danger ahead, but what could it be?

Then Comyn turned to his vast unpaid debts. Somerset's bank account showed the money passing out into casino hands.

At last, he turned to his relationship with his father-in -law.

"Did you realize Lord Gower might have cleared your huge debts with a stroke of his pen?"

"I suppose so, but I didn't approach him." "Why not?"

"Because the old man would never do it! He loathed me for gambling his daughter's dowry away. -But that was our money not his. She didn't care"

His eyes blazed defiance at the thin bewigged figure across the width of the court.

"How did you feel about his attitude?"

Again, the tone of reasonable enquiry seemed more like an interview with a friendly doctor rather than a deadly prosecutor.

The earlier questions had been kindly put, so the defendant was eager to build on the apparent sympathy between them.

"He was nothing to me."

"Then why did you visit him on the day he died?"

Just for a moment, Somerset blinked. The jury leant forward, aroused from torpor. Even the Old Bailey ushers paused and listened.

"I went to collect some items from the house that belonged to me." "What items?"

"Just some clothes and effects I had left from previous visits."

"Why not send a servant for this task?"

Somerset smiled at the jury. "I can do simple tasks myself. Besides, I knew where the things were."

He was gaining confidence with every question. "Did you find them?"

"Misfortunately, I could not find them all."

A gasp swept across the courtroom. The jury turned to each other and Comyn smiled briefly. It took a few seconds for Somerset to grasp what he had blurted out.

"That is to say, I couldn't find everything but it was no great loss..."

James Comyn took up the letter exhibited and read again the quote from the murderer.

""Tell the jury why you truly went to Lord Gower's house at such an hour?"

"Why do you keep asking about that visit? I've told you why I went and that is enough!"

Red in the face with rage, Somerset gripped the edge of the witness box and glared down at the barrister.

Comyn remained silent for a few seconds - the clock on the wall ticked ponderously in the small silence.

"This was your letter and murder was your mission that night!" The bravado of the man was snatched away in one instant.

He had no words to combat the truth. His body sagged with despair and he muttered some denial which nobody could catch.

Henry Pitcher was like a stone statue, he betrayed not the slightest sign of the effect this had upon him. One word had convicted his client. He asked several harmless questions in re -examination, but nothing could be done.

The jury retired at 3.00 p.m. and returned at 3.30.

The foreman, a thin grey man stood to give the verdict. "How do you find the Defendant? Guilty or Not Guilty?" He paused and faced the man in the dock. "Guilty."

Somerset sobbed; not from remorse but from the horrible truth that he had betrayed himself.

Comyn scribbled on his brief and looked away from the dock while the Defendant was taken down. Henry Pitcher leant across the barrister's row and patted him lightly on the shoulder.

Then he turned to his junior "Time for a drink I suppose?"

THREE SHEPHERDS

Zadok stretched and yawned on his pile of sacks. A persistent flea tickled his gut so he scratched fiercely with his grubby nails and pinched it with his fingers. Inside his loose jerkin he stroked a curved knife with a sharp blade. A good friend.

Outside the barn he could hear the townspeople chatting and putting up the shutters for the night. Tomorrow was Shabbat. No one leaves a door unlatched in Bethlehem.

"Curse on the pack of them," he muttered, "what's the loss of a chicken or a lamb, you bastards, you've plenty to eat."

He stood in the shadows, careful not to be seen, as he calculated his chances of a quick cut-and-run on some old man or a woman.

No luck; so he slipped down to the inn where there was always rough company and no one asked your name.

In front, there was a space where the poor congregated. The door was always open but they knew only paying guests could go in. The place was bursting with customers, so he reckoned a bit of business might come his way later in the night when the young men or the merchants got too stupid and stepped outside.

"Any road, there's a good chance of a scrap of food from the waste bins. A full house means a lot of meals and plenty of leavings."

Among the crowd, he marked a young family, just arrived. The woman was pregnant and they were too poor for this place. He turned his back in case they looked his way. If a chance occurred, their donkey might be worth something and the less they saw of him the better.

He squatted close to the outer door to get first pickings from any bucket passed out, his sack pulled down over his face. He was only nineteen years old but had lived like this all his life. Only his long sharp nose and spiked beard were on show.

"Get away from my pitch."

A voice spat in his ear and a fist like a hammer drove into his kidneys. Zadok turned and found himself struggling with a black man with a scar across his face. For a second they wrestled fiercely until it dawned on them at the same moment.

"Zemal! ..."Zadok."

They were not friends but they shared the same destiny. They were the outcasts of this community and lived on the edge. No crime was wicked for them except the one that got you caught.

No hand would help. Everyone knew this, so life was a contest, each man against the rest.

"Make room for me." The black man shuffled a little and Zadok squeezed next to him.

The couple with the donkey had gone out of sight round the back of the building, to the stables.

Zemal leant over. "Three merchants lodged tonight."

He said no more. Zadok understood. He wiped his knife on his sleeve and glanced meaningfully at the other man.

Zemal wore the garb of the Bedouin tribe but the white jellabiya was grimy now and his turban pulled down over his straggled hair gave him a wild look. He was a tall man with a fierce gaze, older than Zadok.

He came and went without warning and had no job, so the town treated him with suspicion.

The crowd outside was restless. The midnight of the Shabbat vigil was approaching and no tasks had been given to the Gentiles jostling outside.

Tomorrow it would be too late, since all righteous men would stay away from work. Who would guard the flocks if not the outcasts?

The bell chimed the end of the vigil. Ishmael the merchant waddled out of the inn and surveyed the crowd. He wiped the grease from his mouth and threw a piece of meat into the air to see the wretches jump and fight amongst themselves.

"Three men to watch the flock."

He looked around to check their faces.

"Here!" - "Here!" - the voices rang out from every direction.

Zadok and Zemal pushed away the feeble ones and stood at the front.

"They're safe with my men." Zadok stood tall and indicated Zemal.

"We've worked for you before, Master, and we are three shepherds."

"Three?" Ishmael looks puzzled.

"My other man is in the stables mucking out."

All of this was a lie. Zadok never saw this merchant before - never herded sheep - had no third man. But he knew the hour was late and the owner too tipsy to pay attention.

"Here," Ishmael handed him a notched stick, "this is the tally taken this day, if you lose even one I shall send for the Romans and the justice of our mighty Emperor."

This raised a cynical laugh among the crowd who knew Roman justice. Zadok tipped his head in salute and took the tally.

"Well done, you blaggard!" Zemal laughed with admiration, "so where is number three?"

"We'll find one soon enough."

At the back of the inn, the stalls were full of noise and movement. In one, the little family with the donkey had installed themselves, sharing with a few animals. Zadok passed them by. Further along, in an empty stall, a pair of legs stuck out from a pile of filthy straw. Zemal grabbed the feet and pulled. A figure dressed in rags emerged as stiff as a corpse. A kick stirred the body and a bucket of water produced a miracle. He was alive!

"Nachman the beggar!" Zadok lifted the groggy man to his feet. He was short and stood on one crippled leg holding on to the wall. He smelt of manure, vomit and stale sweat. Two mean little eyes frowned and squinted at the pair of robbers.

"I'm doin' no harm here," he pleaded, "just resting for a few minutes. I'll be off presently."

"Come on, you'll do as you are." Zemal pulled him upright and half carried him out into the dark yard.

Wrapped in sacks, the three men climbed slowly up the path to the sheep pen in the high meadow. It was a fine night and a sky full of stars greeted them. Occasionally, a shooting star streamed in the firmament. A small hovel alongside the sheep fold offered some shelter from the wind and cold. They stumbled in and sat huddled together.

It was too cold to speak and the silence of the hills wrapped them in a spell which was hard to break.

A howl from a wolf pierced the crystal air.

"Listen! How near was that?"

"Too far to care." Zadok snuggled down into his sacks.

Again, the sound carried on the still air and Zemal looked out towards the sheep fold.

"Better check and show ourselves or he'll linger around for his chances."

He spoke as if the wolf was one of them, ready to seize anything he could. He smiled as he reflected how true that was. As his eye got used to the dark, he looked longingly back down the hill to Bethlehem. Lights shone in many houses and even in the stables he could see a faint glow from one of the stalls.

Above him a star brighter than a diamond glittered and flickered in the dark blue of the heavens.

"Zadok! Come out! See this. What does it mean?"

The radiance was so bright that it penetrated the little hut. Zadok scrambled out and peered up. A primeval fear of the unknown gripped his mind. What could it mean? Was it the Reckoning? The End of the World? Stumbling into the field, he got down on his knees in the way he had seen the Pharisees pray. Zemal dropped down too and prostrated himself, head to the ground. They remained there for some minutes. From the hut, Nachman the beggar peeped out wondering what had caused the commotion. Shading his eyes against the starlight, he stared at the men.

"Is it the Messiah?" he asked.

"What Messiah?"

"The Chosen One sent to redeem the World!"

"Who told you that?" Zadok was impatient with the old fool.

"My mother told me that one day He would come."

Zemal rose from the ground and pointed his finger at the star.

"It's moving!"

Surely, slowly, the star was descending in an arc towards the town.

No one said a word. Everything was still. Even the sheep stopped bleating. Its rays formed a path of light down to the stable behind the inn. Zadok was the first to gather his senses.

"Quick! There may be something in this for us."

He plucked Zemal by the sleeve and hurried off towards the ray of light. Nachman, scared of being left alone, stumbled after them.

The light shone on the stable door; they pushed it open gently. A stall was filled with light. It radiated from the manger where a baby lay asleep. There was no fear – a feeling of peace surrounded the little figure - the young mother covered his tiny limbs with a cloth – she smiled and Zadok smiled back. He said nothing and stood transfixed. Zemal found himself kneeling at the side of the cot, his hands joined in prayer. What prayer?

He didn't know any prayers - but his thoughts rose towards the heavens as if pleading for mercy.

Only Nachman the beggar stayed outside. He feared the unknown and mistrusted the light which dazzled him.

After a time, Zemal got to his feet and tenderly touched the sleeping child. His eyes filled with tears and he moved quickly out of the stall and stood sobbing in a dark corner of the stable. He could not explain the change which generated these tears. Maybe years of sin and countless crimes were leeching out of him?

Zadok realized the little family must be protected. Whoever this child was, his life was fragile and precious.

"Stay out of sight," he spoke for the first time to the young man standing beside the mother, "until I can be sure you are safe from harm. Any strange birth or unexplained event will attract attention."

The man nodded and gripped his hand in thanks. Slipping out of the stable, Zadok moved to the kitchen door at the back of the building. Within a minute he was back with a pot of stew still hot from the hob. The young couple never asked how he got it and he didn't explain.

From that night, Zadok was the guardian of this little family, hidden from the eyes of the town. There was talk of a search by Royal Guards. Strangely, he felt exalted by his new duty. He stood guard when some richly-clad strangers arrived seeking the Child. They brought costly gifts and he stood at the door in case curious eyes looked in. For a week Bethlehem was the centre of his world. He enjoyed the feeling of belonging, a sense of true worth for the first time in his life.

In his turn, Zemal set off for Nazareth to make ready the home to which the family would return. His life was given over to the care of the family of the starlight. He never thought why he was chosen, nor dwelt on his past. He was content.

Nachman the beggar watched in disbelief as the two robbers followed a different way. He stayed outside and went back to the sheep fold. In due time, he collected the pay for the night's work.

Days later he sought out King Herod's Guards and told them what he had seen. A Royal decree had ordered the elimination of all newborn males. They rushed to the inn and ransacked the stables but the family had gone.

EPILOGUE. Zemal stayed in Nazareth, tending the livestock of the village and hiding his past. For many years he watched the boy from the stable grow and come to manhood, but he never said a word about the Star. He was satisfied to be of use. He died worn out by labour but he never complained.

Nachman was taken by the Royal Guard and tortured to reveal the names of the family who escaped the Massacre. He died under torture and never gave their names - because he never knew them.

Zadok went to Jerusalem. Away from the stable, he fell back into crime and cynically took whatever he could rob or steal. It was his revenge on the society which rejected him. Caught and condemned some thirty or so years later, he was crucified along with two other men. As his cross was raised, the prisoner next to him said:

"My Friend, you will be with me tonight in Paradise."

He turned to look, and for an instant found himself back in Bethlehem. The radiant Child at his side. He gave up his life with a smile.

BITTER CHOICE

Omar hailed the bus as it groaned along the dirt road. It came to a halt beside him and he pushed Bashi and the baby up the step and tried to squirm his way in too.

"No!" the driver shouted. "Look! We can't take any more."

He pointed to the interior to show how the old bus was crammed with people and the roof covered with sprawling bodies.

"But these are my family, there must be room!"

A voice from inside replied, "Get off! You can see it is impossible!"

Omar ignored this and pushed harder. Bashi had managed to slip in beside an old woman who held the baby while she found a space.

Another voice spoke: "I'm telling you to get down!"

He saw, for the first time, the face of a man in uniform staring down at him from the roof. He had a revolver in his hand and Omar heard the click of the safety being released. It was a sound familiar to many Syrians like himself who had lived in Aleppo all their lives.

He stepped back from the door and as he did so, the driver revved the engine and the bus began to move. He grabbed at the door handle but it slipped out of his grasp. Running alongside, he slid his hand inside an open window, but his fingers lost their grip as the bus gathered speed. After twenty yards he tripped and fell onto the road in the swirl of dust thrown up by the moving bus.

After a minute he picked himself up and moved quickly to the verge as a convoy of pick-up trucks roared past. They were full of armed men following the bus away from the fighting.

"Bear up, Brother." A voice spoke nearby. "Those dogs are not worth your anger. Armed men running away from battle! Such dogs!"

The speaker was an old man who sitting on a plastic chair in front of a shell-damaged house. The door was missing and inside was a bare room with a trestle bed. The windows were sheets of plastic covering hollow frames. He motioned Omar to sit beside him and when he did, clapped his hands and calling a young girl to bring tea.

Omar was dazed by the turn of events. One minute the family had been united and on its way to safety – the next minute he was alone and still in danger. His money was in Bashi's purse and he thanked Allah she would be able to buy help and shelter.

"What shame!" said the old man sipping his tea. "And you, too, will leave?"

Omar explained his wife and baby were on the bus and how he had been turned away.

"This is a sign," the old man nodded his head. "You must take notice, my son, it means that you should not leave Mother Syria at this time."

On his forehead was the callus of a devout believer: a vivid trace of his lifelong prayers.

"How can you say that? You know nothing of me!"

He regretted his outburst at once, but the strain of the journey had taken its toll. The old man looked down and shook his head sadly. His thin brown face was creased and worn. Around his neck an amulet of quartz caught the light as he moved his body. He sipped his tea and said no more.

The young girl came to the table and sat beside Omar.

"You must listen to the Mahdi," she said. "He can feel the future."

"How can a man feel the future? Do you mean, see the future?"

"No. The Mahdi senses the waves that come from the body and can tell what will happen."

Omar grunted impatiently at this nonsense and thanking them for their hospitality, he moved out into the road to wave down a car approaching. He noticed the old man watched as he left, raising his hand as if blessing him, or was he sending him away?

The car stopped; a big Mercedes estate car with signs on the side: "al Jazeera." It seemed familiar but he could not recollect why. The driver wore some form of khaki uniform. He lowered the window.

"What do you want?"

He wore dark glasses and it was impossible to read his expression.

"I got left behind – my family are on the bus bound for the Turkish frontier – please help me!"

From the back of the car, a woman leant forward to look at him. She too wore khaki like the driver and her head and face were uncovered.

"What happened?" He explained how he had been kept off the bus.

"Come in," she said and spoke to the driver. He reached out with his left hand and opened the rear door.

Omar got in, brushing the dust from his sandals. The rear of the car seemed full of equipment but he saw a seat for him next to this immodest woman. She wore a man's shirt which was loose at the throat and her black hair was uncovered and held back by a hairband of bright blue. Her legs were bare and she wore short trousers like a European female. As they moved off, she was fiddling with a piece of equipment that he recognised as a voice recorder. There was camera equipment behind the back seat.

"Why do you want to escape Syria?" she asked. Omar was mystified by the question. Who would want to do otherwise? Who would stay to be bombed and terrorised out of their home? He did not know what to say; he knew any reply might trigger a rejection. Was she an Assad Syrian? Or an Iranian supporting Daesh? Whichever way his answer courted danger.

"My Lady, I just want to be reunited with my family." He spoke quietly and with a humble tone to placate her. He looked down, afraid to look her in the eye. He needed all his control to mask his anger at her stupid questions.

She did not reply, but just said, "We will follow the same route as your bus, so you will soon catch up."

The car moved along at speed, driving through the straggling mass, moving past several broken down trucks and refugees with push carts; but they never stopped again.

She seemed to ignore the scene outside her window and when Omar looked back he saw the dust cloud thrown up by the car blew debris over the long queue walking beside the road. He could do nothing for them but still felt ashamed that foreigners ignored the plight of his countrymen.

Gradually, he began to relax and enjoy this miraculous intervention. He dared not speak but occasionally glanced at her. She spoke on a cell phone in a strange language although she had addressed him in Arabic. The chauffeur glanced at him in the rear-view mirror and Omar could tell by his look that he despised him. However, he smiled at the driver in the mirror. The man stared straight ahead and ignored him.

Soon, they reached a check point and a Syrian soldier held up his hand to stop them, his AK47 clanking against the car door. He eyed them with the usual suspicion; he spoke to the driver and peered inside. He looked hard at Omar but the driver slipped something to him and his manner changed. Saluting smartly, he waving them through.

By now the woman had told him that she worked for the TV and radio station. He did his best to ignore her lax appearance.

"We can help you and your family, if you co-operate."

Although she spoke in his own language, he had no idea what she meant. Co-operate? What did that signify? What could he do in exchange for this favour? What did she want?

Ten miles further on, they approached another checkpoint. There, parked beside the road, was the bus surrounded by soldiers and the passengers. Omar could not see Bashi at first, but then he caught sight of her sitting in the shade of a tree a little way from the others. She was feeding the baby.

The car stopped and he jumped out and ran to her, gathering her in his arms. She smiled with relief, but looked past him at something behind him.

The driver was filming them. He moved round them examining them like specimens. Omar stood up.

"Why do you take our images? Don't you see we are private persons?"

He could not find the right words to express his feelings. The man went on filming.

Then the man said, "Get closer! Get back together for a moment."

"No! Go away. Leave us!"

The woman from the car came bustling up to him. "You want our help, don't you?"

"Yes. But what is this you do?"

He was bewildered; she explained why they were filming him.

"We will send out this picture to the whole world and then we will help you to get safe. This is to show how Assad treats his people."

Omar felt sick. This irreligious woman with her Western ways had raised his hopes and now the truth emerged. What would happen if the Syrian police saw him on this foreign programme? What would Daesh do to him if they found out he was supporting a foreign news company? The consequences either way were frightening.

"Please! No! Leave us alone! I cannot do this."

Still the camera turned as the man swooped in to film Omar talking to this woman. Now she covered her head with a scarf as if she was pious, so the film would show her modestly dressed. What a hypocrite!

She asked him his name and he hesitated. An irritated frown showed on her face.

"Come! This is what we must do. You want to be with your family don't you?"

For a moment he reflected. He was already with his family. But the hard truth of his situation bore down on him. He thought of Bashi and the baby; he watched the bus queue forming with the men climbing onto the roof;

the crowd still pushing and shouting to find room. He turned to the woman: "Where will we go?"

She used her cell phone again, pulling the scarf from her head, in an irritated gesture. After a short conversation, she explained: "We will find you a place to stay in Homs where you will be unknown. This is the best I can do."

Bashi looked up into his face. Her eyes searched for reassurance.

"Will our life really be better struggling with these crowds? My baby needs food and rest."

He was weary with the struggle and reflected: is it right to flee one's country at time when it is on its knees?

The old man's words came back to him – his contempt for the fugitives – his proud boast, "Mother Syria."

Omar straightened his shoulders. He put his arm around his wife.

"We will stay in our country," he said, "because it is our homeland."

The woman put on her scarf again and the camera whirled.

"Why do you stay in Syria?" she asked indicating he should speak to the camera. Omar turned to face the lens:

"I am a Syrian and this is my homeland. We want peace and a chance to restore life. Even if the fighting continues for decades, we will be here and we will survive."

He felt better than he had for weeks. As he took Bashi and the baby in his embrace, the cameraman nodded in reluctant respect and said:

"Inshalla"

THE DARK LAKE

The ferry was due at 10.30. A cluster of people arrived at the little ticket kiosk as the boat came into sight. Patrick could see the tourists in their sandals and bright plastic cagoules and a number of business men in sharp suits together with some women who looked as if they were locals. His eye was attracted to a girl waiting in front of him in the line. She was slim and dark and her hair shone in the morning sun. Everything she did was graceful yet she seemed natural and elegant. She waited calmly for her turn, reading a magazine.

At the head of the loosely formed queue was the portly figure of an English tourist peering into the window of the kiosk. On the other side of the glass the ticket clerk seemed to be shouting at him. The clerk, a small old man in a faded blue cap, waved his hands to assert himself. The tourist shouted;

"Give me back my card or give me my tickets" His voice easily reached the back of the group. The fat man put his face close to the grill and spoke louder than before

"Due billetes por favor and get a move on"

The group waiting for tickets began to murmur. The pretty girl looked at Patrick and raised her eyes to heaven. He had to do something or they would all miss the ferry. Walking up to the ticket office he spoke politely and quietly to the English tourist;

"It seems he doesn't understand exactly what you want"

The fat man took off his black straw hat, his puffy face scarlet with anger;

"I asked this stupid man for my tickets and offered him my credit card but he pretends he doesn't comprehend me"

Patrick turned to the ticket man and offered the fare in cash. With a shrug of the shoulders the clerk mumbled some profanity and issued the two tickets the man asked for. The plump man in the hat snatched the tickets and pushed his way towards the boat. All this took a little time to complete and the crowd surged forward as soon as the grumpy Englishman moved on. As Patrick struggled to find a place in the shoving mass of people he felt an arm pulling him forward to the front and a soft voice whispered in his ear "Bravo." The fragrance of scented hair brushing close to his face made him turn. It was the lovely girl in the crowd and her slim arm was moving him forward.

"Grazie Signor" she spoke in a soft accent "you are very considerate and deserve your place in the wait"

He understood her meaning and bought his ticket not knowing if it was correct or not, his eyes and senses distracted by the presence of the girl. He filed onto the ferry and looked to see where she was but in the bustling crowd he could not find her.

The crossing to Garda would take an hour so he enjoyed the fresh air and gentle breeze as he leaned on the rail of the top deck. The lake seemed calm and blue. The mountains pale and grey, making a backdrop for the colourful villages along the edge of the water. He turned to find the girl just a few feet away leaning on the same rail. She pointed to a village.

"That one is Liseze; you will enjoy it if you stop on the way back"

She smiled and he said in English

"Thank you for rescuing me at the ticket booth, I nearly got lost in the rush."

Soon they talked like good friends. She was Carla and she was attending a course of Advanced English at the Academy in Sirmione. He explained his interest in the churches of the area. As the crossing continued he found her charm and "natureleza" was unforced and they talked as if they had been friends for years. When she laughed it was clear she was content to be with him and he in felt thrilled to be with her.

One thing puzzled him. She wore high heeled shoes, slim black elegant shoes which made her unsteady on the ridged wood of the deck. On more than one occasion as they moved about the ship he had to steady her as she slipped on the footing. He was happy to hold her and somehow it confirmed their new found intimacy.

The ferry arrived at Garda. The bright cafes and hotels lined the wharf and the lively scene was inviting. Carla spoke to the ferry captain. He smiled and saluted her and they chatted for a minute. She hurried back to Patrick.

"He says Hotel Catullo is the place to eat. Shall we try it?"

Patrick felt elated. Without a word, she assumed they would spend the day together. He could not have wanted anything better and they walked to the lakeside restaurant. Occasionally, their hands touched. It seemed natural.

Over a meal of linguine, with wine she chose, she spoke of her ambitions

"When I have finished this course I will complete my degree." she said "And you, what do you want to do next?"

"I could take up my old job and design projects" Patrick grinned at her wrinkling his brow with mock horror "but I want to do something new and exciting"

She smiled and put out her hand to him "I can see that you are at a cross road, maybe that is why you came here?"

He felt his life might be at a turning point when he looked into her dark blue eyes. He took her hand and for some minutes they sat in silence with unspoken thoughts. Talk came easily to them and they delighted to find so many things in common. He asked if she would like to visit the churches in the town.

"Of course,I want to share your interests too" and they strolled into the cool shade of the 18th century church. He pointed out details which he knew from his research and she adding occasional comments from her local knowledge. It was perhaps the most perfect day of his life. She murmured her thoughts of the things they could do the next day.

"Would you like to see Verona?" she asked "on Thursday the cathedral has a recital in the evening which I want to hear"

His only desire was to be with her and his assent gave her as much pleasure as himself. Her beauty seemed to exalt him, her skin so clear and soft, her curves, her generous nature all combined to transfix him. It was a feeling he never had for any woman he had ever known. He felt a confidence that this was what he had waited for all his life. She whispered how happy he made her and linked her arm in his. He kissed her and held her close, feeling the warmth of her body against his.

The time came to return to Sirmione and they made their way back to the jetty with other travellers.

The lake had taken a different colour, more greyish in hue and the sky clouded over. As the ferry approached, he could see the captain looking towards the North of the lake where the clouds were gathering but the waters of the lake were as still as the ship came to the quay. The captain asked then had they enjoyed their meal and Carla replied with a remark that set the crew smiling. Patrick saw how they responded to her beauty and a slight twinge of jealousy came over him. He recognised this was natural as he was falling in love with such a desirable girl, but that was no consolation to him.

The crew became more active as they moved out into the deep part of the lake. Three men went onto the top deck and seem to be testing the hatches and generally checking the lashings of the life rafts. He saw all the rafts were on the top deck and wondered where they were located for the inner cabin. He and Carla and most of the passengers enjoyed the upper deck open to the sea and sky. As they cleared the harbour he noticed a slight swell as the ship began to roll; just a slight movement but different to the steady action they had felt on the crossing.

Carla moved close to Patrick and she put her head on his shoulder as if to sleep. The warmth of her body stirred his longing for her as they sat together. Gradually, the other passengers left the deck and they were the last outside. It was a chance to be alone they appreciated.

He was the first to feel the difference in the roll of the ship. It seemed more uncontrolled and some water dashed over the bows casting spray all the way back to where they sat. Carla laughed and ran for the stairs leading to the saloon and he followed. Just then one of the ship's officers climbed past them and checked the upper deck.

"Waves waves" he pronounced it like "wa fes wa fes "and they laughed secretly at his strange accent. Soon they felt a change and the ship began to rock and plunge as it met the larger waves head on.

"Attenzione Attenzione!" For the first time, the tannoy boomed out through the ship.

"He says he will try to turn back" Carla said and for the first time she turned pale and clung to Patrick's arm. The other passengers were silent as if they waited for some dreadful event.

The ship began to twist in an irregular way and more water crashed over the cabin as it moved across the direction of the waves. There seemed to be no control. As the boat rolled it plunged downwards and then stood up clear of the sea in a wild spring that ended in another plunge into the grey mass. This time, water crashed through the front screen of the saloon in a wave of such force that it plucked Carla from her seat and pulled her from Patrick's arms. She was flung against the doorway leading up to the upper deck. As the ship righted Patrick screamed out to her

"Come back to me"

His eyes locked on hers as she struggled to gain ground on the skewed deck. He could see her feet skidded on the wet surface of the deck. She clambered forward but one of her shoes jammed in the deck. As she struggled he leapt forward to catch her and pull her to him.

At that moment a grey mass of water smashed into the cabin. The ship was abeam the storm and the sea began to cast the hull from side to side in an increasing metronome of movement. The rolling barrier of water took her with its full force driving her out of the saloon into the sea beyond. Her screams faded into the noise of the storm and she was gone.

Dazed and frantic Patrick staggered up to the top deck where he had seen the life rafts. Clinging to rails as the sea fought to break his hold, he reached one of the rafts but the lashing was as tight as steel. He looked back at the sea as it raged behind the ferry but he could see no human form in the mass of waves curling in behind the vessel. The captain wild eyed and frantic screamed into the wind and sprang to the radio but it was impossible to stop the ship or turn back against the waves.

Slowly the violence of the waves decreased as the ship wallowed round to run with the sea. They clawed their way into Sirmione with the siren wailing for help. Within an hour the biggest ship in the fleet had been sent to scour the lake but nothing was found. Patrick sat dumbly on deck as police and others rushed on board. Among the frightened passengers was the fat Englishman who had argued at the ticket office. He looked weary and had lost his hat. As he passed, he touched the young man's shoulder in a mute gesture of sympathy.

Waving away the officials who approached him, Patrick had to be led from the boat to his room in the town. He said nothing, he ate nothing, but sat in his room. The captain arrested by the Maritime police claimed Act of God to explain his conduct but could not explain why the rafts were locked to the rails. Patrick cared nothing for all this. When asked to provide a statement for the inquest, he gave a brief account of the final journey. The police treated him with sympathy and he was not obliged to give evidence. He left Garda the following day. He told no one of the tender memories which haunted him for the rest of his life.

How can you predict what Fate has decided? A day may start in sunshine but end in shadow. The lake recovered its calm, limpid and reflecting the mountains. No memories rippled its surface.

HEALTH AND SAFETY

This Report concerns the full facts of the incident giving rise to my claim as per Reg 23 of the Safety Act 2005.

Inspector Bill Due and I were proceeding down Oxford Street W 1 on the 13 th of this month, dressed in full uniform and white helmet when I saw a male pedestrian carrying a ladder on his shoulder.

"Hold on" I said "You can't go about with a mounting appliance on your shoulder, it's not safe." I showed him para 4 of reg 21 to prove my point.

"What's it to you?" he says.

"I'll tell you what" I said "I am one of her Majesty's inspectors and I know what's right."

That put him back a bit and he set the ladder down. Mr Bill got out his pocket book to issue a formal warning (under para 4(a 322) but I intervened, in a compassionate way (as recommended by the Ministry.)

"Alright Bill, this time a Caution will do." I smiled, "but don't let me see you do it again. The Regs say a ladder needs two operatives and a hazard notice."

We moved on and I heard the sound of respectful thanks as we turned the corner.

Two minutes later Bill pointed across the street. There in plain sight was a window cleaner standing on one leg as he wiped a shop window.

"Stop that" Bill showed his authority with a massive cry. "You can't do that."

"Do what chum?" said the criminal and he continued to wash down the glass with no sense of shame.

"A worker who is not braced upon both feet risks his health and balance." Bill quoted word for word from the Handbook--a brilliant performance off the top of his head

"How do you think I do every job?" the scoundrel said without trace of respect.

"This will never do" I intervened "Disregard of regulation 10 (4a) is a punishable offence and I am reporting you."

I took out my red Report book and proceeded to take down his details. Funnily enough, he had the same name as David Beckham. When I commented on it he just shrugged. But I got his address and when he gets home to Brighton pier he will find a summons waiting for him.

We took a break about eleven in a caff off the main road and enjoyed a well-earned cuppa. It was a pity we had to issue a warning about unguarded kettles as it left a very unhappy lady at the counter but we didn't deserve the words she muttered as we reached the street.

We strolled down Mount Street, taking our time to show ourselves to the public in case anyone felt need of us in an emergency. I looked up and could scarcely believe my eyes. Above me was a horse chestnut tree with branches spreading over the pavement.

"Stop! Don't move" I shouted. A boy of about ten was in the act of picking up a conker. I snatched the chestnut out of his hand before he could do any harm.

I bent down and stared him in the face.

"Don't you realize conkers can hurt people? Have you never been told of the kid whose eye was put out in a conker match?"

The little whelp began to cry and people crowded round to see what was going on.

"Stand back" shouted Bill "Nothing to see here" and he held out his arms to keep them away.

I emptied the little beggar's pockets and the crowd gasped as six or seven bright new conkers spilled out onto the floor.

Several voices shouted out "Leave him alone, you workers" but Bill and I know our job and ignored this vulgar talk.

I stamped on the conkers and sent the little tyke off with a word of advice. As I turned to caution the objectors, my foot slipped on the conker mush and I fell on my back. Someone in the crowd spoke up but I didn't catch the words, I was in agony-something sympathetic, no doubt. Bill called an ambulance and I spent the next three weeks in Chelsea and Westminster Hospital.

This is the full account of the accident which has resulted on my need for a convalescent period as defined by Memo 743 of The Health and Safety Union Work Conditions.

I claim 14 days convalescence and sick pay for time lost on patrol.

A. Skyve

Health and Safety Inspector.

THANK YOU,
MR ROTHERSTEIN

"Come in my dear Coleman." The fat man rose from his seat and extended his hand across the large leather-lined desk.

"I got your letter and of course, I am happy to see you."

He sat down again and pulled a box of Cuban cigars towards him, selected one and removed the band before hesitating and pushing the box towards the man.

"How stupid of me! Do have one if it suits you."

His visitor was still standing, but with a wave from the banker he took a seat on a hard wooden chair. He declined the cigar with a small shake of the head.

"Things have changed from when we last met and I am sorry to read of your troubles."

His fat cheeks sucked in as he lit the Corona from a gold lighter on the desk. Coleman waited till the cigar was fully lit, before he said: "I only came because I felt you would recall our time together at Oxford and might wonder how I was getting on."

His fingers gripped his bowler hat on his knees and he smiled faintly. Rotherstein had seen men like this before. Men who couldn't survive the Depression on their own.

Always looking to cadge a loan from us who survived.

He sucked in the fragrant smoke, his lips large and red. When he puffed on his cigar they protruded, and left a wet mark on the surface of the tobacco.

Coleman was in his late thirties, although his pallid complexion and thinning hair made him look older. His hands played with the hat nervously and he had difficulty in looking directly at the banker.

"I wonder if I can just say a few words about my situation? You know Madeleine and I split up two years ago and the boy is with me."

"Ah yes!" cut in Rotherstein. "How is the lad? Must be twelve or thirteen by now?"

"Yes, twelve, and getting ready for his Common Entrance."

He hurried on: "That's mostly what I wanted to see you about."

"Very sorry about Madeleine," said Rotherstein, "such a lovely woman but a little extravagant would you say?"

His small dark eyes glittered as if to say: *You fool.*

"I had to settle quite a lot of unexpected bills and it hit me hard."

His voice faltered a little as he mentioned his dilemma. He looked down and brushed an imaginary speck from his hat. Then he put the hat on the floor.

"You said in the letter your Travel Business folded?"

The question was floated gently and Coleman looked up.

"Well, yes, the Depression has hit hard. No one is touring in these times and there is no money about. What I really want is a job." He leant forward eagerly and gripped the edge of the desk.

"I mean, you know I can do lots of things – remember how I toured with you in twenty-two? I did all the translations – French – Italian – even some Arabic in Morocco."

Rotherstein raised his podgy hand in a gesture to stop the gush of words. His ruby ring shone in the light.

"Of course I remember! It was my celebration after we left Oxford. You offered to chauffeur me didn't you? What good times..."

Coleman smiled brightly and said: "If only we could go back to those days. Summer with you and Maddie and not a care in the world."

The banker shook his head sorrowfully and tipped an inch of ash into a large ashtray.

"The Depression changed everything," he said, "I know, I know."

No, you fat bastard you don't know. You sat on your bum and called in all your debts. Then bought up business for a song.

"Well, I'll tell you what I will do," said Rotherstein. "Suppose I write to some friends of mine and tell them about you. Would that help?"

The tired, thin man looked up and his eyes widened. "Would you? I'd be so grateful!"

Rotherstein grinned to himself as he watched his reaction. "Of course! Leave it with me and we'll see what happens."

He rose and came round the desk and took Coleman by the arm, ushering him out.

"I can't tell you how much this means to me."

"Think nothing of it; I'll get on with it as soon as I can. Goodbye." A few minutes later he rang for his secretary.

"Take a letter to Mr Salamon.

'Dear Salamon

Thank your dear wife for a delightful evening on Thursday. Our meeting was a great success and the offer you suggested worked like a charm with the shareholders. We can now run with this one for a few months before pulling the plug and cashing in.

I wonder if you could use a "£5 per week type of driver"? I have a man who is down on his luck and might suit you? Do drop me a note if you can find the time.
Yours ever etc.'"

A week later a handwritten note arrived:
"My dear Raphael
This is just the sort of harassment we get these days from the English Middle Classes who prey on us mercilessly.
Your man needs to buck up and get a job at any level to justify his existence. No help here I'm afraid.
With very best wishes
Simeon"

Rotherstein read the note and tore it up. He never replied to Coleman. He forgot about it.
Coleman went back to his digs and carefully hung his only suit in the wardrobe. He brushed his bowler and put it on a hook behind the door. Sitting at the table under the dim shade he pulled out his typewriter and rolled a piece of copy paper into the machine.
"Dear Mr Armfiel
Thank you for your solicitous enquiry as to my welfare. I regret to say everything is far from well with me..."

NOTE: *This sad story is based upon two letters and a postcard dated 1931, between a Mr Rotherstein and a Mr Coleman which I found in a second-hand book.*

A LETTER TO ALICE

Dear Alice,

I am leaving tonight on the troopship Arethusa to join up with the boys who are fighting the Turks in Anatolia. I don't know where it is but I'm told it will take us about two weeks to get there and it will be hot!

I couldn't go without letting you know my feelings for you since we have been going out for a while now and I hope you will not mind my writing to you like this.

Jemmy has been a good friend to me and I think of him, not just as your brother, but my best friend. He reminds me of your lively smile and bright shiny hair, so when I am far away I will see you, Alice Jenkins, through your brother.

General Haig tells us that the Turk is a ferocious soldier, but we have better equipment and will have every support. I hope he is right because at the moment we have not got tropical kit and our main battery guns are not in the convoy. So when will they arrive?

Jemmy says that you kept that rose I bought you at the summer Fair in Doncaster, but I think he is joshing me. If you did – well I'd be as pleased as punch but I expect it is just his joke.

I left my best things with Mother in case we have a hard time an she will find some cash in my tin box that you know about. Dad is no good for cash since he got that lung infection or whatever it is that he got down the pit and he just sits around all day wheezing, poor old feller.

Anyhow, the colonel says we'll be back home by New Year, so we can be together ,if you would like that.

Don't know when I can send this, but will try to post it when I can

Don't forget me.

Your special Joe   xxx

(By Order of The War Ministry. This letter found on the body of Private Jonathan

Worboys. 4327898   1st Yorkshire Light Infantry. To be delivered to the addressee in accordance with General Instructions 18/3476)

THE BROCCOLI DEBATE

The Council of Vegetables met in an emergency meeting at the Soup Kitchen.

The Grand Pumpkin asked for silence and glowered at a couple of radishes twittering on the back shelf.

"I have to announce" he said in his pompous pumpkin voice "that a desperate crisis has arisen in the Kitchen and action must be taken."

Whispering began among the lettuces who fluttered with anxiety.

"What's the problem Fatty?" The Mares Potato bellowed. He had tried to throw his weight about on earlier occasions but the rest of the bunch shouted him down.

Pumpkin ignored the interruption: "The Chef proposes to add Broccoli to the Cauliflower soup and call it Brocoflower Medley."

A wave of noise washed over the assembly. Peas and broad beans squeaked-avocados shrieked and a babble of runner beans wailed loudly.

"What desecration" said a superior Carrot "our Professional Standards will be in ruins. Imagine if he tried to make a carrot and onion cake, or carrot and potato soup. The idea is appalling."

"Not so fast, you skinny red snob" said the Potato "I happen to know there is a thing called Potato and carrot soup sold in supermarkets."

The Carrot sniffed "I don't spend my time in Supermarkets." He turned away with a toss of his green shoots.

"Come to Order everyone "said Pumpkin "Shall we hear what Cauliflower wants to say about it?"

Cauliflower rose to his stalk;" Let me say I have nothing but the best regard for my purple friend" here he nodded towards the Broccoli

"But facts are facts and cauliflower soup is a perfect creamy colour accepted by the most discerning palates. There can be no purple in it and the idea is" he hesitated before going on "PREPOSTEROUS"

The last word he shouted and three new potatoes fell over in alarm. There was a silence for a moment and all eyes turned to Broccoli who sat wrapped in his broad leaves a few inches away.

At last he spoke "Who among you has won praise for his health giving minerals? Who can deny the plaudits showered on my fellow Broccoliers?

The Press rave about the benefits of my steamed stalks. Only yesterday Nigella swore my Flowery heads were medicinal. The value of this blend will be remarkable."

A rustle of agreement ran round the courgettes and cucumbers.

"Hang on" shouted the raw Potato "you've been planting yourself in all those North London Allotments-no wonder you get all these Trade endorsements!"

"But that is not the issue" said the Grand Pumpkin "We must decide whether we will boycott this idea or accept it."

"Ban It! Ban It!" chorused the cabbages and spring onions "We want no hybrids here."

"But you've already made a soup together" pointed out the Squash.

"What do we want? No new soups.-when do we want it?-Now" chanted the cabbages and they drowned out the voices of the petit pois who tried to speak.

"Let's have a vote of fronds" said Pumpkin and he counted up. The whole basket waved their appendages.

"Right" he said "no blend of Broccoli and Cauliflower it is"

The cooks arrived for work, read their instructions and began to prepare the vegetables for the soup of the day.

"Look at this Bob" said the sous chef "all the cauliflower's gone mouldy."

"Bin it then "said Bob "get weaving on the broccoli."

"No luck there it's shrivelled and stringy"

"Bloody Hell! We'll have to do carrot soups again."

They couldn't hear the giggles in the vegetable racks.

TAKE MY PULSE

"Yes Padre, come in I don't mind. Sleep? I don't sleep; I lie awake in my cell and think of Carla. No one disturbs me now the appeal has been turned down. They leave me alone and that's the way I like it. People say you blank out bad feelings but it's a lie. The trial is a dim memory but I recall every moment I spent with her. The burning jealousy, the way she laughed when I complained; how she set up with the manager when I was out on the job.

Sit down, you may learn something, if you pardon my saying so.

Last year, I began to work for Danny Yeoman. He was the boss of the delivery service I worked for in the old days, before I went away. He took me on again and I thanked him for it.

"We all have a past Jonny, time to start again, not look back"

I believed him.

Most of the time he gave me long distance jobs which paid more but took a lot out of you, what with the hard drive and the loading. But I didn't complain. The merchandise came sealed in brown packets and he never told me what was inside and I never asked. I guessed, since I never delivered to the front door but always round the back, out of sight. God's honest truth, I didn't care much, as long as I got good wages and no trouble.

After a few months I met Carla at the local bar. To my mind she was different to the rent girls I'd got used to. She had long black hair and the whitest skin.

Her figure was something and she knew it. The way she dressed made most of the guys light up but she smiled only at me. In those days she never flirted and we began to see a lot of each other.

She set up a flat for us a few doors away from the yard.

"Jonny, it'll be handy for you and it's not too far from the bar."

For two months we were good, sex and all, if you follow me.

Danny put me on a series of trips to Newcastle, Glasgow, all over, working me to death but paying top dollar. I never gave it a thought till I noticed the loads were light and the guys at the other end began rejecting stuff.

Coming back a day early was my big mistake. I wandered down to the bar about eight thirty that evening and found the truth. Carla was nowhere; Danny was nowhere, and the barman knew nothing, so he said. I stayed because I didn't want to go up to the flat and face the facts. I saw how it worked; half the week I was out on the road and Carla was down the yard with the boss or in the flat. About half nine, Danny strolled in like a prince. He swaggered to the bar before he saw me in the corner. His expression changed.

"Why the hell are you back so early? What's up with you?"

His mean little eyes darted about the room to see if any of his men were handy.

"I'm back cos the customers are complaining about the goods."

We spoke about this for a few minutes and I told him I was going up to the flat.

He smiled: "Wait a sec, have a drink. Maybe I was a little hasty just then."

The barman brought another drink and he sat with me as good as gold for another ten minutes. I wasn't surprised when Carla walked in and sat on a stool next to him.

"Didn't expect you home so soon" she said "what happened on the road?"

She offered no kiss no hug, just a question. No one treats me like that, Padre.

They despised me and used me. I'm not a sentimental type but life has its rules and they broke most of them. So I did what had to be done. I went back to the flat and packed her things. She stormed in about an hour later.

She laughed at me then she flung herself at me scratching with her long red nails. I pushed her away but she came at me again shouting "Danny"

He burst through the door; he had the baseball bat from the bar in his hands. Once, twice, he struck me. I fell to the floor. He kept hitting me and I crawled out onto the walkway outside. The door slammed shut. I managed to reach the stairs, tumbled down, picked myself up and ran.

Later that night, with a bottle of petrol, I came back. I know you are a man of God, but there has got to be justice here on earth I reckon. I waited till the lights went out, then I torched the place. They never got out... well they couldn't, the door was barricaded shut.

Nothing more to be said, I did what had to be done. Who would punish them if not me? You look for salvation but I needed justice.

Am I fearful? Do I look it? Take my pulse and judge for yourself.

BLIGHTED EXILE

A spanking breeze brought the Renown into harbour with a dash of old navy spirit. As she settled to the wharf, all hands were busy making good and 'showing the flag' to the amazed audience on the quay. The crew were dressed in best rig, and when the Admiral stepped ashore a flurry of officials hurriedly made their way down to pay respects to such a distinguished visitor.

Admiral Lord Cochrane, sixty-five years old and plump as a turkey cock, wore his full uniform and every medal he'd received in fifty years' service. A naval man might have wondered at some of the ribbons and insignia on display. There were purple sashes and jewelled stars which never came from England. Upon his fore-and-aft cocked hat sat a bright jewel, glistening in the blazing sun.

The Mayor and three Aldermen ran down to the quay, pulling on their ceremonial robes as they reached the waterside.

'Our joy is as great as our surprise, m'lord.'

The Mayor bowed and doffed his hat. 'Had we notice of your arrival, we would have shown our respect in more timely fashion!"

Cochrane looked about him for a face he might recognise. He expected a greeting party of at least a colonel, or higher rank. The frigate had been in the offing for about twelve hours, and any bright naval officer would have spied it well in advance of his arrival.

I suppose this is an example of damned army slackness. Still, must make the best of it.

'No need of ceremony, my dear Sir.'

He heaved himself down the gangplank and waved a vague salute to the Union Jack hanging limply from the flagpole on the dock. He wiped his face with a cloth and doffed his hat to reveal bright red hair, undiminished by age, in stark contrast to his greying mutton-chop whiskers.

The island harbour was Jamestown, St Helena; the most isolated of His Majesty's dominions in the South Ocean. It had no claim to distinction, save for the outstanding fact that the Emperor of France, Napoleon Bonaparte, was held here in exile. The garrison providing the guards and sentries amounted to no more than two hundred officers and men; the total less than the crew of the warship which moored so neatly.

'I'd be obliged if you would make my arrival known to His Imperial Highness and, of course, to the Governor.'

Cochrane looked down on the official with a kindly patronage.

'Is it possible to find some shade? I find this sun a little too much for an old man!' He waved his hat like a fan and followed a servant to the veranda of the Custom House to await a formal welcome. He sat, rather like a broad, multi-coloured Buddha, on a rattan sofa and accepted a glass of pale wine. He grimaced just a little as the poor-quality drink rinsed his throat like a medicinal potion.

The Admiral was a remarkable man. At the end of the Napoleonic wars, he'd found himself 'on the beach', with no fleet and heavily in debt. He enlisted in the navy of the New Republic of Chile, taking command of the hastily-formed fleet to fight the old regime of Spain, which still held power in South America. His panache and experience achieved wonderful results, and the strange medals and jewels he wore were awarded by the grateful new nations he helped to create.

Reluctantly drawn down from Longwood House, Governor Sir Hudson Lowe presented himself.

'A very good welcome, my Lord! May I ask what brings you to this godforsaken place?'

Very little intuition was needed to guess that he hated the posting.

·Cochrane scrutinised the Governor with a shrewd eye and hesitated before replying.

Sir Hudson had been chosen for the thankless privilege of shepherding the Beast of Corsica, by a Whig government which wished to relieve itself of one of its most active opponents in the House. His only claim to the post was that he would walk over hot coals to get to a peerage. Even he, who sacrificed his health and his wife to this unhealthy climate, could not keep the edge of bitterness out of his voice. His narrow face, with its tightly drawn skin, was like a pale mask from which his dark eyes stared through. His pallor was a living contrast to the weather-beaten visage of the seafaring lord.

Lowe kept his chin stiff and his head up, trying not to reveal his resentment of the freedom and reputation of this 'freelance mercenary' recalling how Cochrane appeared to have passed through life with every privilege and had made a name for himself across the wide world of Europe and the Americas.

Cochrane spoke. 'There is a matter of a confidential nature that I must put before the Emperor.'

The Governor stiffened at the peremptory tone of the request.

'We do not address him with that title in this place, but if you wish, I may be able to arrange a meeting. Of course, it will be my duty to attend.'

The Admiral's face began to resemble a boiled beetroot.

'Nonsense! This matter is of a personal and confidential nature, and I have sworn to deal directly with...' he hesitated, 'Napoleon, and in secrecy.'

The Governor controlled his temper. Clearly, such a confidence was out of the question, in the strictest sense, but what harm would be done? A friendly word in Whitehall was always valuable. Discretion would be needed.

'Let me consider it with the prisoner's advisors. If they agree, it may be possible.'

A warm smile crinkled the corners of the Admiral's eyes. 'Then do me the honour of dining aboard this evening! It is time I had some civilised company instead of rough seadogs.' His raucous laugh set a flock of parakeets in flight. Lowe bowed with just sufficient a nod to express his consent.

The evening went well. The officers of the Renown, kitted out in their various dress uniforms, were presented to the Governor. Among the group, Lowe was surprised to find most of them were ex-officers of the British Navy, cast aside at the end of the war and finding employment in the New States: Uruguay, Chile and Argentina. A dinner of fine fresh turtle soup, fish cooked in Chilean Muscadet, followed by brandy plundered from a French man-o'-war, had a soothing effect on Sir Hudson. The various young men in the strange uniforms came from good families and took considerable trouble to amuse him, promising to send messages to Lowe's family at home and charming him with their society chatter. Cochrane's eyes gleamed, his plan was working well. Before the evening was over, Sir Hudson believed he had won a new friend at Whitehall.

The necessary consent was granted.

The following morning, Cochrane came ashore to find a guard of honour formed around the ancient carriage which served as the Governor's coach. An aide-de-camp waited on him and they set off at a snail's pace up the long hill to Longwood. The house sat among trees at the top. A gloomy brick building with little favour, its appearance was only made bearable by a deeply shaded verandah stretching across its width A slight mist hung in the air, and Cochrane felt the damp seeping into his uniform. He began to see why Lowe described the place in the way he did.

A French officer greeted them, and showed them into a drab drawing room to await the prisoner. The room's dismal brown walls and faded, slightly grubby furniture betrayed the fact that this was no customary reception room. In one corner, a curl of damp wallpaper crept free of the wall; dank air from the mist outside filled the room.

Knowing he would find it difficult to rise when the Emperor came in, the Admiral remained standing, leaning a little on his dress sword for support. A curtain covering the opening to an adjacent room twitched, and sensing he was observed Cochrane took up a pose to impress his observer. Suddenly, the curtain was drawn aside and Napoleon stepped into the room placing his hat on a side table.

'Mon cher Amiral, un grand merci pour votre visite.'

The man who stood before him was familiar to every soldier and sailor in Europe. Yet now, seeing him in real life, he seemed puny to Cochrane. He was smaller than he had imagined and was dressed in field grey, with no decoration. The contrast between the corpulent seaman and the Emperor of All France could not have been greater.

Cochrane bowed and spoke in English. 'I have voyaged round the Cape to present the respects of the Liberated Nations to you, your Highness.'

Napoleon shrugged and held out his hand. 'What am I? An Emperor of this rugged island of...' he looked for the word, 'brumes? Fogs?'

He nodded to the aide-de-camp and the young man withdrew, leaving the two great men alone. Napoleon took a seat and motioned to Cochrane to sit facing him.

There was an awkward moment as both men regarded each other, weighing each other up, recalling what they knew of each other

'You may know,' Cochrane eventually began, 'I have commanded the fleets of the Liberated Nations to drive the Spanish from the New World.'

The Emperor nodded with a slight smile. Memories of Austerlitz and Jena, victories which crushed the combined forces of Europe, came to mind. Was the fat sailor trying to compare himself with a man who had been King of Italy and Emperor of France?

'The people of the Spanish colonies must know their debt to your lordship.' Napoleon conceded with a gracious wave of his thin hand.

Cochrane bowed slightly and registered the condescending remark.

He moved on. 'I deplore the fact that your Imperial Highness finds himself in such straitened circumstances.' He glanced around the dank room with a look that took in the contrast between this place and the gilded chambers of the Louvre, which Napoleon had been forced to leave.

The Frenchman never blinked as the thrust went home.

'I must tell you of the aspirations of the new nations,' the Admiral said. 'They long to find stability and safety from the predators in Madrid.'

Bonaparte listened politely, imagining the picture of this gross figure as an agile seaman, clearing the decks of enemy ships. He recalled that in an earlier age he described this man as 'Le Loup de Mer' - The Sea Wolf - who had been a thorn in his side during his conquest of Europe. Now the corpulent man in front of him was an old hulk; what purpose did he have coming here to speak with him?

'I feel for their aspirations,' he sighed. 'Was it not the same instinct that drove me to free the French people from the serfdom of a wicked regime? It is a natural desire, but needs a strong unity.'

The Admiral sat forward in his chair, his podgy hands pressing into the flesh of his knees as he saw an opportunity to make his case.

'Do you realise how much the people clamour for help? They believe their destiny lies in the hands of a man who can bring order to the several nations.'

Napoleon raised his hand in mock protest. 'But San Martin has gained the prize, no doubt much due to your fighting spirit.' Cochrane sensed the tinge of sarcasm in the remark, but pressed on.

'President San Martin knows he can not engage the confidence of all the nations in this great quest. What is needed is a man of destiny, one who can unite the peoples of South America and lead them to a new world power.'

Napoleon sat immobile as a figurehead, his eyes fixed on a patch of blue sky far above the scudding clouds framed in the window. Then he turned, and asked,

'Will no one take up the mantle? One of the brilliant young men of the south, perhaps?'

Cochrane leant forward, so that his curly red head was on a level with Bonaparte's ear. His voice rasped with urgency.

'It needs a great man."

He held Napoleon's black eyes with an unblinking gaze. 'I am commanded to offer you, Emperor, the golden crown which fate has snatched from your head.'

The words rolled off his tongue with practised ease; he knew vanity was a weapon which could win as easily as a blade.

Bonaparte sat motionless for a time and then cupped his face in his hand. His large, domed head, with the wisps of dark hair still plastered across his forehead, became the focus of Cochrane's attention. He wondered at the figure of the man who had held all Europe to ransom.

When he lifted his head, Napoleon's eyes transformed his face. The light of ambition glowed with a startling intensity once more. The tired, weary figure was banished; confidence lit up his countenance with new life.

'Is this the Will of the Nations?'

'I have come a thousand miles to bring this message.'

'Then let God's will be done!'

Napoleon rose and approached the Admiral, as if to embrace him. Cochrane tried to rise but his weight defeated him and he struggled to get out of his seat.

'Stay as you are. I salute you with joy and gratitude.' The former Emperor took Cochrane's hand in his and held it for a moment. In his turn, the Admiral blessed his luck: he had avoided a Gallic embrace.

They remained in conference for an hour. Napoleon laid down an outline of the tasks required to establish this new Empire. Cochrane listened with attention then indicated he would return to St Helena after the Council of Nations ratified the plan. Meanwhile, secrecy was all, of course.

'Trust me, Highness; you face a task of magnitude but great significance. A world of new opportunity awaits you!'

Bonaparte stood, put on the simple tricorn hat and faced the Admiral with a look of supreme confidence. Stiff backed, he seemed taller.

'It is clear I must accept the challenges that fate has prepared for me. The Nations will not find me asleep in my island den! When will you return?'

'I intend to return within three months. I will send a courier before we arrive and we will follow at the date he will specify. Be sure, Monsieur L'Empereur, we will bring you in triumph to Santiago.'

'But the troops? How can we avoid bloodshed?"

'I have no doubt we can complete this exercise painlessly. My men are, after all, Englishmen too. They will not fight their own kind."

With due ceremony, the Admiral withdrew, and after attending on the lGovernor he set sail again for Chile.

Three months to the day, a frigate of the Chilean navy appeared in the offing outside Jamestown harbour. The Captain came ashore with a sealed order for the Emperor's eyes only.

It was never delivered. The Emperor had died three weeks before, of an unknown gastric illness.

FOOTNOTE: The basis of this story is true. Cochrane devised a scheme to create a new empire in South America, and offered it to Napoleon (who was just fifty-one). The officer bringing the plan arrived three weeks after Napoleon died. The cause of death has never been established.

URN RETURN

California is all sunshine and bronzed bodies. Style is the message. If you haven't the cash, then you fake it -just like your tan.

Jake had lived in Maribou with his partner Jim for fifteen years. When Jim died it seemed for a while as if the sun was going down on Jake. He had no cash. You see, once you live in a condo facing the coast, you tend to forget little things like mortgage and realty fees. Jim dealt with all that and Jake never gave it a thought.

In the Chapel of Eternal Peace he had never felt so alone. His light blond permed hair and his pale blue suit with a matching tie set off his tan rather well, but no one else saw it. The coffin slid smoothly behind the curtain, the music swelled and the sound of the hungry furnace was almost imperceptible. He felt a tear welling up and he wiped it away with his silk bandana.

A kindly official led him out into the sunshine.

"If you would be so kind as to wait here I will be back in fifteen minutes and we can complete formalities."

Jake strolled to a bench facing away from the chapel, he examined Jim's file of papers for the first time. There were several letters, documents and a cheque book. The funeral director returned and ushered him into a large air-conditioned office beside the chapel.

"This won't take long" the man smiled in a kindly way "just run your eye over this invoice and if you'd be so kind..."

His voice tailed off as he offered Jake a pen and indicated a line where he should sign. The paper seemed out of focus and all he could read was the Final Total which glared out at him.

"*Christ! this is murder*" He thought "*Jim, you'll ruin me.*"

There was no money in his own account. His thoughts darted to the file lying beside him on the seat. He drew out the cheque book and wrote the cheque as if in a dream. Jim's signature was easy -he'd done it before so many times it seemed natural.

"Very satisfactory." The kindly man scooped up the cheque -he never looked at the printed name on the cheque-and having shuffled some documents passed copies across the desk.

"That is all done, Sir"

He stooped down and picked up a small cardboard box which he placed respectfully on the desk.

"How would you like the departed packaged?"

It took Jake a few seconds to realize all of Jim was now contained in a cardboard box nine inches square.

"What do you usually do?"

"Generally, the family will choose one of our urns. They vary from economical to the Executive Range. Can I show you a catalogue?"

"No!" Jake's voice rose a little "I'll take them as they are. Thank You."

The man stared at him for a moment and passed the box over the desk. He seemed a little less sympathetic.

Walking down the lawn-lined path from the chapel, he saw neat rows of identical tombstones with small urns of various sizes planted upon them. He chose a small bronze coloured vase and wrenched it free from the base. Stuffing it under his jacket, he scanned the quiet parkland but no one noticed. He dropped the cardboard box behind a bush and Jim's grey ashes drifted away unobtrusively. The area where the urn had sat bore no sign to distinguish it from the rest, but as he hurried away, he wondered for a moment why the headstones were so small. He shrugged his shoulders and moved on.

Down the hill from the funeral home he turned into a bar and put the little casket under the bar stool. He called for Bourbon over ice -a double -and reviewed his options. Provided the bank didn't find out Jim was dead, the mortgage charges were no problem. Still, the cash couldn't last forever. The germ of an idea began to grow. Jake spent much of his life turning a penny from scams. It was only after he met Jim in a gay bar in San Fran that he given up the trade.

He punched a number into his cell phone.

"Hi Walter! How are you? Listen, I need some advice. Can I come over?"

Walter was an expat Englishman who worked the same bars as Jake had done. He knew all about Limey customs and habits. His apartment was downtown beyond 22nd street, about thirty minutes by cab.

Walter opened the door and Jake realized this was his day off. He wore a pair of crumpled silk pajamas and slippers. His toupee sat on a stand in the hall and he held a tumbler of whisky in his hand.

"What's so special? You know I'm off duty."

"This is nothing to do with the bar. I want some advice.

They moved into the apartment and Jake explained his idea.

"Could be good" Walter smiled "Let's see."

The two pored over the letters from the file.

Walter delivered his verdict. "I reckon this could work. All we have to do is finesse the English party and cash in!"

Jake paid no attention to the plural pronoun, his mind raced ahead. He took out the little bronze urn and put it on the table.

Walter was silent for a moment.

"Where d'you get that thing?"

"I won it" said Jake and after a pause "For Christ's sake! They gave me a cardboard box to hold Jim's ashes! Bloody Savages!"

"What's inside it?"

They prised open the ornamental lid with some difficulty and peered in at the grey dust which half-filled the urn.

"Well" said Walter "Jim won't mind, will he?"

Jake said nothing but jammed the lid on tightly.

"First thing is to connect with the Brits." he said.

"We got to write about the Urn an' all."

"Ok" he said "But listen, we share the scam.Ok?"

Walter agreed and set about drafting a letter.

"Dear ......

I have the sad duty to tell you that my best friend James Hardcastle passed away last week and I attended the cremation yesterday. His last wish was to be united with his Kin in the land of his birth at Leeds Town in York Shire England. Unfortunately, he left no funds to carry out this last duty and we wondered if his English friends could help with a first instalment of 350 (US Dollars) towards fees involved?"

"That should start 'em off nicely." Walter said confidently.

Jake riffled through the letters in the file and found one from a Dr Ann Massow on Leeds University note paper. He reckoned an academic lady would be just the mark for this scam, so the letter was sent and they sat back to see what happened.

*

Leeds Faculty of Beaux Arts was based in one of the older buildings in the university campus. Post was collected each morning and dispatched to the Members of Faculty at once. Within a day other members of the Arts Group had learnt of the death of Jim Hardcastle and a meeting was arranged to discuss action. Dr Massow passed the letter to the Rector.

"I knew Jim Hardcastle," said the Rector. "We worked together when he was a rising star in Creative Writing. Remind me, when did he go to the States?"

There was a small silence before one of the women spoke up.

"If you recall, Rector, there was the incident with the dog..." her voice faltered and faded.

"Oh! I see!" he cleared his throat and went on quickly. Time had not expunged all recollection of his student days with Jim. "Perhaps we should do something. I'll get my secretary to write back."

The reply reached Jake within a week and he went down to the Gaiety Club. Walter was working, sitting with a large bald headed man in one of the booths. His magenta frock was low cut and Jake had to admire the way it set off Walter's deep brown hair style. After a moment's badinage, he managed to escape the embrace of the stout party and came over to the bar.

"Got a bite!" said Jake "Here read this." He handed the reply over and they both scanned it together. The MoneyGram was made out to Jake for 350 US dollars.

"That's my boy!" Walther gave him a dramatic hug and looked over Jake's shoulder at the fat punter in the booth. He gave him a wink.

"Now we gotta stir it up a little. Meet me later and we'll chat."

Then he sauntered back to Fatso and Jake left.

Next day a letter was winging across the Atlantic explaining the problem with the Customs and the excess they were charging for the dispatch "of funereal equipment containing depositary substances"

*

Dr Lambert, the Rector, frowned as he read the new letter. The business about Hardcastle and the dog still rankled. The Press had never given up their search for the truth and the awful scandal could flare up at the slightest hint. It would be better if he dealt with this himself. Some of the staff had a prim attitude towards experimental practices by young men.

"After all, we were all young and made mistakes ... still unusual ..." he thought.

He came back to the present with a start and decided another contribution had to be made. This time he paid it direct from his own account.

*

The $500 dollars paid nicely for a trip to Acapulco. Both partners enjoyed the exotic pleasures of low life

Mexico. "Do you reckon we can scam again?" Jake looked across at Walter as they sipped Bacardis.

"Naw! This is a quick in and out. Pull the plug and send the tin."

Some days later, Jake packed the urn in a polythene pack and consigned it to Fed EX.

*

The Rector's secretary received the parcel and prepared the ceremony for his approval.

"I think full academic dress is justified don't you?"

"Oh yes ! Celebrated Alumni deserve recognition.... and besides" she added "I've lined up the Northern Echo to report."

Lambert smiled discreetly and adjusted his gown. This would be a chance to flaunt Leeds' academic prowess to the world.

The Hall filled with the undergraduates and Press as the Faculty entered in solemn procession. On a dais high upon the stage the urn had been set up on a bed of pale silk. The spotlight was strong and he noticed, in passing, how small the urn seemed on its bed of silk. He spoke for twenty minutes on the values of Jim Hardcastle and his experimental work in modern English Prose. As he finished he took up the urn and held it for all to see. The last remains of a modern master. Under the strong light he began to read out loud for the first time, an inscription etched on the rim of the cup.

"To my darling PIXIE the best Pekinese in the world."

IZZAT OR
FAMILY CONFLICT

The class at Skirmdale Academy cleared out as the bell rang, with a clatter of slammed chairs and loud voices. Faiza and her friends grouped outside in the playground and gossiped about the usual things: the stupid boy in Year Four who came on to Jane Parker; Miss Turner's new hairstyle (Sandra said it looked like one of the Clangers); then a quick flick at Snapchat before they moved on to make their way home.

Faiza lived three streets away and sometimes her elder brother would be waiting for her outside the school gates. Jamal was tall and grew his beard in the way of Allah -Peace be upon Him - to show that he had become a full member of the Rashid family. At nineteen he refused to work in the factories. He said he could manage on Social Benefit.

The front door of 17 Aldgate Road was always locked, so Faiza banged at the upper panels where the paint had been scratched away with age. Her mother opened the door without a word and shuffled back to the kitchen. Time had not been kind to her. She arrived with her elder sister from Pakistan, twenty-seven years ago. Her father sent for them when his second wife died and they came as family to share his life in Huddersfield. Her marriage had been arranged back in Pakistan, and her new husband, cousin Karim, came two years later. She had three children and kept house for the family. She never needed to learn English, just a few simple words; she could not be bothered, in any case.

'What have you done today?' The question in Urdu was not a cheerful enquiry; Faiza's mother never enjoyed happiness, ever since a young bride. Obedience to the code is what she had been taught and there was little room for gaiety.

'Nothin,' Faiza replied in English, partly out of laziness and a little to taunt her mother.

Later that day she phoned Aziza, her friend, she went to a different school, where strict rules applied and she wore the niqab.

'What's up chick?' Aziza queried.

'Pissed off at home, that's all.'

'Come on over and blend, then.' They agreed to meet at the market clock in Upton Park.

'Bring your phone, girl,'

Faiza said, she didn't have one, her father or brother would suss it out if she did. At six o'clock she skipped out, while her mother watched a video and before her father got home.

Aziza stood next to the clock, talking to a boy from Faz's school. She wore a short skirt over jeans and a bright red top. Her head was uncovered and she had eye make-up on. no sign of the niqab.

'Hi Faz!'

A white boy from a class in the same year as hers stood with his hands in his pockets grinning at her, and so she smiled and chatted to him, free of the rigid code that separated boys from girls in the school world.

'Bought some SIM cards cheap at the market, want one?' Ryan showed them the pack of SIMs and offered them like cigarettes or gum.

Aziza grabbed one and examined it. 'Thanks! Save a few bob.'

She put it in her jacket pocket.

"Come on let's go down the market and get you one!'

She pulled Faz in the direction of the shops and she allowed herself to be led.

"No harm in looking I suppose," she thought.

The shopfront gleamed with shiny phones: multi-coloured ones; glossy Black and pure white ones. Every one the man showed seemed better than the one before. He was a tall Sikh and watched the two girls with amused interest.

'Your Daddy will approve of this one,' he said and held up a plain Nokia.

Aziza wrinkled her nose and shook her head at Faz.

'This one!' said Aziza and picked up an iPhone 6 in red.

'Good choice,' said the man, 'I give you a good price! It's second-hand.'

Faiza was dazzled by it but shook her head. The salesman pushed the phone her way.

'Go on, you can pay me in instalments, say three pounds a week.'

Aziza joined in. 'It's a no-brainer,' she said, 'I paid twice as much for this crappy old Samsung. Go on! If you don't, I will.'

All at once, Faz felt an impulse, so strong that it took hold of her.

"Why can't I have what she has? And she is more Adeb than me, or pretends to be! "

Aziza dipped into her pocket and brought out three pound coins.

'Done!' she said and handed them to the stallholder. 'You can pay me back later.'

He put the SIM card into the phone and showed Faiza that it was already charged. The smooth touch of the phone and the weight of it excited Faz in a strange way. It radiated power and freedom; she held a magic wand which gave her a network of friends and skills she'd never had. The girls sat together on the wall by the library and she learnt quickly how to download apps for the services that were essential: Facebook, Twitter, Google, Facetime and more, giving music uploads and videos. A new world opened and the excitement drowned out her fears about the family response. Until Aziza said, 'What you going to do about hiding it?'

It acted like a dash of cold water. Faiza's eyes widened with alarm. The reality of what she had done ran like an electric current through her body. She began to tremble and clutched Aziza while she tried to make sense of the turbulence in her brain. One voice exulted in her freedom, another screamed a warning and the picture of her brother and father loomed large in her imagination. She felt helpless for a moment and turned as if to take the phone back to the trader.

'No!' Aziza sensed what she was about to do, 'I can keep it for you if you like.'

'Won't your family make a hell of a fuss if they find it?'

'Don't be a zombie. D'you think they'll find out?' The look of scorn silenced her.

They walked back to Aldgate Road and parted at the front door. It was half past seven and Faiza realized her father would be back.

'Where you been?'

Karim opened the door and grabbed her by the shoulder. She pulled away and pushed past him without a word.

'Come back here, Kutta,' but she ran upstairs before he could reach her and slammed her bedroom door. Too tired to follow her, he went back into the kitchen. He swore at his wife, blaming her for the girl's disobedience, then subsided into silence, hunched over the newspaper. He was a bulky man in his fifties, dark complexioned with small brown eyes and thick eyebrows. His hair, brushed back from his forehead, slick with oil, shone in the dim light. He sat astride the chair with his arms on the table.

The woman went upstairs and pushed open Faiza's door. She frowned, it meant something unpleasant.

'You are fifteen now,' said her mother, 'we have decided to find a suitable husband.'

'You're joking! What, some old fart from Lahore? You are in la-la land!'

'Don't speak to me like that. It has been discussed in the family and it is proper.'

'Not with me it's not. Do you think we are in the dark ages?'

'What you mean - the dark ages? This is family - this is Izzat, family honour.'

Karim appeared at the door.

'What have you said?' He frowned at his wife. 'Did you tell her what the family want?'

Before she could reply, Faiza was shouting at her parents, near to tears.

Karim swore and stood with his back to the door, his arms folded across his chest.

'Do you think you can do what you like because you are here in England? Do you think we care what you want? This is family.'

Faiza went to reach the door but her father blocked her path.

'You go nowhere,' he said, 'until all is decided.' He went out and closed the door behind him.

She sat down on the bed and the anger she felt was replaced with a feeling of numbness. She never dreamt for a moment that this could happen to her. Unlike her mother, she lived in the world of today. She went to school with a view to getting some sort of career, just like the others. Maybe a nurse or IT office worker; she never aspired to some of the fancy dreams of girls like Sandra or Aziza who talked about becoming doctors or lawyers. Life moved along evenly with only school exams to disturb the boredom of teenage existence. And now this bombshell. She wished she had the mobile phone with her and blamed herself for being frightened to bring it home. The house phone was in the hall downstairs, so she was cut off up here.

The kitchen door opened and Jamal came in. He glanced briefly at the figure of his father sitting akimbo on the chair and gave his mother a kiss on the cheek, then asked if there was anything to eat. Later, when she had the chance, she took him aside and told him what had happened. Her son would support her and she preferred to call on him to work alongside her, rather than the difficult task of getting her husband to do anything except bluster and hit out when frustrated.

Jamal went upstairs and unjammed the bedroom door.

'What you playing at? You know what the family want, so stop messin'.'

She looked at him, knowing he would give her no support.

'Fine for you, you dropped out of school and look at you! No job, Mister Cool!'

He struck her with the back of his hand and she fell back on to her bed, holding her hand to her cheek.

'Shut it, you stupid bitch. Do what we say or else!'

He left the room and forgot to jam the door in his irritated state. It swung open as he swept downstairs. Faiza crept to the top of the stairs and listened. All the noise came from the kitchen; she could hear her brother arguing with her father and the sounds of washing-up at the sink. She fell asleep fitfully.

She woke to the sound of voices from below; voices she did not recognize. Then several footsteps coming upstairs. The door opened and her father and an old bearded man came into the room. He wore a long salwar kermees and a white head covering. He sat on the one chair in the room and gazed at Faiza intently.

'My child, are you afraid?' His gentle eyes surveyed her and he stroked his long beard.

'Yes I am. Everybody's against me!'

He smiled and held up a hand. 'Peace!. You are mistaken. I shall prevent harm to you, I swear.'

She realized he was the local Imam, although she had never been to the mosque.

'My family! Look at them! They want to beat me!'

Her father stood in the doorway, his hands on his hips,nothing but anger written on his face. The Imam looked up into Karim's face and put out a hand to touch his arm.

'Be still. Let me speak with the child.'

'Let us pray a little,' he said and bowed his head. Faiza sat silently, not wishing to be rude but failing to comprehend the instruction. After a little while, he looked up at her and sat with his hands palm-upwards in his lap.

'What is your fear, my child? We are all travellers in a journey,' he began, 'no one can be master of his own destiny.'

She wanted to say that her destiny was to live freely, but the words wouldn't come. She sat dumb.

'Let Allah - peace be upon him - guide you, my child, so that you see the goodness of family life.'

The meaning of this phrase was obvious. She found no comfort in this old man's words. He was just a mouthpiece for the hateful orders of her father and mother. She stared at him for the first time. Folding her arms tightly across her chest, she shook her head. He turned away and got up wearily, his eyes on the door.

'Bless this house, inshallah, may peace return!'

Karim opened the door and the old man walked out shaking his head. Faiza pushed the door shut behind him.

Next day, her mother tapped at her door at seven o'clock. What chance did she have if she stayed at home? Her family meant to force her into a life of their choosing. Her mother's life of drudgery filled her imagination and reaffirmed her certainty that she had to break away.

By nine o'clock, she had dressed and came downstairs carrying her backpack. She gave one last look at the scene and stepped outside, closing the door. She vowed this would be the last day she would spend in that house.

Girls and boys gathered in separate groups outside the school gates. When the bell went, she filed into class and sat at the usual table. But soon she understood that nothing would be the same. Where would she go? Who could help her? The great gap between her past family life and an unknown future loomed like a dark presence behind her.

At break Aziza turned up and poked her head through the railings.

'I've left! I'm never going back.' As the words came out, Faiza heard them as if spoken by another person. Could this be her own voice? There was a moment of silence. Aziza put a hand over her mouth.

'My God!' she said. 'You done it!" Aziza, wide eyed, clung to the railings to keep her balance.

'You got any cash? Where'll you stay? What about school, they'll find out!'

Faiza turned away, she had no idea where she would go; she had ten pounds in her pocket and some jeans and T-shirts in her bag.

'Have you got my phone?' Before Aziza answered, she sensed what she would say.

'Don't do it! You can't get away like this with no cash and no place to go!'

'Where's my phone?' Aziza fished it out of her pocket and handed it over.

Before the bell went, she walked out of the gates and set off for the town centre. Aziza had disappeared.

She looked out for Nair, an Indian boy she had met at a party in Aziza's house when her parents were away. He had chatted to her and told her where he worked but she had never seen him since. At the back of her mind she thought he might help her in some way, although she had no firm idea what that would be. She saw him on a fruit stall unpacking a box of oranges. He stood up and smiled.

'How goes? Haven't seen you here before!' She had forgotten his bright eyes and smile. She smiled in return.

'I've left school and wondered if there's a job going?' she said.

He stepped down from the display and wiped his fingers on his overalls.

'How old are you?'

'Sixteen,' she lied.

He glanced over his shoulder and then took her arm and moved to a corner of the stall.

'I know Hassan; he works in Leeds and might have a job for you. You'd have to move to Leeds though.'

'That's no problem, I have relations in Leeds.'

'Stay here. I'll give him a bell.'

Her face flushed with excitement; already she felt the bonds dropping from her limbs like a prisoner on release. He came back grinning;

'All OK. If you go down this afternoon he can see you.'

He scribbled an address on a paper bag and handed it to her. She took it and touched his arm. She didn't know what to say.

It began to rain as she got on the bus to Leeds. Glancing out of the window, she wondered if this would be the last time she ever saw Huddersfield. The prospect made her shiver. The journey took about an hour, and when she got off the bus she found the address Nair had given her easily, just four streets away from the depot. A large old house with worn paint and a front garden half filled with rubbish.

It was not what she expected. Her imagination had pictured an office in a business district; Nair had described Hassan as a big businessman. The man who answered the door peeped warily around the edge and spoke sharply to her in poor English.

'What you want?'

'I've got Mr Hassan's name and he has a job for me?'

'Wait here now.'

After a few minutes a big man came to the door. He smiled and held out his hand to her

'Salaam, sister. Nair rang me about you; come in, come in!'

Unlike the man who answered the door, this man was tall and heavily built. He wore a dark suit and open-necked shirt. A gold necklace **hung** just visible around his neck and a ruby ring gleamed on his little finger. He smiled at her and ushered her into the hall. The house smelled of hashish and she came to a kitchen with a table and some metal chairs.

'Sit down, my dear and have a drink.'

The big man poured out mint tea from a small pot and passed it over to her. She sat at the table and realized for the first time she was hungry and thirsty. The tea tasted sweet and she felt more relaxed.

'Now, you want to work?'

'Yes, I'm ready to - I can cook and I have a certificate in Computer Studies,' she found herself tripping over her words and sipped the tea to stop herself from chattering.

'That's good, that's good.' He seemed to show little interest in what she said because he looked up at the ceiling and scratched his head. 'What I need is a girl to act as receptionist. Do you think you can do that?'

'Of course,' she leant forward, 'of course I can do it!'

He smiled warmly and opened his arms. 'Well there we are then! No problems. Let me have a word with Melinda. Of course, I can't pay you for the first week that will be a trial. Is that OK with you?'

He didn't explain who Melinda was and Faiza did not want to question him; he appeared so emphatic and confident she felt lucky to have got a job at all, so she just nodded and waited. 'You will go with Lalith to the house where Melinda is and stay there. You will be comfortable with her and the girls.'

His smile was broad and with a wave he dismissed her into the care of the grubby servant. They crossed a busy road and came to a parade of shops; some of the shopfronts were blank but he went up to the door between two lit windows and knocked loudly. Faiza noticed one of the windows was a massage parlour and then the door opened and the man pushed her forward. The woman at the door turned back inside and walked ahead of her up the stairs to the living accommodation above.

As she climbed the stairs, she spoke over her shoulder.

'Hassan told me you was keen to work. Is that a fact?'

She never turned to speak but kept ahead of Faiza until they reached the landing.

She looked for the first time at the woman in front of her.

'I'm Melinda,' the woman said, 'and I run this place for Mister Hassan.'

She was about forty years old and dressed in a T-shirt which appeared to be one or two sizes too small for her large, sagging breasts. Her skirt was black and on her legs were black lacy tights. Faiza noticed there were runs in the tights and through the gaps, pale flesh pushed through like small blisters. Her face was pale; she had been an attractive girl at twenty but time had been hard on her and she knew it.

The living room above the shop and faced the road. Dirty net curtains drooped from the windows and the lights from passing traffic crossed the room like the occasional beams of a lighthouse. Three young women sat on a velvet sofa facing the door. Faiza smiled quickly at them and one of them returned her smile. She was a small stick of a girl with wide oriental eyes and black hair.

Her phone rang, which startled her, and she hurried out of the room to stand on the landing. It was Aziza.

'Thank God! I thought you were caught! Where are you?' The words came rushing out in one breathy stream of sounds.

'OK. OK, I'm in Leeds.'

'Who are you with? Are you OK?'

'I'll tell you everything; can we meet tomorrow?'

'Are you serious?' An anxious note crept into Aziza's voice, 'I can't get to Leeds mid-week without huge problems - school, family an' everything.'

'I've got somewhere to live but no one knows me and I need some clothes and things.'

She could hear her tone of her voice and felt bad about the tinge of desperation. 'Still, I'll manage.'

Aziza sounded excited. 'Listen, we can meet on Saturday afternoon. I can get the bus and meet you about two o'clock. OK?'

'Yes please, can you bring me some of your gear? I need Primark stuff and things, you know?'

She did not want to admit she needed to dress in European clothes. It seemed unnatural, disloyal.

One of the girls showed her the room they were going to share. It was just big enough for two single beds and a chair.. The bedding was creased. A smell of sweat and cheap scent rose from the bedding and the general state of the room, with a jumble of clothing lying on the floor, depressed her.

How to survive? How to avoid her family? How to be somebody? She lay on the bed in her street clothes and soon fell asleep.

Next morning she awoke and went down into the bathroom. There was a rubber shower hose jammed on the taps and she used it to wash. A towel hung on a hook and she pulled it down to dry herself, cringeing as she saw the smudges and dirt marks on it. She dressed again in the same clothes as yesterday. By the time she reached the kitchen, Melinda had arrived and was cutting bread and brewing tea.

'What do the girls do?'

Melinda rolled her eyes. 'What you think they do? It's a massage parlour!'

Faiza had seen there were massage parlours in Huddersfield as elsewhere. She knew men used them for sex, but had no idea how they worked.

'Come down with me,' Melinda said, turning to the door, 'I'll show you what's what in a few minutes.'

She bustled downstairs and unlocked the door of the shop below. It was dark inside and when the lights were switched on, Faiza could see a desk in front of a purple screen with 'Divine Massage' written in large letters.

'This is where you'll be. You keep the diary and take the cash - obviously in advance - if they want a receipt they can have one but not many do.'

'What do I charge?'

'All-in massage, fifteen quid - any extras the girls will sort out. OK?'

Outside, the street was quiet and a few minutes passed while Faiza adjusted to her surroundings. Nobody came in; nobody left; it was like living in a purple-shaded cave. There were four cubicles with doors of white panel board. Inside each one was a flat table with a papersheet across it. Rose coloured bulbs lit the cubicle and a large roll of paper towel hung from the wall. She could detect the smell of bleach and it reminded her of the lavatory in her own house, bringing her back to reality with a bang. She shut the door.

'Where the hell are you?'

A shout from the front brought her running back down the passage. Mister Hassan stood hands on hips in front of the desk. He seemed even larger than before. He stood with his feet wide apart and looked down on her.

'MeL! Get down here!' She came down, her heels clacking on the steps.

'Look at this bint! What you running, a charity shop? Get some clothes for her!'

He turned and leant forward till his face came within inches of Faiza. 'You gotta show out a bit. You need some make-up and do your hair more classy. What's your name again?'

'Faiza.'

'No. You're Jasmin in here. You got it?' She nodded, mute with fear.

'Get this place sorted out, use some spray or somethin'.

Then he walked out, got into his car and drove away.

She sat behind the desk and examined herself in the shop window. She saw a slim girl in a gaudy T-shirt staring back at her. Her eyes were dark pools in a faded face that looked like the shadow of someone she knew. Tears of self-pity welled up and she brushed at them with her fingers

The door opened and a man walked in. He was about fifty years old. He wore a black bomber jacket open at the front with his belly pulled in by a belt. His hair tied back in a sparse ponytail, exposing his broad forehead and large ears. He grinned in a familiar way and Faiza noticed how his lips were loose and wet.

'What's your name, love?'

'Jasmin,' she replied.

Melinda pushed past her.

'Hello Sam! Lovely to see you. Tai-Ming's here. She'll look after you.'

A plump girl clattered down the stairs. She wore high heels and black fishnet tights. Transformed by a wig of long black hair and wearing a loose blouse open at the front, she went straight to the cubicle and shut the door.

'Did you get his cash?' Melinda gripped Faiza's arm.

When she shook her head, the grip tightened and she gave a tight-lipped frown.

'Next time, do what I say!'

The day moved on slowly. Then, as the evening went on, the girls worked more regularly as closing time neared and the pubs were turning out. Melinda came down at one o'clock in the morning and switched off the purple light which advertised the 'parlour'.

'Go on girl, get some sleep.'

She pulled out the banknotes from the drawerand stuffed them into her dressing gown pocket.

That night was a long one. The room was hot and the air stifling. Thoughts whirled round in her mind, about the sordid unfamiliar life in this foetid building..

The confidence which had sustained her when she left home drained away and the isolation, even among this group of women, made her tremble.

Early the following morning, she went downstairs.at eight o'clock ; none of the girls was awake. She sat in the kitchen, enjoying the quiet solitude. Counting her money, she had five pounds and a few coins left. Enough to get away. But where to? She rang Aziza. By now, it was nine o'clock and the phone rang for some seconds.

'Hello Faiza!' At last the voice she longed to hear!

"Ziza!' She gulped with emotion, 'What shall I do?' She couldn't keep the emotion out of her voice, even though she had told herself she would be strong. Faiza poured out the story of her situation in bursts of speech. By the time she finished, both girls were sobbing in sympathy. Aziza's tone was firm,

'We'll find a way to pull you out.'

'But how?' She wrapped both her arms round herself. instinctively.

'What if they find me?'

'You hang on there - I'll buzz you when I get to Leeds and we'll skip.'

At once, she felt better. The sound of Aziza's voice put new heart into her. She went downstairs and switched on the purple light, then arranged the desk as if she was setting up for the day. By eleven o'clock, she could not sit there for a minute longer. At last the buzz on her phone went off and she ran to the front of the shop away from the stairs.

'I'm at the bus station.'

'I'll be with you in a few minutes; the shop is just a few streets away!'

The excitement made her dizzy. At last she would be out of this place. She jumped up and ran for the door. Out in the street, she raced towards the bus station with the wind in her hair, never looking back and arrived out of breath. A crowd of people was just getting off a bus and she found it impossible to make out Aziza among the mass of people. She used her phone, and Aziza told her she was in the cafe. Her voice seeemd strained and hesitant as she spoke, but Faiza ignored it and hurried to find the cafe. It was a dingy cabin on the corner of the building and very busy.

In a corner seat **sat** Aziza hunched over a cup, gripping it tightly. She looked at Faiza wide-eyed with an expression of fear on her face. It took a moment for Faiza to register the scene, then she saw Jamal and her father sitting at the next table. Jamal jumped up and stood in front of her.

'You're not going anywhere - sit down and shut up!'

He pushed her down into the bench seat next to her father, who said nothing but seized her wrist and held it tightly. Tears welled up in her eyes and she looked across to Aziza who sat still as stone, frightened to face her. Aziza's face was pale and she put her hands to her face as if to hide the cruel deception she had played. After a short while, she got up and ran out of the cafe without a word.

It was that movement which brought Faiza back to reality. She clenched her teeth in a tight-lipped smile and stared at her father.

'Do you think you can make me stay like a slave? I got away once and I'll do it again!'

'No you won't! We'll see to that.'

He shook his head and stared at her with narrowed eyes.

'The car's outside. Get in!" He gripped her wrist harder and Jamal took the other arm and they lifted her out of the seat and propelled her out into the street. A few heads turned as they moved stiffly out of the café, but no one paid much attention to the little group.

Jamal drove and Karim sat in the back with her. Nothing was said and she **sat** dazed at the speed of events. Her head felt heavy and fatigue seeped into her body as the journey continued. What good did it do to fight them? All energy drained away as they reached home and she stepped out of the car, tripping as she entered the house. Jamal caught her and pushed her down into a chair in the front room.

'Stay there and Mam will come to you.'

He left the room and she heard the lock click in the door. Time seemed to pass slowly. As she sat, she could not resist the thought that this home, these smells and familiar noises, had a comforting effect. In her mind, she resisted the restraint the family had imposed on her but beneath that reasoning, it was hard to suppress the instincts that resonated in her body. The itch of the grubby clothes she had worn for days, the lingering smell of sweat and cooking that clung to her skin, these filled her with disgust.

The lock turned and her mother shuffled into the room. Faiza noticed, for the first time, how grey her hair was and the stoop which had developed, unobserved. She had a glass in her hand and held it out to her.

'Here, drink this, it will do you good.'

She spoke without rancour in a flat tone as if Faiza had been away at school for the day and returned hungry. She took the glass and knew it was her favourite lassi - the one made with coconut. Before she could stop them, large tears formed in her eyes and brimmed over on to her cheeks. Some even splashed into the drink. Her mother took out a handkerchief and wiped away some of the tears. Even the smell of her mother's handkerchief brought back feelings of loss and longing. For some minutes, she sat with her shoulders bowed and looking at the floor. She waited for some word from her mother or some gesture which could bridge the gap between them. A hand slipped into hers and held her fingers entwined. She sobbed aloud and put her face against her mother's shoulder. They stayed like that for uncounted minutes.

The door opened and her father stood looking down on them. He had a belt in his hand. His wife stood up quickly, pushing herself between the man and her daughter. She spoke rapidly in Urdu and pointed to the belt. He wrapped it round his fist and tried to push the woman aside. She stood firm, she could see the veins in his neck tighten and he clenched his teeth.

'Get out of the way, you bitch! Or I'll whip you too!'

Still she stood squarely in front of him. Fazia shrank back against the chair, watching his red eyes as he raised the lash. He brought the belt down hard across his wife's shoulders and she reeled back but regained her balance and stood defiant with eyes wide, challenging him. He had never seen this before and it brought him to a standstill. For a moment he stood with the belt raised as if to strike again.

She shook her head and gazed up into his face, her eyes looked directly into his.

'No punishment in my house. You try again, I kill you.'

Her words were spoken quietly and firmly, He could not misunderstand what she meant and he stared at her in astonishment. For a moment he confronted her, then he walked quickly out of the room and they heard the front door slam.

Faiza looked at her mother in wonder; a woman who had spent years of subservience under a tradition she had always obeyed. It had taken a fifteen-year-old daughter to bring her to independence. She rubbed her shoulders and gave a wry smile at her daughter.

'Go get changed and have a bath. I make dinner in half an hour.'

THE EARTH MOVED

I turned on the monitor and saw the bulbous face of a Neb appear on the screen. He was reading something with his front feet propped up on the desk.

"Come in, Commander. Report your position."

He swivelled two of his eyes towards the screen but I saw his third eye was still scanning the script out of sight below the desk. Nebs are inquisitive creatures and we have to watch them carefully to stop their minds wandering.

"All good here Chief," his voice came through the translator box with a cheery tone.

"Just passed Orion and looking smooth."

I hate this nebular slang but the machinery cannot convert it to proper Martian speech so I have to put up with it.

"Give me co-ordinates please."

I tried to keep the irritation out of my voice but who knows what it sounds like at his end of the system. The trouble is, we can't fit into the flight deck of the space craft, so we have to employ these Nebs to fly the thing.

"Well, I reckon we're about halfway to Earth at this point of time" – Where does he get these expressions from – "and may land in about two hours."

"You do realise that this is a vital mission, don't you? The fate of the Martian race depends on a good landing and restocking with nutrients."

I hoped that might stiffen it up, but its blobby shape wobbled a bit and I took that for a nod but maybe it was just wobbling. It's so hard to read their minds.

"Pass me to the Supplies Director."

It rolled its upper eyes and leant forward in the control seat, reaching for the transfer button.

Another round moon shaped face appeared on the screen, this time it wore a blue earing and I recognised Neb Three.

"Step back from the monitor," I said, "I can't see around you, and stop shouting into the microphone."

His voice was blaring out from the translator and his words seemed slurred. As he moved clumsily away from the screen, I caught a glimpse of a canister he was pushing out of sight.

"Have you been drinking, Officer?" There were red patches on its cheeks and the top of its head was pulsating.

"Not a drop, Shir. I was just checking the shtock and slipped – thatsh all." The voice seemed slightly indistinct but I put that down to the translator.

He gave a salute with one of his flaps and then sat down suddenly on a barrel of neutrant stacked against the spacecraft wall.

"I am watching you. You realise I will be reporting every detail when the mission is concluded?"

I thought it said, "Whatever...", but the transmission cut at that point and the screen went blank.

By my calculations, the ship should have been within an hour of Earth's surface and I sent out the exact co-ordinates needed to bring the craft down on the ground.

Then the task would be simple enough for the least efficient of Neb workers. All they had to do was scoop up as many Earthlings as they could find and head back to Mars quick as a flash.

When the screen revived, I saw the shape of the planet looming in front of me. It was bright and mainly blue which meant that there was plenty of water and oxygen on the surface. Just what we wanted; well-nourished Earthlings to fill our containers and restore our fading organisms.

I watched as the screen filled slowly with the image of this wonderful planet.

I could hear the babbling voices of the crew in the background shouting with excitement in their primitive Nebbish way.

"Now! I shouted into the intercom. "Activate the landing sequence!"

There was a flurry of action in the space capsule and much shouting and squealing among the crew, but the image of the planet seemed fainter with every minute that passed. Soon the blue orb shrank in size and faded from the screen.

"What the hell has happened?" I shouted down the intercom.

A Nebbish fat face loomed up on the screen. Its blob wore a stupid expression.

"Well," it said," I think the Earth moved."

ITHACA REGAINED

Give me leave O Muse to tell the story of Odysseus the king of Ithaca. How he fought the malice of the dark God Poseidon. This is a tale full of courage misfortune and love. I seek your blessing and approval.

As Odysseus set off joyfully from Troy over the white flecked sea, he gave no thought to Poseidon nor the hateful progeny of that Immortal Being. He was a hero and returning home. Yet Fate brought him and his crew to the shores where the Cyclops lived.

These huge one eyed monsters were cannibals who relished human flesh, and the worst of these beings was Polyphemus son of Poseidon.

It was hunger that made the crew and their Master take refuge in his cave.

O the horror that came from that mistake!

When Polyphemus returned to his lair and found the crew –he had no mercy for wandering guests. He ripped off the heads of two men to make his evening meal and rolled a great stone across the cave mouth to trap the rest. Trapped and in fear, still the wily Odysseus kept his Senses.

"Drink with me, Polyphemus, so that we may mend this harm which has come between us."

"Gladly" said the creature "but first tell me your name so that I can make you a gift as you depart"

"My name is Nemo --which means No one" said the Cunning Traveller.

"Then Nemo shall be the last man I eat" roared the Giant his laughter made the sailors tremble.

Odysseus offered him bowls of sweet wine and he soon fell into a sleep, vomiting out wine and gobbets of human flesh.

Just then, Odysseus, urging his faint-hearted men, plunged a wooden spear into the giant's eye--it was a shaft tempered in the fire and as it blinded Polyphemus it made a sound like hot iron makes when plunged into a bucket.

The creature cried out for the others to help him-

But they asked:

"Who has done this to you?"

"Nemo has done it –No one has done it"

"Then it is a sickness" they replied "and the gods will mend you" so they left him alone.

The fearful crew and their master crept away from the roaring giant under the bellies of thick fleeced sheep though the giant searched each sheep's back- seeking his revenge.

As Odysseus pulled away from the shore (thus it is that Pride can mar the brave)--- he could not resist calling out:

"Ho! Monster --see how the Gods punish you for your cruel Gluttony?"

This threw blind Polyphemus into a rage and he tore off the peak of a volcano and hurled it at the ship. So nearly did it swamp the vessel that the crew begged Odysseus to stop. Then they struck the grey waters with their oars and sailed frantically away.

Woe to the Man who defies the Gods. Had Odysseus no regard for the fearful might of Poseidon? Did he imagine that the injury to such a son as the Cyclop Polyphemus would go unpunished?

Now the angry God of the sea stirred the waves with his trident staff and the ship of the Wanderer was battered and smashed –losing all direction and cast after several days on an unknown beach.

Struggling ashore with the crew, Odysseus sent out a party to find refuge. When they reached the centre of the island they found a stone palace set in the middle of a forest glade. All about were wild animals, lions, panthers and wolves-- but not such as terrify mankind—these creatures frolicked and fawned on the visitors and made the men wonder at the charm that had bewitched them.

From the house a beautiful voice lured them on. There sat the most beautiful woman they had ever seen, Circe by name, weaving at a loom and dressed in delicate graceful garments such as the goddesses love.

"You are welcome to my home" she said.

She bade them sit at table and served them herself. It was a meal of cheese and maize enriched with honey which they fell upon hungrily.

How could they know that she had poured a charm into their wonderful feast? How could they have foreseen that their fate was to join the enchanted animals which wandered in the glade outside?

Yet pigs they became and wallowed and grunted helplessly.

Meanwhile the Master of Craft followed on. As he approached the enchanted grove, he drank down a charmed potion which he had kept for protection. mAgain Circe showed herself to him dressed in a robe of silvery sheen with a gold belt round her slim waist. Warned by some instinct, the Cunning–Master drew his sword and ran at her as if to cut her down. Immediately her aspect changed and she begged him to spare her.

Offering him both herself and her palace, she charmed the Wanderer and banished from his mind all thoughts of homecoming.

And so for months under her incomparable charm he remained, a self imposed prisoner enjoying all her delights and ignoring his duties. At last, tiring of his love and mindful of his increasing sadness and nostalgia, the Goddess relented and gave him his freedom. Generous and bountiful, she released his men from their spell and gave them all safe conduct to the ship. So bountiful a lady --so fortunate a captain! With a following wind, the blue-prowed ship sailed away with taut white sails and oarsmen at rest.

At Dawn's first streams of light, the proud beaked ship approached two islands. There was no help for it but to make a passage between them. On one side Odysseus could see the cave of Scylla who waited eternally to torment seafarers. Fables told of her six long necks and heads set with triple rows of teeth.

On the other side, almost unseen, lay the vortex of Charybdis --she who sucks down a whirlpool three times a day and from which no man nor ship returns.

Choosing to pass by Scylla of the six heads, the Master raced through groaning with terror but not before the monster had seized 3 of his men as he had passed. O how their shrieks echoed from the cliffs above the ship!

"Odysseus" they screamed-- but it was the last time they used his name. And so grimly but surely the weary crew stretched at their oars and moved on.

After days of hard labour at the oars, the ship reached the island of Hyperion, the sun God. Here in rich pastures grazed the fat cattle that the God cherished.

"Make no mistake" warned Odysseus "these are sacred and it would be more than our lives were worth to slaughter them."

Then he left to explore the island leaving his steersman in charge.

Within minutes, the men exclaimed

"Our Master is a man of stone-yet it was not he who broke his back at the Iron clad oars. After so long a torment surely we can feed ourselves as hungry men?"

At once they took and slaughtered the fine fatted cows and began to feast. When Odysseus returned he could scarcely believe the madness of the crew—

"Did I not warn against the slaughter of Hyperion's cattle? How you have repaid my trust!"

At once he forced them to rejoin the ship and they embarked without a moment's delay. Just then Hyperion's golden globe rose in the east and cast a piercing ray on the fateful scene. What punishment could fit this crime? How fearful the anger of the Gods when men transgress! The sea rose like a pillar of solid rock and the wind lashed the frail craft against this anvil. The keel was split from the planks of the ship and the crew was flung into the whirling menacing foam. Not one man was saved- only Odysseus was able to withstand the power of the storm. He it was, who clung to the riven keel and was carried unconscious to a distant shore more dead than alive. There he lay for days, alone and exhausted.

Crusted with brine, naked and broken, the Prince of Schemers awoke to the sounds of happy laughter. Before him stood a Princess with her handmaids.

"If I dream then wake me not" spoke the artful Traveller, "Yet if this is not Elysium, then where have I landed -beaten and hurt as I am?"

"I see from your speech" said the Princess "that despite your pitiful state, you are a man of breeding."

And with that, she bade her servants to bind up his wounds, bathe and oil him and find him the finest garments. She was Nausicaa of the slim-ankles --daughter of King Alcinous and in the custom of her country, she gave help to travellers. Soon Odysseus found himself conducted into the palace of the mighty king. Here he told his name and the story of his journey-but left aside his conquests over the Cyclops and his escape from Hyperion's fury, fearful that his conduct might alarm the king.

"I weep for you" exclaimed Alcinous "that such a journey has separated you from your wife and child. But do not seek to enter your homeland as a prince or king. Ithaca is tormented by a pack of evil suitors who, encamped on your island, seek to win your wife Penelope. She stays aloof but seems to sanction their plunder of all that you possess. Soaked in the finest wine and fed on your best meats they look to kill you and your son Telemachus."

With these words alive in his ears-Odysseus begged that he be given passage to his homeland. Alcinous assented and leaving Nausicaä with glistening tears, all--daring Odysseus set off to reach his homeland. Like a team of stallions who jump to the touch of the whip, the oarsmen of Alcinous sprang to their task. The great ship plunged forward and a great white wave foamed in her wake, urging her onwards. Odysseus fell into a pit of sleep such as he had never enjoyed while the swift strokes drove him homeward.

As the morning star began to usher Dawn's tender light, the ship reached Ithaca and daring Odysseus jumped ashore. Not as a prince but dressed in rags of sheepskin to test the ground that was truly his. His way took him to the lonely hut of a shepherd who confirmed the harsh truths already told by the king Alcinous. Ithaca was besieged by wanton, greedy suitors who vied with each other to impress the lovely queen. Yet custom prevented her from renouncing them so that they feasted and rioted at her expense.

What rage and suffering was this to the proud king! Yet could he vanquish them without the powers of the gods? At that moment Athena –Merciful Goddess! seeing the Hero Safe from the ever-vengeful wrath, set the feet of Telemachus striding to meet his father. The pair so long parted met now with one purpose. With joy they greeted each other and sat long hours to make their plan.

How like his father –the young warrior became! Nimble-witted Odysseus fashioned a plan which would accomplish all their desires. First, he sent Telemachus back into the city to arrange with his mother that a final choice would be made to find a husband who could reign in Ithaca. In her turn Penelope called a council of all suitors and her retinue. Solemnly veiled in a golden headdress she proclaimed that the man who could string and draw the mighty War Bow of Odysseus would be her king.

What Chaos! What Vanity was here! Of all the Princes of the Hellenes, none doubted that <u>he</u> would be the one to gain the Crown!

The night before the test, a great feast was held at which, as custom had it, all manner of people high and low were invited. Seated near the Suitors in their finest tunics sat a rough Traveller clad in goatskin with a shepherd's cap on his head. He collected alms from the company but when he reached Antinous- one of the Principal Suitors –Antinous threw a cow's foot from the rubbish at him

"Here Beggar-I make you a special gift!"

Twisting with agility, the warrior-beggar avoided the blow. He smiled and locked the image of that man in his heart.

Strangely, as the feast progressed, with the finest of food and wine prepared, yet the Suitors were plagued by strange apparitions as if the bread was tinged with blood and the walls dripping with gore. Such was the Gods' message to these malefactors.

Later that night, the Beggar –the Prince of Schemers- unlocked the mighty War Room and a collected for himself and Telemachus, the best of bronze swords and spears. He hid them in the courtyard where the contest would take place.

Next day, drowsy with heavy heads from the wine, the Suitors assembled for the competition. Penelope-of the long neck--swathed like a Goddess in a purple robe with gold and silver ornaments –held up the bow which glistened in the morning light as its ivory and bronze shape slipped from its sheath. She placed it with its quiver of deadly arrows on the ground before the assembly.

Covering her face with a veil of gossamer she left the scene and waited in her palace for the choice the Fates had prepared for her and her Kingdom.

Without hesitation Suitors tried the bow-but failed to string it. Then Antinous, braggart and bully, took his turn. He groaned as he fitted the string but his strength failed as he tried to draw the bow.

"No man alive can do what I cannot do" he shouted "This must be a trick to defeat us"

The Suitors murmured in assent.

It was at that point that the beggar in sheepskin rags stepped forward to try the bow already strung by Antinous. A jeer went up from the crowd but with the first arrow, mighty Odysseus pierced the breast of Antinous and through him two other men beyond him.

"On On" he cried "This match is played and won. You Cursed Dogs! You pillaged my kingdom-you wooed my wife on the sly-now your doom has come"

And the great king cast off his ragged disguise and with his son, set about the massacre. Bronze swords-spears and arrows flashed with speed through and through the screaming mass. Not one of the unworthy was left, nor the servants who had taken the coinage of disloyalty. At last, slaked in blood, weary with killing, the father and son paused. None of the suitors survived.

For many long years the graceful queen had bravely kept her love of Odysseus alive yet the Heavens themselves knew how many tears she had wept over her lost Lord. Besieged by suitors –loaded with cares of state –she had battled on. Now came news of the man who could wield the great Bow of her king-and the terrible news of the killing in the courtyard.

Despite the urging of her son, cautiously she came to see the man. She sat apart from the Victor of the contest, looking into his face.

"Since you are the Victor I shall keep my promise to wed you--but I do not accept that you are my Odysseus, since you bear scars and injuries I do not recognize."

Then she proposed that the marriage bed should be moved outside the royal Chamber for a new beginning. Seeing this as a trick devised to test him –Odysseus laughed at her cunning.

"No man can move that bed My Queen" he smiled "I made the frame from a living olive tree –see how it still flourishes to give us shelter"

At this Penelope knew at last that they were re-united and her tears fell. Nor was it shame on the King's part that he held his purple robe before his eyes and shed many sobs so that his cheeks were wet with tears. Then with many tales of adventure and tragedy the happy couple talked on into the night until sweet sleep embraced them.

Such is my tale of Odysseus – great Lord of Ithaca. So Muse –commend me for my pains- and forgive me for my errors. Such is my story--- and it is done.

THE PEACE DEAL

"Where are my socks? The question was so familiar and irritating Norma simply ignored it.

"Norma, where have you put my socks?" He persisted.

"*How the hell do I know*?" was what she said in her mind

"Look in the top draw." Is what she actually said.

They had been together for seven years and she realized recently the pattern of their lives had never changed. How had this happened to her? Thirty two years old and she knew she earned her place in a law firm in the City. Yet it was startlingly obvious where she had gone wrong. At the age of twenty five she frightened herself with the idea she was too brainy and plain to find a partner. She looked around to find a man who would do and James would do-just. No one to be blamed but herself and this situation was ordained to happen sometime. Her boredom, his work ethic and their drab home life added up to a grand nothing.

James sighed; *she was the most annoying woman. Why should she moan about trivial things like socks? What did she want from me? I work well and nobody can say I play the field, though the office is full of totty. If I expect a clean house and a bit of laundry-is it expecting too much? Maybe I should think about myself a bit more. Could buy a few suits and try a dating agency?*

He sighed. But she knew what to do. She would socialise more and maybe take advice from a girlfriend.

Would Amy do? No! On second thoughts, she was just the kind of friend who would enjoy her discomfort.

Ask Francesca at work? She was a sympathetic type and always useful for advice on legal matters-but unmarried and single, would she really understand the dilemma? Better not; no use advertising one's mistakes in the office.

Then she got the idea. A week in a health spa. She was owed some leave and things were quiet at work. Weymouth seemed ideal.

She announced at breakfast "I think I will join Jenny at a Health Spa next week. You can manage can't you?" There was no Jenny. But she drove down to Weymouth.

Who's this Jenny? he wondered. Still, a week to explore options seemed a good idea. He joined an on-line dating agency that day and began to draft his "Profile"

—eligible thirty's professional-*No, too prosaic*

–Romeo seeks Juliet-*no, too corny*

–Quiet art loving gentleman-- *too cranky*

Why not-Tired City Type needs Stimulus-*at least it was true.*

So he tapped it in and waited. Twenty four hours later he was still waiting. Then pinging through the ether came- "Life coach -thirties-can revive city type" James stared at it -Life coach? No sex mentioned -- had he slipped accidentally into some gay network? Had he sent the wrong message? Tentatively he rang the phone number listed....

Norma soon adopted the regime at The Elysium Spa. No name tabs-uniform track suits in purest white cotton and a timetable of exercises to be carried out. She had packed a dozen Snickers bars in case of starvation but the food was good and healthy. Among the staff, she found the cheery welcome and hearty cajoling to be an effort but one instructor stood out. Ray had the quiet confidence of a physically fit teacher. Lean and tanned, his slow smile and steady hands, as he helped her with yoga, seemed comforting without being too sensual. After the second day, she was taking most Yoga sessions in his class and chatting afterwards in the Relax room. On the third night she left her door unlocked and he slipped in to practise his special yoga moves which she joined in enthusiastically...

The voice on the phone was female, much to James' relief. She was called Anita and they chatted awkwardly for several minutes before he managed to bring himself to ask her if she would like to meet. She agreed. He reckoned Costa Coffee on Southside was an innocent place to rendezvous but it was crowded and noisy. He had forgotten to identify himself and peered at every new female arrival as 11 a m passed. A tall black girl with long straight hair came in and glanced round the café. She was dressed in figure hugging biker jacket and trousers. With a glance she swept the room and drew everyone's attention. James pulled his anorak closer round his skinny body and plucked up enough courage to wave in her direction. As she weaved between the tables all eyes turned to follow her.

"I can see you need stimulus. Hello I'm Anita"

James was gobsmacked. Girls like Anita never approached him and he never imagined he could interest them.

"You look stunning" he blurted "I'm James"

He had already told her his name on the phone but what do you say when you meet such a girl? He was gasping for ideas and his mind went blank.

"Well, that's a good beginning" she laughed and at once he felt easier and his edginess vanished. Soon they were exchanging stories and enjoying themselves. He tentatively asked if she would have lunch but she told him she had work scheduled that day, but tomorrow was ok. They arranged to meet at his address in Clapham for the next day.

James felt terrified and excited at the same time. He bought sushi from Pret and changed the bedsheets. One o'clock and Anita arrived. She wore a track suit and her hair was pulled back in a bun. She had shades with very dark lenses. He noticed her tee shirt seemed two sizes too small and she saw he noticed it too. Once the sushi was finished, in an inspired move, Anita produced a flask of sake.

"This is how a Life Coach teaches her students."

From then on James found himself in a spiral of warm sake and sex which ran from missionary to cannibal in quick succession. By four o'clock he was a shadow of his puny self but she left as lively as she began....

Weymouth was wet and throughout the week Norma stayed inside the Spa. Ray was in demand by a number of clients, mostly women, but he still paid an occasional visit to her room for yoga purposes. At the end of the week he agreed to come back to London with her for the week end. On the drive back, she felt fitter than ever before and calmer about life. She appreciated her way of life was incompatible with the life Ray knew. But what about James? She decided a long talk would solve any problems. She drove straight to the Clapham flat and went upstairs...

Inside the flat James was laying a table for a takeaway with Anita. Even he could manage knives and forks. As Norma came through the door, he blinked with surprise as he saw her and the figure of a man behind her.

"You never told me when you were getting back" he said weakly "I've a friend coming round in a couple of minutes."

"Well that's fine -this is Ray, we met at Weymouth." Ray glanced at James and said not a word.

"Let's eat together" said Norma brightly.

The doorbell rang. Anita swept into the room in full Beyoncé mode. She sized up the assembly in a flash.

"How lovely" she cooed, "Are we all here for the same thing?"

Ray smiled one of his professional slow smiles and his bright eyes sparkled at the new guest.

"My my" purred Anita "James has just finished a course with me, haven't you?"

James began to feel uncomfortable. This evening was not turning out as expected.

"Norma, I need some help in the kitchen" he whined and pushed her out of the room.

Ray hardly noticed her leave and Anita was turning her Life Coach beams at full power on Ray.

"Look, Norma can we get out of this set up?" James looked beseechingly at her. "In all honesty, I can't keep this up -she's like a fierce animal and I can't cope."

He sounded so desperate that Norma saw in a flash she had him at her mercy. *No more feeding him, no more ironing for him, he would do as she pleased.*

Was this better than a few weeks of good times with the lusty Ray? Yes.

They heard the laughter and the sound of whispers from the other room. Ray and Anita had already forgotten them.

"Peace Deal?" begged James. Norma smiled.

ALL SOULS DAY

Outside the bedroom window, early morning mist clouded the trees. I climbed out of bed and wiped the crust of ice from the inside of the casement. Pulling on jacket and trousers over my nightclothes, I slipped my feet into rough boots. It was time to light the fires and wake the other servants. I skimped my firelighting and kicked the bootboy awake, then skipped downstairs before he could catch me.

The night before, the vicar said "Tomorrow is All Soul's Day I shall want to be up before six o'clock to set out for Marlock. Harness Bess and get the pony cart ready in good time."

It was a command as usual. Why would he ask anything of the workhouse child lodged in his garret?

Bess looked at me in surprise when I opened the stable door. Her soft brown eyes held more affection for me than any human I knew. As soon as I had the harness fitted, we trotted round to the front door and waited. I was proud of my skill with animals and looked forward to a journey into Marlock. It was the nearest town to our village and an adventure for me.

The vicar was a tall man with a long face. I never saw him smile. His angular jaw and heavy brow gave him a grim look and when he spoke you felt you must have done some wrong, tho' you hadn't. He came down the front steps and pulled himself up into the cart. "Walk on" he said as if I was the pony and we set off briskly into the frosty air. The road to Marlock took us through the woods and as we made our way it seemed we were passing through an arcade of crystal pillars.

On both sides the trees were a pattern of frosty branches almost meeting over our heads. Occasional showers of soft snow drifted down and settled on the pony's back.

"Wake up! Keep to the middle of the road or you'll have us over..." In a second, the wonder of the morning vanished and I was again the undeserving orphan who could do nothing right. I took up the reins with a firmer hand so that Bess moved on obediently along the centre of the road. My hands were inside the sleeves of my coat but the frost was reaching them and my fingers stiffened as the cold crept up my sleeves.

The priest huddled down inside his great coat and pulled his black hat down tightly over his ears. He sat immobile as a block of marble wrapped in a cover of canvas and fur, not watching the road ahead but slouched with his eyes shut.

I did my best to keep Bess in a straight line but the road was rough and occasional sheets of ice made her slither for a few steps as she regained her footing.

"Keep her steady, you little dullard or you'll have us over."

He grabbed the reins from my hands and pushed me out of the way. The pony gybed at the unexpected jolt and pulled on the bit. Racing off at a mad pace, bouncing off the verges, skewing across the road, out of control. The vicar heaving at the reins and shouting. Then Bess tripped and went down.

The rig bounced high in the air. It flung me into the brushwood hedge. The parson catapulted out of the cart onto the road with a thud and a crack you could have heard back home. Bess dragged the upturned cart to a stop about fifty yards away. She looked back with an insolent eye and then began to nibble at the frosty grass.

It took me some time to gather my wits and find that I was bruised but not broken. The vicar lay inert, his face down on the icy surface of the road, his arms spread out as if embracing the cold hard stones.

I stumbled over to him and knelt beside him. His hooded eyes seemed to look at me with reproach but they never blinked.

A trickle of blood oozed from his ear and when I stooped to listen to his heart I heard nothing but the wind across his face and not a sound from his body.

I remembered that at church on Sunday, Parson told us that All Souls' Day was the day when souls of the departed went to heaven if we prayed for them.

So I prayed that his soul had gone to Heaven.

Then I pulled his wallet out of his coat, his gloves off his stiff hands and set off for Marlock with Bess. I hope it was a good day for the soul of the vicar.

It was a good day for me and Bess.

A COUNTRYMAN

Peter Cheney loved the countryside. He farmed a few acres in the best part of Suffolk and enjoyed the company of his gundogs and friends.

He was seen out hunting on mid-week days and was known to take a straight line in any country. He never told a lie, but when asked about the 'flashy' horse he was riding that day, he just said "Well, she went well today." Few people knew he was showing one of the local copers nags which they wanted to get rid of and only he could ride.

At any party he was a charming success. Nobody doubted that he enjoyed the attention of a succession of ladies within the county set but he was a welcome addition to any dinner party.

He gambled a little but never cheated, although how he won large sums on rank outsiders that showed a turn of speed on race day was never clear.

He drank with the best and enjoyed spending a night in the local pub with the local poachers and riff raff. Those nights often ran on in to daylight when the chums would try out a little sport in the famous coverts of Lord Dashwood who lived nearby. His shoots were famous throughout the county. One early morning in August, in the woods around the Dashwood estate, the calls of the cock pheasants drew Peter from his bed. Like Circe calling to Odysseus, it was irresistible. Gun in hand and dog at heel, he circled the wood and took a brace of pheasant in the first half hour. It was only after he had taken an early hare that he saw Gregory the Dashwood gamekeeper striding out of the trees.

"Good day to you Mister Cheney. Up bright and early I see."

His eyes focussed on the game bag with feathers peeping out of the flap.

Peter put on his best smile. "Just pottering"

Gregory looked him in the eye. "Yes Sir, hope you find another hare or summat."

Peter called his dog and strolled away without a backward glance.

*

That evening, the Dashwoods gave a grand dinner party. Hermione Dashwood paid particular attention to her social duties. Everyone who was anyone hoped for an invitation to one of her dinners.

At eleven that morning, she rang Peter in great distress.

"Peter! You must help me out! One of the men from my party has fallen ill! I need you to come and eat with us."

Nothing could have been better; he knew Dolly Gilruth would be there and wangled a place next to her at the table. It was going to be a grand evening.

The company was all he expected. Dolly was there catching his eye whenever her husband was distracted. Dashwood was particularly charming and attentive and the dinner was going splendidly. They ate Beluga with small blinis to begin with and then the butler processed to the head of the table with a troop of maidservants holding trays of game arranged in a delightful way. There were pheasants, woodcock and grouse in silver dishes for every guest.

The elderly man servant came directly to Peter's chair. He had a domed silver tray which he held aloft with a dignified air. Guest turned to stare as he bent to offer the dish to Peter. He lifted the lid.

"Lady Dashwood ordered this specially for you, Sir"

On the dish lay fish and chips in newspaper.

"She thinks you would like a change of diet Sir!"

DEWI MORGAN

Inside the cottage, a wet tweed coat hung from a washing line and steamed pungently over the coal stove. The tang of drenched ferns rose from the damp material, mixed with the sharp smell of urine. Sprawled in front of the stove, a weary old dog licked his sodden fur.

This was the home of Dewi Morgan. Seventeen years of solitary life had made Dewi what he was. He lived in the hill farm on Dolgellau. He had everything he needed; he only went into town when necessary.

When he did, people said,

"There he is the hermit of Maindiff farm."

They treated him as an outsider. Once, Dai bach, son of the baker, told his father how he wanted to become a hill farmer.

"Don't be stupid," said Dai, "you don't want to end up like Dewi Morgan do you?"

Something about his look troubled the village. His dark wild hair and small eyes squinting under shaggy brows. He was a big man and moved slowly.

"Like a bull in a field," said Missus Evans, but she never had a kind word for anybody.

One November evening, two of the Thomas' boys were out on the hills looking for a missing calf. As night closed in, they lost their way and found themselves in the fold below Maindiff.

"I'd better give a shout," said Dylan and they both shouted out into the rising wind.

Up in Maindiff, Dewi heard a faint noise but ignored it. His dog bristled and growled to warn him, so he went to the window and scanned the darkness.

This time the sound was distinct and he went to the door, taking his gun with him. It came from the track leading to the sheep fold. As he stepped out his dog slipped past him and made his way down the pitch.

"Who's there? What d'ye want?" Dewi gripped the shotgun and pointed it down the hill.

"We got lost Mister Morgan" said a small voice and out of the mist he spied the silhouette of the two small figures standing together.

"Come up here at once," he shouted, "what are you doing on the hill at this time?"

The boys climbed up clumsily, Griff still holding his brother's hand tightly.

"How did you boys get up here at night?" demanded Dewi. Dylan explained how they had followed the calf and got lost.

"Well, I can't take you back down tonight; you'll have to wait till morning."

Griff, the younger one, looked up at his elder brother for guidance and Dylan said, "But our Mam will be looking out for us."

"Can't help that," said Dewi "I have a sick cow here and need to be at hand, you'll be safe here till the morning."

The man set about preparing his evening meal at the griddle over the open doors of the stove. He brought pieces of lamb and kidneys to the flame and threw herbs and a few onions onto the pan. Soon the frying meat and the tang of the onions spread out through the entire room.

"Here!" Dewi pushed a plate in front of the boys and indicated where they should sit. They scrambled down and sat at the table expectantly. The meat sizzled. Dewi brought it to the table, sharing it out between them. Gobbets of beef, still bubbling, gave off an aroma that dominated all the other smells; the damp clothes - the wet dog and even the pungent sweat from Dewi's clothing.

There was a silence except for the whining of the dog as they chewed their meal.

A clock chimed on the mantelpiece and the farmer glanced up.

"Now I'm going to the barn to quench the cow and check the stock, so you'd better find a covering and bed down."

"What did he mean "Quench the cow"? Asked Griff.

"You know," said Dylan, "when the cows need flushing." He found it difficult to explain.

"What's flushin' then?"

"When a cow is ill, you do that." Dylan was reluctant to admit he did not know what it meant.

"Let's have a look." said Griff and he crept up to the door and peeped out.

There was a lantern in the barn and the boy could see Dewi moving about and the sound of splashing water. The cow made a lot of noise and Dewi was swearing.

In the dim light, it appeared as if the cow's hide was slathered in grease but they realized it was soaking wet. It pulled away from the rope halter tied to its neck and the farmer had difficulty in keeping away from its hind hooves.

He saw the boys peering in through the open door and shouted. "Get me some more water. I can't let 'er go now. Get me some water!"

Dylan grabbed the pail on the floor and ran to the pump, Griff stood wide -eyed in the doorway.

Three times Dylan refilled the bucket and soon both boys were as wet as Dewi struggling with the cow. At last, the cooling effect of the quenching calmed the animal and Dewi relaxed his hold and stepped away.

With a weary step, he trudged back to the kitchen, peeling off his sodden clothes.

He hung his shirt and trousers up by the fire and stood half naked to warm himself before the stove.

The two boys slipped into the kitchen and stood shivering, their jackets and trousers dripping water onto the slate floor.

"Don't be daft! Come nearer and take them things off." It was an order and they did what they were told.

Stripped of their coats and trousers, they sat in their undershirts near the fire.

Dewi looked at them. "Take off the rest of your things or you'll catch a fever.

Dylan did as he was told and stood in his underpants next to the farmer who made room for him by the stove. Griff stood mute with his hands in front of his crutch - he had no underclothes and kept back from the farmer.

Just then, a loud knock hammered on the door.

"Morgan, are you home? Open up!"

Dewi rose slowly and went to the door. His naked torso was pallid in the light from the lamp and he peered out of the door, holding it ajar.

The door was forced open and a group of men made their way into the kitchen.

The two boys, one naked and the other barely covered, stood up as the men filed in. One of the men grabbed Dewi and forced him up against the wall.

"You Bastard! What have you been up to?"

Dewi struggled with the man and two others rushed at him and between them tried to force his arms behind his back and Dai the baker struck him across the mouth with his fist.

"Dirty tramp! Look what you bin doing up here! Naked and stripping them boys!"

Griff said nothing but Dylan began to tell them how they got lost, but no one listened. They were crowding round Dewi, punching him and swearing at him.

He was shouting and struggling as they flung themselves against him. He twisted and turned and his great strength made it difficult for the group to keep a hold on him. His pale skin showed red where the blows had landed but he kept up a roar and fought back fiercely.

It was then that Tudor Evans the builder took up a shovel from behind the door and struck the man on the back of the head. Dewi dropped like a felled tree. As he went down, his head struck the kerb of the stove base. and blood seeped from the wound. He lay still.

The sudden silence was as if they were all turned into statues. Nobody moved and nobody spoke. Tudor Evans put down the shovel and looked about him.

"You all seen how he attacked us. I had to do it, didn't I?"

He looked into the faces of the group. They muttered but no one spoke up.

Dewi lay a still as a stone. Dai bent down and felt his neck with his fingers.

He said slowly "I think he's gone."

Evans looked at the baker. "Dai, we'll need to do something here." He indicated the body at his feet.

Somebody at the back mentioned the police but Evans turned sharply and said,

"What you think will happen if we don't sort this out? What about the two boys? Do you want them to be held up for shame? Do you want to be charged with manslaughter?"

The men stood silent. Then Dai the baker got up and rubbing his hands down the side of his jacket as if to wipe away the memory of the struggle.

"Pick 'im up and we'll put him outside near the pump, then we can call the police."

In the kitchen, they dressed Dewi as best they could. His bulk and stiffening body made the job difficult. They could not hide all the bruises but his jacket and trousers hid the worst of them.

"Now listen," said Dai the baker, "we came up here to look for the boys. Understood?"

They nodded.

"and we found him with the boys naked. Right?"

"Well, right enough," said Pugh the butcher, "but what about his fall?"

Dai baker held up his hand, "Look, the only way to clear this up is to leave him outside as if he'd slipped and fell."

There was a murmur of agreement at this. Without another word, three men hauled the body out into the yard. They put him face down against the pump and arranged his clothes as best they could.

Evans looked at Dai, as the men returned; a look as clear as a beacon. Dai nodded without saying a word. He pushed his way into the little bedroom where the two boys waited.

Sitting on the little bed, he looked hard at the two of them.

"Mr Morgan took our clothes,"

"Yes" said Dai baker, "yes he did, and we don't want everybody to know that, do we?"

It was hard to find the words and Dylan sensed Dai baker did not want to hear them, so he lapsed into silence.

"Be good boyos and we'll make sure no one finds out about it, that's best isn't it?"

The baker smiled broadly and patted Griff on the shoulder.

"Now," said Dai brightly, "let's get you back home nice and tidy. Put on your things"

He brought the boys into the kitchen and nodded to Pugh.

"Come on boys," said Pugh, "off we go, time to get home to Mam."

He ushered them out of the house and took them home down the hill.

On the way, Dylan asked, "How is Mister Morgan?"

Pugh walked on. After a minute, he spoke.

"We want to protect you boys," he said, "better not talk about Dewi. He's had an accident, so he won't be a trouble to you again."

Pugh knocked at their house door.

There was much hugging and tears as their mother clung to them and blessed the men who'd found them. Soon she put them to bed even though it was almost morning.

"There, my angels, you've had a bad night. Get some rest and come down later."

They got into bed and pretended to sleep.

"What did he do Dyl?"

"He made us take our clothes off, didn't he?"

"Yes." And Griff lapsed into silence. The shame of being naked in front a stranger was a terrible thing, so it seemed.

They never talked about Dewi Morgan again. No one ever asked them about what really happened.

Much later, when he was a grown man, Dylan went to the graveyard at Dolgellau. He sat beside the grave of Dewi Morgan and whispered something.

No one heard what he said except the birds and the swaying trees.

WEST BAY

Past midnight, a storm hammered and rocked the walls of Jack Brad's hovel on West Bay. He lived alone ever since he kicked his wife Maggie out for stealing his wages,

"She'd steal the coat off a beggar if she could, the crafty witch."

A sudden noise brought him wide awake. The sound of a fist on the door. There it was again. No cry or shout, just the pounding again and again.

"What's your business?"

"Open Jack!"

He ran to the kitchen for the twelve bore and quickly thumbed in two cartridges.

"Mind, I got me gun and stand back from the door!" The shadow moved.

Easing the bolt back, he jarred open the door pushing against the wind. In the whirlwind stood a tall figure wrapped in oilskin with a hat jammed down on his forehead.

"Let me in Jack, I've got summat for you and I need a place to hide it."

It was Crask, a scavenger, who lived under the high cliffs which hunched around the Bay. He cradled something in his arms and laid it down on the work table and turned up the wick in the lamp.

"Put down the gun, Jack and I'll let you into a bargain."

Crask leant forward, put the object on the table and twisted his lips into a half smile.

"Just you and me, mind, and down the middle!"

Jack breached the gun and stood it in the corner.

"Show us what you found an' I'll think on it."

The scavenger bent over and began to untie the cloth which wrapped the prize. It was a fine cotton material, with some dark stains. Crask had some difficulty in untying it and ripped at the bundle.

At last, the object rolled onto the table. It was a woman's hand torn off at the wrist, the fingers curled as if in a spasm of agony.

"Jesu! What have you done?" Jack shrank back, eyes wide and stood against the wall.

"Calm yerself," Crask held up his hands, "I found her on the strand. In the dark, no one saw her jump."

West Bay folk knew how the great cliffs drew unhappy souls to the brink and certain death.

"But the hand!" Jack stared at the blanched fingers and the delicate wrist.

"She fell on the rocks, it was natural. But see,"

He pointed to the fingers; two rings glittered, even in the lamplight they glowed brightly. "Must be worth a good amount."

Jack stood back as Crask pulled at the rings. He held the palm with one hand and twisted the finger. The grey skin swelled up as he tugged; a little circle of resistant flesh formed around the finger as he twisted and pulled. Eventually, he freed them and put them on the table.

The hand curled again and lay palm up with one finger outstretched. Jack covered it with the bloodstained sleeve.

"Look at that!" Crask hugged himself, looking down at the treasure with a fixed gaze.

"Get it out of here!" Jack looked him in the face and pointed to the hand, "Just take it, in the name of Christ! It belongs to the poor creature on the shore."

Crask stirred from his reverie and nodded. He took his hat and without a further glance, pushed the grey bundle into his coat pocket.

"What about the rings?" "Hold 'em till the morning and I'll collect them when it's safe." He swept out into the wind before Jack had time to speak, leaving the door wide open and the wind swirled in, howling and tumbling the furniture about the room. Struggling to the door, Jack put his back to it and bolted quickly. The silence seemed strange after the tumult. In that quiet moment, he looked for the rings. The table was empty. The chairs were tumbled over and he scrabbled on the floor where they had been. The rings had gone. The floorboards beneath the table were bare. He pushed aside the table and chairs to scour the floor. No sign of them. His eyes darted into every dark corner of the room.

He covered his eyes with one hand and sat hunched against the wall. In his mind's eye, the hand with its curled fingers was still there, beckoning to him with one outstretched finger. He cursed Crask and his greed. Then, in a moment, he saw the truth. Crask had pocketed the rings after he stuffed the hand into his coat.

He clenched his fists and scrambled to the door, pulling his greatcoat from its peg. Outside the darkness covered him instantly. As he ran he shouted but the wind whipped his voice away from his lips. Above him, the faint outline of the cliffs hung over him; he stumbled along the shingle making for the steepest bank of the Bay where he expected to find Crask. A dim shape was moving among the stones below the crest. As he ran, thunder rolled around the sky and a flash of lightning, gave an instant of clarity to the scene ahead. The figure of a man stooped over a bundle on the ground. Another roar of thunder filled the sky and he sprang at the man gathering him in an embrace to choke him. They struggled shifting from side to side as they fought, tripping on the lifeless corpse that lay under their feet.

Again, a crack of thunder burst out of the heavens and without a sound, the cliff began to move. Silently, swiftly the face of red clay dropped to the beach and covered the struggling men. It spread out into the shingle in a rolling carpet of stones and earth covering everything in its path.

The next morning, curious folk came out to see the damage. Jack Brad's hovel stood open. Inside, in a crevice by the door, they found the two rings. Maggie, Brad's wife, peered in like all the rest. Her sly gaze took in the scene in a flash.

"Them's mine," she said quickly, "I lost 'em years ago."

LIVE THE DREAM

The shop bell rang as he pushed open the door. Mister Shah put down his cup and smiled across the counter.

"Usual bets Charlie?"

"Give us a fiver's worth, I feel lucky!"

This had become a custom on pay day and gave a bright spot to the end of the week. What If? Like every other punter, Charlie Spence shared the dream to win a piece of the jackpot. It didn't matter that he had tried for the last three years and won sod all--it was the dream.

Tucking the slips into his back pocket, he went out into the grey evening light, heading for the Cross Keys. He spent half an hour in the pub sipping a pint and watching the bar maid; she was gorgeous and she called him by his name as if she was a girlfriend. He liked that. He's never had a real girlfriend in all his twenty-eight years, but sometimes he visited the 'house' in Palmer Street.

Back home, his Mam bustled at the kitchen stove and laid his dinner on the table. Charlie chewed through the meal, half his mind on Dorothy the barmaid and half on the prospect of another dull week-end. Then he subsided into his usual state and turned on the telly.

The man on the screen was young and tanned and his smile got on Charlie's wick but when he began to deal with the National Lottery results, Charlie straightened up and pulled the slips out of his pocket and added them to the pile on the sideboard. This was the weekly ritual and he felt for the pencil they kept next to the slips. He wrote down the numbers as they tumbled out of the canister. The smiling face of the star loomed large as he approached the screen and wished everyone good luck. He announced the total of prize money with a wide gesture as if taken by surprise. The tv audience screamed with simulated joy; then the commercials came on and Charlie switched off.

He took up the note of the numbers and began to check the top slip. He checked again. Yes, there were seven out of eight numbers right!

"Bloody Hell!" He sat still for a moment, and checked again--still seven numbers.

Like a greyhound, he was off to the corner shop.

"Look Ali! I got seven numbers!" Within a half hour the Lottery confirmed it and Charlie knew he was a winner. Shocked and unsure of himself, he sat in a corner of the pub and pondered what to do. Nothing seemed real, the win, the voices of the Lottery Team as they burbled on, the unspecified amount of his prize.

He looked at Dorothy, and wondered about her. She looked unreachable. She smiled as she pulled pints; her eyelashes fluttered, her breasts strained against her blouse and her glossy black hair swept to and fro He shook the image from his mind; she was too hot for him. He got up and went home. The wind blasted him along the dim street and into the house.

Next morning was Saturday and he slept in. The wonderful news cossetted him in a warm glow. It was his secret which he longed to keep hidden while he absorbed the news. How much was it? When did he get paid? How would he handle it? Gradually these thoughts began to whirl inside his head and he got up and dressed. The morning air was keen and he walked briskly up to the papershop. Missus Ali was filling the paper racks.

"Quick! See how much you've won!"

She handed him The Sun and his hand trembled as he turned the pages. There had been eleven tickets with seven winning numbers and the payout was £120.000. His first reaction was disappointment. His imagination had fixed on millions not thousands and the figure seemed puny against his expectation.

When he went home, he said nothing to his mother. His secret was so special that he wanted to keep it to himself as long as possible. He felt that once his parents found out, everything would be different.

The phone rang and he jumped to it.

"Is that Mister Spence?" said a posh London voice, "Mister Charles Spence?"

"Yes."

"We've arranged a presentation at the London Hilton for the winners." And he gave a date.

"Will I get my money then and there?" Charlie's voice rose a little as he spoke.

"Yes indeed!" Said the suave voice, "you can be sure of that. Of course, bring the ticket with you!" Charlie didn't like the tone of the laugh at the other end of the line. He put the phone down.

The date was early next week, the Tuesday, and his mind whirled with what to do. For the first time, he had to make choices. Should he take someone with him? What should he wear? Would he have to stay down there? Life had been simple and orderly up to now as he had no need to make decisions, even if life flowed on disagreeably.

At Sunday lunchtime, his father came in from the Legion with a look on his face. He stabbed a finger at Charlie.

"What's all this about the Lottery?" Veins stood out on his neck and he looked flushed.

"Happens I won some cash on the Lottery. What's it to you?" Charlie could hear his voice as if someone else was talking yet he could not help it; years of frustration were bubbling up inside his head and he was incapable of stifling it.

Monday morning he stayed home. The tyre-fitters could manage without him. Instead, he walked to the Cross Keys as soon as it opened. Dorothy was there.

"My My!" she said, "tell us all about it? What you goin' to do?"

He looked down and away for a moment, unable to meet her gaze.

"Got to go down to London tomorrow to find out."

He didn't want to tell her how much because she might be disappointed.

"That's nice. Fancy a trip myself!"

He looked up to see if she was teasing him but her blue eyes gazed at him with interest. She leant forward across the bar and he had to look up into her face to avoid gazing at her breasts. It was difficult and she knew it.

There was no one else in the bar and he bit his lip.

"Do you want to come with me?" His words were out of his mouth before he realized it.

"What to London?" her eyes sparkled and she tilted her head back, "What would your Mam say?"

"What's that got to do with it?" He felt a surge of defiance rising inside.

"Just asking! If you want me to, I'll come."

He could hardly believe it. Dorothy! Who never chatted to him. Dorothy! Who every bloke in the pub fancied!

"What you got to do then?" Her eyes grew serious and she looked at him in a different way.

"Well, they give out the prizes in a fancy hotel, so I suppose they want photos and things."

"Listen!" She gripped his arm, "You got to spruce up. I'll sort it out, shall I?"

"Like what?"

"We'll get you a new suit and shoes ---the works."

His confidence began to grow; things he had not considered were being dealt with and the prospect of the London trip seemed less daunting.

That afternoon, they bought the new suit and a pair of smart trainers. He felt taller and took sidelong glances at Dorothy as they left the shop. She tucked her arm in his as they walked along.

Next day, they met up at the station and arrived in London at mid day. She found the way to the big Hotel and he was grateful; the bustle and excitement was almost too much to take. She looked ace, with her hair done up and the high heel shoes. He knew people were looking at them and felt like a new man. When they arrived, they were put into a group of other winners and herded into a large plush room.

A plump man in a dinner jacket stood on a platform and held up his hand.

"Welcome ladies and Gentlemen and congratulations to everybody! When your name is called, please come up to the platform and show us your slip and we'll take it from there."

A steady line of people formed. Nobody wanted to push forward, so it took several minutes for Charlie and Dorothy to reach the stage. The beaming man leant down and held out his hand for the slip. Charlie passed it over. Dorothy smiled at him and smoothed her glossy locks languidly.

A puzzzled smile passed over the gentleman's face and he looked again at Charlie's slip.

"This is no good," he said, pointing to the slip. "Do you know what this is?"

Charlie looked up at the little man. Was he trying to take the piss?

"What d'you mean?" Dorothy frowned and moved forward.

"This is last week's ticket. You've got no prize with this!"

He waved the piece of paper in Charlie's face.

It couldn't be true! It was on the top of the pile in the kitchen where they were always kept!

"See? Look at the date!" The horrible man pushed the scrap under his nose.

Dorothy grabbed it and peered at the date, then she turned and slapped Charlie so hard that the people at the back thought the stage had collapsed. He hardly felt the sting. His mind was numb and he stepped back from the crowd and sat on one of the little gilded chair which stood against the wall.

His new suit was tight under the arms and he felt sick and hot. The show went on as he sat there, mouth agape till a hand touched his shoulder and he looked up. It was Dorothy.

"You daft Pillock!" She said, "I should have guessed you'd fuck it up somehow!"

She looked down at him and a corner of her mouth lifted. "Come on we better get out of here." She hoisted him to his feet and they left. No one noticed them.

Outside, the bright lights of Piccadilly glowed in a friendly way. He rubbed his eyes and looked sideways at her.

"If I say sorry, does it make a difference?"

She grinned: "No, you're still a noggin, but we're in this together aren't we? Till we get home, I want to enjoy myself--let's get a room!"

That night Charlie lived the dream.

WARRIOR WOLF 1132

The early sun sent a brilliant shaft of light pouring across the blue green ice. Warrior, the pack leader stretched his back and sniffed the pure crystalline air. He left the den and set his mark against the nearest rock to claim his territory.

From the mouth of the cave, a few muzzles drew in the air sensing the new day and the weather. No other wolf stirred but they watched him as he circled the area raising his head to the sun and blinking in the bright light. He let out a call in one long lingering howl, challenging the world.

When the snow came, the pack moved down from the high country to hunt the deer and caribou feeding on the rich grassland. Now with the freezing winds, snow drifted lower and their food became scarce. The herds moved on down the valleys and now the pack had to deal with other predators driven by cold and hunger competing for the same prey.

For three days Warrior led them on trails but they made no kills.

Hunger and vicious temper brought a wild challenge from Tyrant who dared to fight him for supremacy. If he could find no food then what right had he to be leader?

The contest had been savage and now Warrior limped where Tyrant mauled him. The rest had stayed quiet and silently prostrated themselves in submission. Tyrant's body lay outside untouched. Warrior snarled at any attempt at scavenging the remains; the challenger deserved respect.

This new day promised better hunting. The breeze blew from the south and fresh scents mixed with the powerful smell of the pinewoods. The whole pack began to stir with excitement and they crowded round Warrior whimpering and looking to him for a lead. Lean and agile from the hunger which gnawed at them, they would not stay still but he did not move until he filtered the wind and found animal scent.

They set off in file stepping in the prints of the leader and drawing in the new scents of vegetation and life as they went. Small tracks in the snow led them to warren of pine martens and they ravaged the mound as they dug for their meal.

Briefly, they rested. Certainly, they were desperate for food; two of the dams were heavy with swollen bellies and needed nourishment.

Warrior went on alone to spy the tracks and movements ahead. Something big and smelling strange was among the trees some distance away. Creeping flat on his belly he moved forward scenting and looking between the trees. The stench grew stronger; acrid and meaty with a wet tang. The noise of gnawing teeth added to the mystery as he edged closer to the sound. He moved so quietly he disturbed no stones or branches on his way.

At the far side of a small clearing a brown shape appeared. Standing man-tall, a grizzly bear was stripping bark from a tree and grinding it into a pulp.

Warrior withdrew and ran quickly back to the pack. The scent he brought with him told the wolves of his contact with a large animal. They whimpered in fear undecided what should be done.

He nipped Trojan and Hunter and they yelped but followed him as he set off in the direction of the bear.

The rest trailed him in a subdued way, fearful but obedient.

As they approached the clearing, the sound of the bear became clear. Its musky scent was strong and exuded violence. They formed a pack at once. The weaker males and the females circled the clearing and lay just out of sight at the snow's edge, under the trees.

Warrior stepped forward to confront the bear. Breaking off at once from its work on the tree, it turned to stand facing the wolf. Its maw gaped with anger, its fangs bared. It roared furiously and stormed across the clearing on all fours in a rush to seize the wolf. Warrior jumped aside at the critical moment and the bear skidded in the snow, swiping wildly at the dancing wolf.

Behind it, Trojan sprang at its hind legs attempting to unbalance it but it was agile and twisted quickly to engage him. The bear struck out with a flailing paw and the wolf was flung into the trees, bleeding from his flank.

Hunter jumped and sank his teeth into the fleshy back of its neck snarling and twisting his teeth to get a better grip.

All this time Warrior waited stock still, observing the struggle and gauging his next move. He moved like lightning when he saw the bear stretch to reach Hunter with its bright claws. He sprang at the creature's throat from the front and clung there as the giant flung himself to and fro to remove his attackers. Standing at full height the bear struck once -twice, teeth flashed, wolf-blood spurted- claws tore at flesh and roars of pain echoed through the clearing. Warrior took another hold gripping its lower jaw; snarling with anger, twisting this way and that to stifle the huge beast.

Hunter hung on to the back of the bear. Battered by the claws of the animal and slammed against the tree, his strength faded and he lost his grip and fell to the floor. Now the contest became terminal. Warrior knew only his courage could keep him in place as the beast tore at him, raking his flesh. He tightened his grip and felt for the first time the bear was weakening.

It staggered from side to side and moved erratically while continuing to grip the wolf with its mighty claws. Then it fell forward, dragging him down with it... Still Warrior kept his grip on the jaw, though the weight of the huge animal pressed down on him. Gradually, the strength of the beast slipped away and Warrior clung on sensing the struggle was ending. With a sigh the bear slumped forward shrouding him in a heavy covering of fur. The pack rushed to reach him and tore at the corpse, pulling it from the body of their leader. They whimpered and nuzzled the unconscious form as Warrior lay motionless on the bloody soil.

Some minutes later, he revived and staggered slowly to his feet, licking his wounds and then lapping snow to cope with his thirst. Hunter and Trojan lay dead in the bushes under the trees. The pack keened as they mourned their loss but soon began to tear at the warm flesh of the fallen bear. There was plenty to feed them for several days and the pack was safe. Warrior limped to the centre of the clearing. He surveyed the carnage and the triumph. Then he lifted his head and howled to the risen sun.

COUNT FOSCO AND
THE HOLY CHALICE

Fra Angelo had arrived in Milan seeking a new shelter where he could be safe and protect The Relic. Shuffling slowly along the wide arcade, the old man seemed lost. His wispy hair and uncertain steps made the crowd avoid him, choosing to divert their eyes in case he demanded attention. His dark shabby overcoat had a velvet collar rimmed with grease where his long grey hair rubbed against it. Beneath the coat his cassock was black, but age made it shiny and faded. On his calloused feet he wore scuffed sandals. The quick nervous turn of his head revealed his long nose and dark ringed eyes.

As he walked he held his right hand closely against his body as if he had some valuable object to hide. And he did. Within his coat he guarded the Chalice of the Precious Blood of Christ. At the end of the arcade he trod down some steps till he reached a well-worn door and pushed through. Inside was a barrel-shaped room lit by a candle. It contained a chair and a bed with a grating high in the wall to let in some air. He felt safe here for the moment.

By contrast, in Rome, a Cardinal sat on a throne before an audience of robed attendants and military figures. His face was white with anger and his eyes flicked from face to face. "How is it 7 months have passed without a sighting of this priest?"

"Your Eminence, we have twenty agents at work"

"Then explain how it is no result has been obtained?"

The Cardinal' spoke quietly but the force of his words sent a chill through every heart.

"Send me your most astute agent and I will instruct him myself."

And with that he waved his counsellor away and turned to his next task.

Some short time later a tall figure in the uniform of the Papal Guard presented himself before the Cardinal. His face was framed by his helmet but at a sign from the throne he removed it and his dark features were revealed. His hair was long, pulled back into a knot at the back of his head. His cheeks were scarred and a line of bluish wound cut across his nose and upper lip.

The Major Domo announced him:

"Count Fosco, your Eminence, at your command"

"What I seek, Count, is action, not prevarication. With this ring you can provide yourself with 2 retainers and all equipment you need to hunt down the apostate monk who defies his Holiness. I need results."

The Cardinal's eyes glinted as he handed the soldier a ring with the Papal symbol upon it. He knew the fierce reputation Fosco had among the church's enemies.

With a salute, but not a word, the Count took the ring and left the room. Within the hour he set off. His first call was to be the Monastery of The Holy Chalice at Trieste.

Meanwhile Friar Angelo, hidden in his cellar in Milan prepared a coded message to be sent to His Abbot. His report was passed to the one person he was compelled to trust, Maghreb, an Arab trading between the Milan and Trieste. The merchant wore the distinctive Djellabh of the Toureg Arab and with a sly smile he pocketed the paper.

"Within two days good Father" Maghreb promised "I will deliver your letter, inshalla" and he made a sign to ward off evil spirits. He slipped out of the room, stepped into the street and was gone. Two days later he delivered the message and got paid. The fact he made a visit to the Monastery filtered down to the hookah parlours and brothels of the town within hours.

By chance, Count Fosco arrived in Trieste, within a day of Maghreb. His purpose was to question the monks at the Monastery.

"What is it that you seek from me?" The Abbot demanded. "Your presence here is an affront to our community."

"Leave off your high manner with me" countered Fosco "I have Papal authority in my hands and I will go where I choose."

Within a few hours the search was over -nothing was found.

The bars and brothels of Trieste buzzed with life and gossip. Gonzago, Fosco's sergeant, found out an Arab merchant had arrived recently and made a visit to the Monastery of the Holy Chalice. In one of the taverns, he found him.

Gonzago sat beside him with a bottle of wine at hand.

Each man sensed this was an overture to trading.

"Have you come far?"

With a genial smile Maghreb saw a chance to make money.

"Only from Milan" he replied "Ohalla, if I sell nothing on this visit I am ruined." He sighed. Soon the two were drinking. Gonzago made it clear he had money for trade and Maghreb indicated he had information that was valuable.

"Have you heard of any visitors to the Monastery?" asked Gonzago. The Arab smiled and made a gesture with his fingers, rubbing them together in a familiar way.

"Maybe I do know a little about this -but I cannot tell a stranger"

"I pay well for good stuff" countered the soldier "but it must be fresh"

"Fresh as this morning milk" replied the merchant.

Gonzago reported his news at once. Within the hour, The Count rode hard for Milan.

Fosco decided to use his true identity and establish himself with the great families of the province. His first step was to rent a palace in the city. He attracted attention and invitations immediately.

A Papal Count was a rarity and a prize for society and Church dignitaries. He identified those families who showed sympathy for the Order of the Holy Relic or whose devotion to the Church was suspect. It became apparent that the Giorgio family, Princes of Sienna, was his target. The Prince lived in some splendour in a palace outside Sienna. The building had been a castle for centuries but now enclosed a magnificent hall rich in tapestries and fine furniture. No one stood higher in the Province than the Princes Giorgio.

Count Fosco, dressed in a fine silk coat with silver facings indicating his rank as knight of The Holy See, rode through the gates of the Palace.

"My Lord" bowed the visitor "I am here at His Holiness' request to seek your help."

"How could I refuse such a request? Tell me your wishes?"

The aristocrat studied the face of this dark imperious man. The dangerous glitter in Fosco's eye was clear and no doubt this visit was not a social one.

"My commission is to find a priest who has stolen Holy Relics"

He went on to describe and name Fra Angelo and hinted he was to be punished by the Holy See.

"My first duty will be to question the priests who are under your Protection, Your Highness, since they may know more than we do."

The Prince's smile concealed his fear. Fra Angelo was his brother.

"I cannot permit an enquiry without supervision"

"Then by all means join us at any enquiry."

Fosco knew that if he could get access to Giorgio servants or clergy he would compel them to reveal all, despite their loyalty. Pain and fear are powerful aids.

Fosco and his two men between them questioned the staff and clergy of the household. Fosco guessed The Prince would not oversee the enquiry himself.

One of the staff, not a priest, admitted he had seen Fra Angelo in the main streets of Milan. Fosco seized on this and within a day the man confessed he was the servant of the Prince who had given money to the monk. That information cost him his life. Fosco now knew the link he had suspected.

So he moved on -He was like a hawk stooping on its prey and, as each new step brought him nearer to his victim, his energy increased.

Fra Angelo waited for three days before his instincts told him something was wrong. Maghreb had not returned and fear gripped him. Leaving the cellar, he set out for the only refuge he could reach quickly; the home of his brother Alfonso and his family in Sienna. He chose to walk like a pilgrim along the Santiago pathway. Stopping at the refuges as he went through, he attracted no attention. At last, reaching the Palace, he had no wish to bring his arrival to public knowledge, and made his way to the stable entrance of the Palace.

When his arrival was reported to his brother, the Prince; their meeting was not without some friction. Prince Alfonso began with a question;

"In God's name, why are you here? There are men seeking your whereabouts all over Lombardy and Tuscany"

"Where else should I go but to my family?" cried the monk.

"And put your family and my fortune at hazard by your stubborn oath" muttered his brother.

"I will keep away from the palace-I will leave as soon as I find another hiding place" replied the priest.

"So be it" and the prince turned away. He was annoyed and ashamed at the same time. Family loyalty struggled with fear for his own safety.

By that evening Fra Angelo was lodged in an apartment far from the family rooms but with some comfort. On the same corridor was Prince Alfonso's chaplain, a Jesuit, Father Montebano. The next morning, Montebano intercepted Fra Angelo on his way to Mass.

"Welcome to Sienna, Father." The Jesuit spoke with an easy manner. "Have you come far?"

Angelo sensed in the enquiry, more than simple politeness and he mumbled a reply.

"Please call on me for any assistance" smiled the Jesuit "My rooms are at your service" His bland manner unsettled the monk. He realized a safe place for the Relic was needed immediately. The window of his room faced onto the stables. Crossing to the stables he went inside. A pile of sacks lay in one corner. Rummaging among them he placed the Chalice in the deepest one, filled with oats. At least for a few days the sack would not be needed and no one would search there.

Count Fosco intended to dine with Montebano. The Jesuit seemed a useful contact and he correctly saw the cupidity in his eyes. The presence of the Inquisitor became known and his attendance at the evening meal announced to Fra Angelo. With scarcely a pause, the monk fled from Hall and ran to the stable, with no thought in mind but just the instinct to escape.

Fosco's interests were aroused when he learnt a priest, a fellow guest, failed to appear at dinner. It was plainly suspicious. He questioned the Jesuit about the mystery priest. When Montebano revealed he knew little about the man, Fosco could hardly contain his impatience as the meal went on.

Excusing himself, he gave orders at once. Firstly they checked the palace building itself, with no result.

"Go to, you wretches "snarled Fosco, as the two servants returned

"He is here and you will find him."

Prince Alfonso soon learnt Fosco was on his brother's track. He sent for his son Diego and explained the difficult position he faced.

"They must have some suspicion that he has come here."

"Still, I will find a way to protect him" Diego asserted

"Then get him away from here" replied the prince "I cannot risk a quarrel with the Vatican"

Diego called for his lieutenant and decided to take the priest from the palace immediately.

Having searched the palace, Gonzago and his corporal began a search in the stables. Within minutes they sensed there were preparations for some departure. Trained like bloodhounds they moved in to the stables, weapons drawn.

Diego was about to bring out the priest when he realised the searchers were upon him.

"What do you want in here? You have no business here"

"My business is Papal business" sneered Gonzago "and my warrant is to seek recusants"

At this, Diego drew his rapier and aimed his weapon at the soldier.

"Stand off or take the consequences" he shouted.

Unseen, the second soldier crept up behind the young man and clubbed him to the ground.

"Quickly" Gonzago urged, and they ran into the stables anxious to search before Diego could recover. Their best hope to justify their actions would be to find their prey. Inside, Fra Angelo, startled by the commotion had hidden in one of the stalls where he huddled in a corner. It was a poor hiding place and within minutes the searchers found him and dragged him outside.

They took him at once to the Count.

"Why are you here?" snarled the Interrogator "and where is the chalice you have stolen?

Angelo was dumbfounded to be caught

"I am under the protection of Prince Alfonso" he muttered

Fosco smiled thinly.

"That roof will not shelter you much longer; I have my orders and you are taken. Give up hope of rescue"

They rode out immediately with their prisoner to avoid conflict.

Just as Fosco was moving off, a group of armed men led by Diego rushed towards them and barred their way. Shouting and a clash of arms rang out as the two factions met. The mounted soldiers of Fosco, with their prisoner, had some advantage and forced their way through, slashing down on the retainers. Diego gave way as he staggered back weakened from his earlier injuries.

The Prince learnt of the outrage within minutes and sent retainers after the marauders.

"Sacrilege has been done and Fosco and his villains must be arrested and tried."

Fosco rode recklessly through the countryside urging his small troop onwards. Any complaint could be met if he could restore the Chalice. Turning into a small village, he commandeered a cottage on the outskirts. Setting up a chair, they tied Fra Angelo and beat him with the hilt of a sword till his face ran with blood and his bruised eyes could scarcely see.

"Give up the chalice" demanded the Count "it is your only chance of saving your life. Where is it? In Milan or Sienna?"

The priest stayed silent.

"Speak or die" shouted Fosco but still the monk remained mute.

Time was pressing on the Count, who realised Prince Alfonso or his son would be closing in. Violence had little effect on the holy man. He needed to try another tack. He decided to let Angelo go but to watch him closely. Since he was the guardian of The Chalice, he would not abandon it and would go as quickly as he could to recover it.

Once freed, Fra Angelo staggered to the nearest house to seek help. The owner took him by wagon to

Sienna with a promise of payment at the end of the journey. All this Count Fosco observed and discreetly tracked him as he left the village.

Diego and his men soon reached the village and intercepted the mercenaries. Before the two men could draw their weapons, the soldiers were upon them and held them pinioned and helpless.

"Where is Fra Angelo? Where is your cursed leader?"

"He left us here" shouted Gonzago "we know nothing of his whereabouts."

"You Dog" Diego roared "give him up or die this moment"

"We'll give you nothing" snarled Gonzago, but he said no more. With a quick sharp blade one of the Prince's men slit his throat. He fell lifeless at the feet of his companion. The effect was instantaneous: the corporal screamed out that the Count was making his way to Sienna.

"We will scour the high road back to the castle" ordered the young commander.

Fosco was already making his way through the woods back to the Castle. Avoiding the high road he realized the monk had only one destination-it must be the castle. He moved as swiftly as possible, his charger treading its way skilfully between the trees and moving almost as quickly as a traveller on the turnpike.

His surcoat with its distinctive badges he threw away and now he wore only a dark jacket over his shirt. His high black boots were grimy and dull so he looked like a hard pressed wanderer rather than his usual elegant figure. But his Toledo steel and dagger glittered in the dawning light.

When he reached Sienna, he dismounted and stabled his horse at an inn. He reckoned when Fra Angelo had returned, he would need to make contact with someone about the Chalice. But whom?

Like a shadow, Fosco slipped through the lower gateway where only one sleepy sentry stood guard. Going directly to the quarters of the Jesuit, he knocked at the door. Montebano was about to make his way to the chapel for morning Mass.

He stepped back in surprise as he caught sight of the dark features of Count Fosco.

"If you value your position here, you will do as I say" Fosco pushed his way into the room, demanding the priest's aid. Montebano said nothing but weighed up the plus and minus of the situation.

"You will find the thief and keep him close" threatened the Count "and you will tell me immediately"

"I must do The Church's work" he replied "do you order this?"

"Of course I do" snarled the Inquisitor "remember your sacred duty and you will be in favour with the Lord" Montebano understood the meaning at once. Fosco left.

What meanwhile had Fra Angelo done to avoid detection? His first instinct was to recover the Relic and find some help. His brother had mixed loyalties. His nephew was too incautious.

"The Jesuit must help me" he reflected "our vows in common bind us together."

Taking the divine Relic with him he made his way cautiously to the Jesuit's apartment.

"Thank Sweet Jesus, you are safe" Montebano, quick as light, saw that fortune had played into his hands "You must rest and recover."

He sent for food and shouted for his servant to make up a bed at once. The Chalice was placed in the strong box which held the valuables and documents kept by the Jesuit. Fra Angelo's injuries were washed and he fell exhausted into bed. Quietly, Montebano left the room and carefully turned the lock on the outside of the door. He made his way down through the great Hall in his search for Count Fosco.

Diego was leading his tired horse through the main gate. The Inquisitor had been seen but no one knew where he was. Men searched for him in the main building and in the stables. Diego himself reported to the Prince.

"Watch for the Count" he ordered "Arrest him on sight"

Diego stood at the gate of the Palace, his sergeant ran towards him shouting:

"Someone has seen him inside the palace-he's here!"

Sprinting back inside the main yard, Diego drew his sword and shouted to the man to follow him. The noise of hue and cry came to Fosco's ears as he searched. Unlocking the door to Montebano' room, to his amazement, there on a bed was the priest he least expected to see, still heavily asleep. Fra Angelo's bruised face and fragile frame made the Count reflect. If the steps he had been forced to take caught up with him-he could see just one conclusion, he exceeded his commission and would suffer for it. He had to recover the Chalice.

With less than a second's reflection, he sprang on the sleeping man. Putting his dagger to the throat of the priest he shook him awake.

"Give me the Chalice" there was no response.

"I am in so deep that your life is of no consequence to me"

Still no reply. Fosco's eye turned to the strong box at the side of the bed. He looked for a lever of some sort and found the poker beside the fireplace.

After a little effort he prised the lock and lifted the lid. There before him lay a sack covered bundle. At once he realized he had found not only the Sacred Chalice but his rescue from disgrace. The brilliant vessel shone with such a glow that it hypnotised him. For a space of time impossible to count he stared at the Relic. Then he came back to life and pulled it from the box.

From his bed Fra Angelo realized sacrilege was about to happen and he staggered forward to block the Inquisitor.

Fosco laughed as the old man approached him. It was a cry of contempt and derision that pierced the heart of the old man, who gave his life to guarding the treasure. He stumbled forward with an incoherent plea. As he approached, Fosco plunged his dagger into the old man's breast. With scarcely a sound the weary monk sank to his knees, blood spurting from his throat and spreading down his ragged clothing.

With a final slash, his attacker stepped away and gathering up the Chalice and made for the door. By chance, Montebano was returning. He had failed to find the Count and intended to keep the Relic himself. Maybe he would gain more credit by presenting it to the Prince and sealing a concord between the Order and the Vatican?

Suddenly, he was confronted by a figure in black, dagger in hand, emerging from his chamber. In the faint light of the corridor he could not recognize the figure.

"Get out of my way you holy idiot."

Fosco pushed the Jesuit aside. Montebano was no idiot, he realized in an instant this was a moment of extreme danger and shrank back as the figure passed him by. His cunning mind saw at once the benefit of changing sides.

"Havoc" he cried" Sacrilege-Guards to Arms"

His cry rang out through the palace and reached Diego as he and his men searched below in the courtyard. They ran quickly to him and he pointed in the direction Fosco had taken.

Sensing he must gain time, Fosco ran upwards to the main apartments of the building, looking for a passage to escape or to defend himself. Years of experience taught him coolness of mind in combat. His assessment of the layout of the Palace led him to believe there would be a secret passage from the Prince's rooms to the exterior of the castle. This was a familiar feature in many fortresses. Bursting into the Master Rooms, he found them empty. He barred the door with furniture and began his search. Ignoring the pounding on the door, he carefully examined each wall hanging and tapestry in the room, and found a hidden door, just as the principal door gave way and soldiers tumbled into the room.

"Hold hard" shouted Diego as he set eyes on the black figure outlined against the bright red wall hangings. He moved to engage, sword in hand.

Fosco smiled thinly and stood before the escape door choosing to face him rather than run away. The first contact was the thrust of Diego's blade aimed at the Count's heart. With a twitch of his wrist, Fosco deflected it and retaliated by a touch to Diego's wrist.

"You see, My Dear Princeling, that I do not seek to harm the child of this regal household. Leave off and spare yourself."

This enraged the young man and he moved wildly forward slashing at his opponent. Although Diego was an accomplished swordsman, his temper was his weakness.

Fosco had to set down the Chalice as he dealt with this attack and expected to deal further with the guards. Now with no burden, he began his response to his attackers.

First, he slashed Diego's sword arm and as he reeled out of the way, he advanced on the soldiers who approached him. They crowded him and although unharmed, he was forced back into the mouth of the hidden corridor. The passage led down from the room and would be too narrow for full play with steel.

Dropping the drapery over the entrance he gained a few seconds on his pursuers. Running hard he fled down the dark stairs away from the cries and sounds above. His rapid steps led him always down and down but ever in darkness.

His senses dimmed by the gloom, he stumbled at last against a heavy wooden door, its hinges rusted and its latch stiffened by age. With all his strength he pushed against it. It held fast. He doubled his effort but with no success.

At last, with a supreme effort, he loosed the door and saw, with no surprise, 20 feet below him were the cold dark waters of the moat.

At this moment, one of the soldiers appeared at the turn of the staircase. A quick thrust dispatched him and he fell blocking the way of his fellow behind him.

But, raising himself from the floor the man aimed his pistol directly at the Count from a distance of less than four feet. Sensing he could not miss, Fosco sprang from the gaping door down into the water and out of sight from his enemies. Diego pushed past the men at the mouth of the tunnel and peered down into the swirling pool of the moat. Nothing moved below except the eddies of the dark waters.

For some minutes they peered down, anxious to see even the slightest movement which would show if the Fosco lived or died. Eventually, Diego ordered the troop back to the Hall and reported to his father. Servants went outside the fortress to check the moat and surrounds. There was no sign of the man.

EPILOGUE. Prince Alfonso ordered a High Mass to celebrate the recovery of the wonderful Relic. As the Chaplain to the Prince, Father Montebano proceeded to Rome and presented the Chalice to His Holiness. For this, he was accorded the honour of "Protector of the Holy Places." The College of Jesuits voted him Governor General and he presided over the Jesuits for 20 years.

Diego became the Master of Sienna but never regained his skill at arms. In due time he succeeded his father to the title.

No one recalled the saintly man who had given his life for the safety of the holy Chalice and no grave marked his passing. The name of Fosco was never mentioned in the Vatican and no more was heard of him.

The following year an unknown mercenary appeared in the service of the Duke of Medina at the battle of Zaragoza. Scarred with a cut across his nose and lip, his long black hair tied back, this man was the lieutenant to the Duke. This was the man who killed the Moorish king in that battle but refused all honours awarded by Medina and left his service after the conquest. Nobody learnt where he went or who he served.

He was known as Matamoro meaning "Death to the Moors."

THE PECKING ORDER

Mrs Pumfrey was a good woman. Whenever one of the villagers fell sick, you could be sure the Squire's wife would visit and dispense broth or other sustenance. The sight of her carriage outside your door was a sure sign of sickness and often foreshadowed a death in the family. It became so common that a saying grew up in the village;

"The carriage has bin to Jo Gargery's house."

Or "Mrs Pumfrey'll be here soon." meaning a death was imminent.

She never heard the rumour and spent many hours visiting the community while wondering, sometimes, about the meagre gratitude expressed by the lower orders.

Country folk have a good idea of their proper status in life. The Gentry up at the Manor seemed superior to all. The parson's wife had precedence over the farmer's wife and she, in turn, would not consider walking behind the butcher's wife on the way to church on Sunday.

The old order was set awry when a new Vicar came to the village and took up the living at St John's. The village was agog. He was a high Churchman, with a tendency to use "Smells and Bells" in the new-fangled Popish fashion, but people felt they could not complain since he was the candidate of the Bishop of Ely. The new wife supervised the unloading of the large wagon standing outside the Vicarage. The ladies of the High street could observe every item unloaded without seeming to quiz, as many windows looked out on the road.

"Good Heavens!" said Mrs Perkins, the butcher's wife. "I do believe that is a grand piano! What's wrong with a cottage piano? I'd like to know!"

"And what's that great big table for?" asked Mrs Potts, the baker's wife.

The lady in question seemed unaware of the interest and ordered the men about in a voice which reached the listeners clearly. Her dress was elegantly simple, her figure slim and tall. She wore her auburn hair high on her brow and a perfectly made chignon at the back of her head. There was so much to envy about her immaculate appearance that it took no more than ten minutes for the ladies of Dymchurch to decide they disliked her intensely.

"Gives herself some Grand Airs for a parson's wife." Said Mrs Gethin and the ladies from across the High Road agreed silently. But when the new parson called, they simpered and welcomed him with cups of tea and cake as if they cherished his presence. No one mentioned his wife directly, still their curiosity was acute and Mrs Perkins approached the matter with what she believed was great subtlety;

"Mayhap Mrs Peters has a liking for needle work, Vicar?

"Oh no!" he replied," I'm afraid she has no time to sew, you see she is a novelist." He seemed to believe that was a sufficient explanation, but it mystified the village.

"Readin' and writin' is not hard." said Giles Foster the farrier, "Why, my Nancy can do that and feed the bairns and the chickens as well."

But as the weeks went by, Elizabeth Peters became a force to be reckoned with.

For example, she took the front pew at church as of right. But Mrs Pumfrey had always prayed from her front pew on the other side of the aisle without competition, but now she had to move briskly to ensure she went first to the altar rails for the Communion. Very stressful.

She demanded China Tea from the grocer and white bread from the baker, which combined luxury and mystery. Worst of all, she brought soups of her own making to the homes of the deserving poor.

Mrs Pumfrey could stand it no more.

"My Dear," she mentioned to her husband, "isn't it time we had the parson and his wife to dinner?"

Squire Pumfrey took no interest in the composition of his dinner parties and muttered something in reply. Soon the invitations were posted and the date settled. Of course, the choice of guests and the menu was a work of exquisite labour. The Coulsons of Pembury Park and the Dowager Lady Freeborn had been invited and accepted. Lobsters and oysters from the harbour of Great Yarmouth arrived in baskets of straw, well iced, to preserve their costly contents. The wines, from the best vintages, were brought up from the cellar.

On the day of the dinner party, Mrs Pumfrey made sure the drive had been swept and the gravel walk was brushed as neat as a Japanese garden.

That evening, she wore a gown of grey satin, bought that very week from the haberdasher in Norwich. She put on her pearl choker and casually fanned herself with a fan made of peacock's feathers by a French milliner. Her hair had been put up by her maid in what she was told was "ze 'ighest Fashion Madame."

The first to arrive were the Coulsons. Their carriage, drawn by two matched greys, caught the last of the sunlight on its gleaming coachwork and the postillions added colour to the entourage as they jumped down to open the door for the couple. The Coulsons were the oldest family in East Anglia. Many generations had given service to the Crown and everybody knew that they owned more land than the Duke of Norwich. Then old Lady Freeborn made her entrance with the aid of two footmen who carried her from her brougham into the Hall of the Manor House. Other worthies, invited to make up numbers made their appearances in good time. Still, there was no sign of Parson Peters and his wife.

Through the open French windows of the Drawing Room on this summer evening, the party heard the sound of feet approaching across the terrace. The parson and his wife appeared suddenly at the window and walked in unannounced, as if to a picnic or a family occasion.

He wore a simple coat of black with a pure white stock of finest silk and carried his wideawake hat in his hand. His long fair hair was brushed back from his face. He surveyed the company calmly as if accustomed to the highest social occasions and he bowed to Mrs Pumfrey with an elegant short bow.

"Such a lovely evening! We felt it would be a shame to miss the last rays of sunshine, so we walked across."

There was a short silence as the pair arrived, not so much because of their casual entrance but to allow the party to examine the assemblage of the new arrivals. Mrs Peters walked with the confidence of a young princess. She dazzled the men with her enchanting smile and her blue eyes radiated gaiety which filled the room. Her auburn hair fell about her shoulders in glistening folds and quite ignored the fashion that dictated hers should be "up" for such occasions. Her pale skin seemed as fragile as Sevres china with just a touch of pink on her cheeks to hint at a lively spirit.

The ladies noted the dress, fashioned from yellow silk with a style showing the grace of her slim waist and her beautiful shoulders. The men were charmed to catch her attention when she smiled at them; each man felt her eyes were on him alone.

Mrs Pumfrey rose to introduce "The Parson and his wife" and the couple moved round the room with each introduction. The ladies observed more unpleasant details of Mrs Peter's attire; her magnificent pearl necklace; the rings she wore -plain emerald and diamond stones set in platinum. The men stood like simpletons bewitched with the gaiety of her eyes and the charm of her presence.

The party moved on to the dining room and conversation ranged from local matters to the state of the Queen's health. Mrs Peters felt that not enough care was taken with Her Majesty's welfare.

"How thoughtful of you!" said Mrs Pumfrey with a kindly smile, "have you intelligence on the subject?" Her query was noted by Mrs Coulson as an elegant stroke at a social adversary.

"It may be so," chimed in the new parson, "My brother in law Sir Peter Chimes has attended at Osborne on several recent occasions." Mrs Peters said nothing but turned and engaged the guest to her left as if she missed the remark.

Mrs Pumfrey sat in a thunderous silence for a short time and chided the butler over some perceived fault that no one else had noted.

At the same time, Squire Pumfrey leant across the table towards the young wife and invited her to join him when the hunting season started in November.

Her eyes opened with delight. "Nothing would be more exciting," she said, "but at present all we have is old Bones our trap pony who is adorable but no hunter."

"But that's no problem," said the Squire. "I can lend you Bess She can lepp the biggest brook in the county!"

Mrs Pumfrey broke in; "Shall we ladies adjourn and leave the hunting chatter to the gentlemen?" She looked hard at the Squire and he shrugged in mute submission.

Upstairs, the old Lady Freeborn sat in state upon a gilt chair raised a little to ease her poor aching bones.

"I see you are a lively gel," she said as she caught the sleeve of the young wife, "but watch out, there are more snares in the countryside than just to catch rabbits!"

Elizabeth Peters winked at the old Dowager and pressed her hand.

"You and I think alike, Lady Freeborn, but isn't it fun?"

For once the old lady felt again the thrill of a young girl among the company of her elders, shocking the staid opinions of society; it was fun, as she watched their envy; she recalled how exciting it was to turn men's heads.

"Yes, my dear," said the Dowager, "the pecking order needs a jolt from time to time and you and I know it!"

Months later, the Pumfreys and the Coulsons accepted the fact that the Dowager Lady Freeborn was a regular visitor to the Vicarage and they were privileged if they were asked to tea on the same occasion.

STAR SHINE

She pushed her things into a bag and slammed out of the door. I ran after her down the path leading to the jetty and grabbed her arm.

'You can't go like this.'

'Let go of my arm,' was all she said, and she looked out to sea where the boat was approaching.

Two months ago we arrived on Flanna, as excited as children. At last, our dream of life together began. I had given up my job in London and she came from New Zealand to be with me. The island seemed perfect: remote, beautiful and just the place for us to work. Jo was a writer and I was an observer for the Astrophysics Society, plotting the movement of the planets.

The boat called every two months and neither of us looked for company. We had each other – and the stars.

Yes, the stars. People tell of the brightness of starlight seen from the Atlas Mountains, but they cannot compare it to the commanding sight of the Borealis as it swoops and dances over Flanna. Your skin tingles, your eyes are filled with light. Every nerve is on fire and your breath is stifled. When we first arrived, I tried to show Jo how strong the attraction was.

She laughed and said, 'You're becoming hypnotised. It's only the Northern Lights.'

It was an absurd remark. Surely, anyone can appreciate the power of the starlight?

Two weeks later, I had to stay out all night to record the movements. She complained.

'You can set up the cameras to record – you don't have to be there.'

I didn't reply. How was I to tell her that the starlight radiated its power on me, demanding I should be there? When I returned at dawn, my skin purple with the freezing night air, I saw her expression of disdain. I went silently to bed, alone.

She spoke to me the next day.

'James, let's try to do something together. Can you look at my script and tell me what you think?'

I smiled to humour her and pretended to scan her writing. It was hopeless. The words meant nothing to me, just scribbles on the page. I made some anodyne comment to appease her but I saw the disappointment in her eyes.

I wanted to grip her and shout, 'Jo, the stars are the energy of the universe, can't you see? We must absorb their power to survive!'

But I felt her psyche resisting me. I said nothing.

The Society began to be troublesome; they demanded regular reports. I logged the movements of various nebulae but they wanted more. I realised they had no comprehension of the real significance of cosmic influence; they only recorded data, not the power of the universe.

I stopped sending in reports. What was the point? The real work had to be harnessing the energy of the Borealis to increase one's own significance.

I found a way to do this. Each night, I left the croft and stood on the highest point on the island. Above me the whole of the northern sky poured its radiance down on me. The core of my being absorbed the mighty power of the stars. I shouted and screamed with delight. At last I had reached true union with the universe.

I begged Jo to come out and feel the transfiguration on the mountaintop. She shook her head and kept to the house as if it was some shell or carapace to protect her. I left her to it.

Now, the weeks pass and I find my life becoming focussed. I need more time to intensify the energy. You need to concentrate, and trivial matters, like food and sleep, drop away. She never understood this; I tried to explain but she looked away and spent her time writing in her stupid journal.

Then the next boat was due. I watched on the mountain as usual during the night, while she lay wrapped in a blanket indoors. At one point, she came out into the night air and called to me. I heard her voice but the radiance of the stars possessed my spirit once again. I shouted for her to join me in the ecstasy of true light but she never came.

The next day, she left. I tried to talk to her but it was useless.

I miss her presence here on the island. It is lonely during the day. I am fading slowly into the atmosphere, like a jet of flame burning lower each day. Soon I will be a spirit, at one with the stars. I am waiting, I am ready.

THE MARINER'S SPELL

Once upon a time I lived in a seaside village. The sun shone and the sea was blue. The fishing boats rocked to and fro in the little stone harbour and when a gentle breeze blew, they sang a tune as the shrouds tinkled against the masts.

In our garden flowers and fruit trees and soft fruits grew. Raspberries and strawberries hid under wispy leaves. Overhead the trees blossomed with white flowers and the grass was soft as feathers.

My mother fed me with fish straight from the sea, fruit from the apple trees and warm bread from the oven. She cleaned the cottage and beat the carpets every week. Sometimes the birds would sing as she worked and the sound of the strokes blended with the birdsong to make a lively tune.

I learnt my numbers from her and soon I could read a little as she patiently sat beside me at my stool in the parlour. There were stories of giants and princesses and fairies which seemed to come alive as she read them to me. At church on Sunday she sang and I listened to the parson who told us about the devil and the angels.

Then one day a man came to the front door. His hair shone as black as a crow's wing and was forked into two horns tied with red ribbon. In his right ear he wore a silver earring. His glittering eyes were black and shiny. His mouth was large and when he smiled with his big red lips, a gold tooth sparkled.

"I've sailed the seven seas" he said "I've seen the Barbary Coast and drank rum with Captain Blood. I've been with natives with rings through their noses on the other side of the world and seen wimmin wearing grass skirts."

He told me he had been a mariner all his life and knew magic and spells too. I pretended I believed him but I never trusted him. I watched him each morning as he waxed his hair and admired himself in the mirror, smiling secretly at himself. He never fooled me.

My mother seemed pleased to talk with him and she told me that he would live in our spare room which had been empty for years. I did not want this man to share our home. He drank black rum most of the day and when drunk he sang loudly. He smoked a meerschaum pipe shaped like an elephant. Soon he was everywhere in the cottage and the garden. He drank from a stone jar and sometimes fell down after drinking. Mother cleaned him up and put him to bed.

Eventually he moved into Mother's room. He spent more time at home and became louder and drunker each evening. One day he took the money my mother saved and bought more drink. When mother found out she asked for it back and he swiped her with the back of his hand. He pushed me out of the way and stormed out. Mother said nothing but I knew this would happen again and so it did, many times.

One day I asked him for a penny and he laughed at me

"You little dog, do yer think I am an almoner? Get out of my way." And he cuffed my head and turned away.

Mother found it hard to manage with the extra food to buy and less time to do the scrubbing and housework that paid for our needs. She never sang now and the sweet birds that used to sing with her fell silent. I knew if I did nothing, my Mother would wither and her life sink into drudgery.

My tenth birthday came and I found a book in his trunk. The book was about magic. One page had a spell on it which was easy to read and showed how to rid one of a demon. All you had to do was to catch and kill a toad and burn it, crushing its ashes. Then mix the ash with rum and henbane which grew in the fields nearby. I thought about the spell and asked myself if it was a sin to try to do such a thing? At church on a Sunday, the minister had said that only God could judge us. But surely this man was wicked in anybody's eyes? I had seen a picture of the devil and his face with its horns and cruel smile was like the Mariner. God would surely judge this man in the same way as I did?

The rum was easy to find, there were jugs in the parlour and so I caught and burnt the toad and picked some henbane and put the mixture into one of the stone jars he used. That night the man went out as usual and before I went to bed I moved all the jars and jugs away from the parlour leaving the magic jar beside the comfy chair. Sleep was impossible and as I tossed in my bed I wondered how he would die. Would he fall dead at once? Would he die quietly? I wanted to know so I kept awake.

About midnight he came shuffling back to the house. Mother was asleep and I heard him fumble at the keyhole. I crept out of my bed and hid behind the curtain. As he pushed open the front door a gust of cold wind blew out the small candle left burning on the side table. In the sudden darkness he clawed his way towards the chair and sat down. My eyes were well accustomed to the dark and I could see his slobbering red mouth agape and his gold tooth glinting in the half light. He reached out for the jar and with one hand lifted it onto his elbow and took a long swig. He belched and took another pull then sat back. I shifted myself a little to see better and at once his eye turned on me and he snarled

"What ye doin' here? You little dog!" And he kicked out. I scrambled away as he leapt forward, his gnarled hand inches from my face. His sudden move unbalanced him and he crashed to the floor where he knelt gasping and trembling. His tongue stuck out of the side of his mouth and he began to drool and mutter. He started to crawl towards me, his eyes blazing with anger. I turned to see my mother at the doorway her face as white as candle wax. She moved forward just as the man was about to grab me and she took the stone jar high above her head. Without a word she smashed it down on his bushy black head and it shattered into a hundred pieces. He fell and never moved again. We dragged him outside just as he was and left him crumpled on the doorstep.

Mother washed her hands and swept up the broken jar.

"Come, my angel, get some rest, you have school in the morning."

She looked up at the sky and said "I'm sure tomorrow will be a sunny day."

They took his body away the next morning. No one doubted he had died of drink and it was true. The spell had worked in its own way.

That day the sea was blue and the sun shone and the flowers in the garden bloomed brighter than ever.

ABOUT THE AUTHOR

Paul Purnell is a Queen Counsel of forty years' experience in the Criminal Courts, as a trial lawyer. Before that, he served in the British Army for five years. His extensive experience and understanding of the criminal world has provided the inspiration for many of his short stories and the background for his exciting action novels the 'James Ballantyne' series. He enjoys motorcycling and attempts to play Padel Tennis when he has the time. With five grandchildren and his work, there is not much of that.

This collection of short stories reflects his unique take on modern life.

He writes thrillers as well. They are called 'The James Ballantyne' series. The first of these full length novels begins with "The Kazak Contract" an exciting trip into the murky world of Kazakhstan crime. It is available from Amazon and on Kindle or from good book stores.

The second in the series "The Tontine Trap" follows James into a labyrinth of international intrigue and danger. Again, available from Amazon and on Kindle or from good bookstores.

Look out for the third in the series, to be published early in 2019.

Go to paulpurnell.com for updates and follow him on Twitter@purnell14.

Lightning Source UK Ltd.
Milton Keynes UK
UKHW011249110522
402819UK00002B/98

9 781786 233998